I WANT TO DIE IN MY BOOTS

a novel

NATALIE APPLETON

BRINDLE AND GLASS

Brindle & Glass
An imprint of TouchWood Editions
Touchwoodeditions.com

Edited by Kate Kennedy and Nara Monteiro
Copy edited by Senica Maltese
Proofread by Marial Shea
Cover design by Laura Boyle
Interior design and maps by Alex Hennig

CATALOGUING DATA AVAILABLE FROM LIBRARY AND ARCHIVES CANADA
ISBN 9781990071270 (softcover)
ISBN 9781990071188 (electronic)

TouchWood Editions gratefully acknowledges that the land on which we live and work is within the traditional territories of the Lkwungen (Esquimalt and Songhees), Malahat, Pacheedaht, Scia'new, T'Sou-ke and W̱SÁNEĆ (Pauquachin, Tsartlip, Tsawout, Tseycum) peoples.

We acknowledge the financial support of the Government of Canada through the Canada Book Fund and the Canada Council for the Arts, and of the Province of British Columbia through the British Columbia Arts Council and the Book Publishing Tax Credit.

This book was produced using FSC®-certified, acid-free papers, processed chlorine free, and printed with soya-based inks.

This book is a work of historical fiction. Names, characters, places, and incidents are either products of the author's imagination or are used fictitiously.

Printed in Canada

29 28 27 26 25   1 2 3 4 5

This book is for my mom,
and all the women in my family.

This is a novel. As you come upon references to real people, events, establishments, organizations or locales, please note these are intended to make the story authentic—but this is a work of historical fiction. All other characters, and all incidents and dialogue, are drawn from the author's imagination and are not to be construed as real.

Special acknowledgements are given to the Provincial Archives of Saskatchewan for access to the 1924 King's Bench in the Supreme Court of Saskatchewan trial records that inspired some of the dialogue in the final chapters.

BRITISH COLUMBIA
ALBERTA
Medicine Hat
Penticton
Vancouver
Rossland
Milk River
Spokane
WASHINGTON
MONTANA
Deer Lodge
IDAHO
Philipsburg
Butte

Prince Albert
SASKATCHEWAN
Maple Creek
Ravenscrag
Frenchman River
Missouri River
NORTH DAKOTA
Lewistown
Grass Range
SOUTH DAKOTA

WHERE THE CATTLE RUSTLERS ROAMED

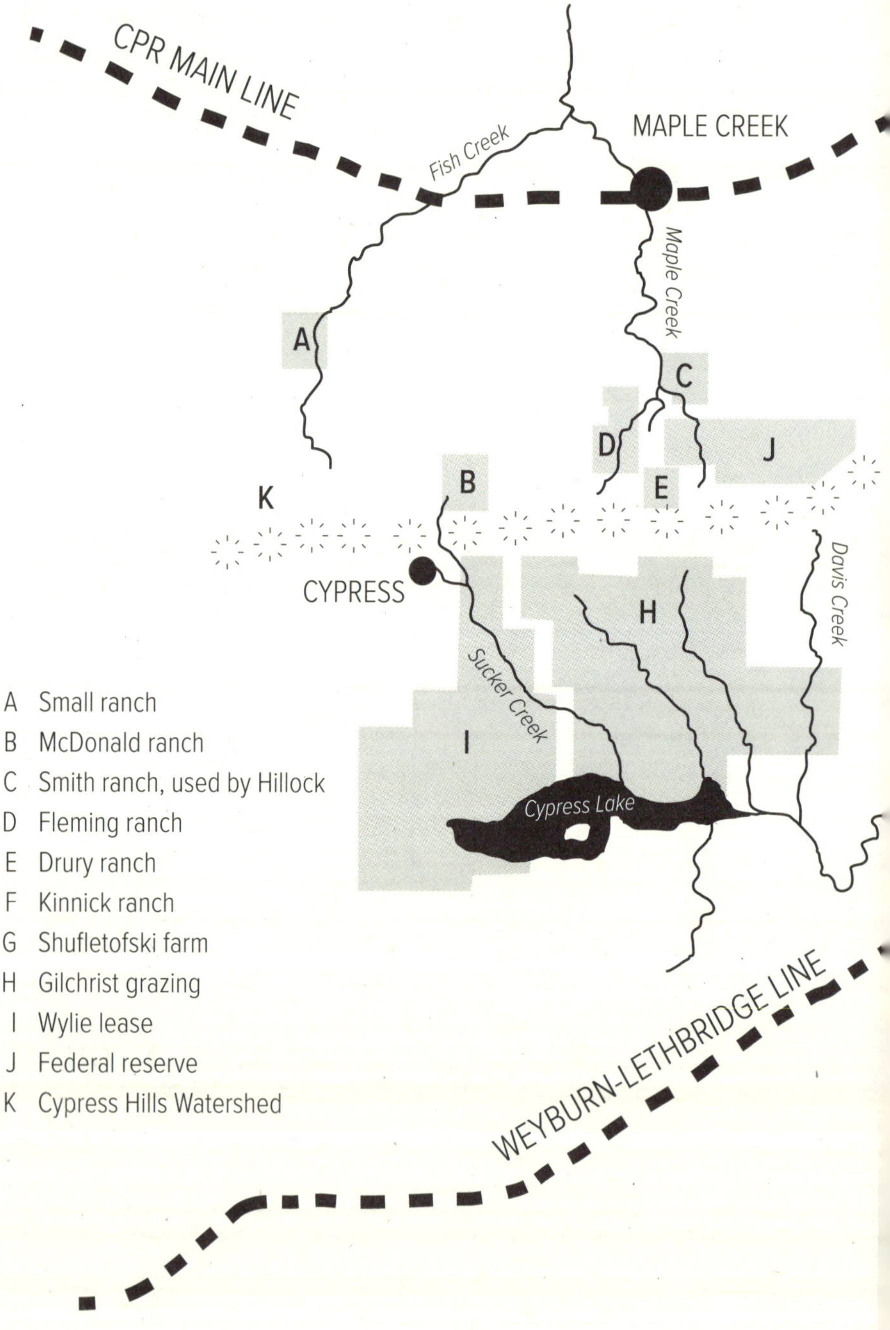

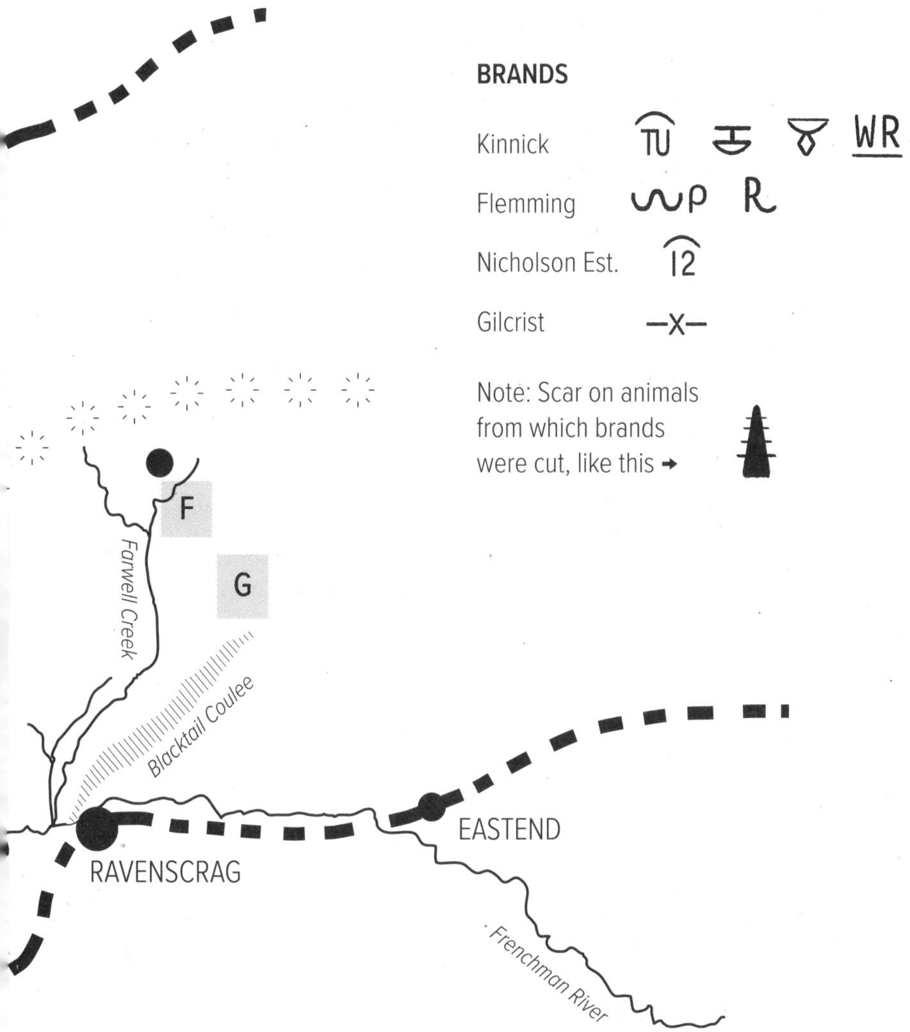

The Leader-Post, Regina, Saskatchewan, 6 December 1924

AUTHOR'S NOTE

I had been researching and writing about the strange incidents and forsaken homesteaders of Ravenscrag, Saskatchewan for nearly five years when I came across a description of a woman I thought I ought to know:

> MRS. B.J. DALE
>
> Mrs. Dale is probably remembered as one of the most colourful people to pass this way. She was most charming to meet and intelligent to talk to. However, if she had a point to make or an argument to win she did not hesitate to let her opponent know she was armed and ready! Many are the stories of her home up the coulee, often referred to as "Robbers Roost," probably rightfully named as it was general knowledge that she was the brains behind a gang of horse and cattle thieves for which she put in "time." Perhaps someone, someday, will write a whole book around her part in the development of this country.
> —*Ravenscrag: Between and Beyond the Benches*

Well, if I didn't fall in love right there.

I began hunting up clues about her storied life. I wondered, how does a woman come to lead a gang of cattle thieves in the 1920s? Oh, but she was elusive. Many names and many ages had been given on official documents. I had to work for it.

Often, though, I felt her and the wild chitter of sparrows at dawn cheering me on.

As I leaned on both the real and the imagined, this woman and her world began to emerge. *I Want to Die in My Boots* is the mostly true untold story of Belle Jane, complete with newspaper clippings that appear as they were printed, mostly in the dailies of Montana and Saskatchewan. And yet, much is fiction in this tale we haven't heard before, about women and horses and Canada's West.

On horseback and on foot, in her boots, here are the adventures of Belle Jane as I imagined them.

part one

FULL OF STARS

LOST

A dark gray mare, white face and dot on right side aged four years, also black horse white face cut on head aged seven years. $10 reward. Apply to Rev Spillway, Maple Creek

PROLOGUE

1917

IN THE MOMENTS WHILE Belle Jane sat on the biffy, the sky darkened to such a steel that her legs disappeared. She could've been the magician's assistant as he performed that trick, sawing a woman in half. It often felt like her legs were *of* her, travelling her body, but getting commands from some other mind. The legs: to the wood pile, to the fire, to the kettle, to the coop and the cows. To the stove, to the table, to the dishes and the socks. To the axe. To the horses, to the creek, to the weanlings. To the pedals, for the children had asked her to play "Ta Ra Ra Boom De Ay!" or "Come Josephine, In My Flying Machine!" Again, if she'd please. She stroked her calf muscles, lithe and thick. That's what she was, thick.

But Belle Jane's legs could not help her now, as she pushed and huffed. It was stuck, twisted with her angst and her mind could not quite locate it, instruct it.

Below, a sting of cool air and the rank of urine. Greedy flies with their not-teeth, like the old men at the Chinese restaurant. Last spring, bluebirds had nested in the roof, right above the walls she'd papered with golden hummingbirds drinking at peonies. Someday, she would have plumbing and electric lights. Someday, she would die.

In the midnight hours, even when the legs knew it was not right, they went to the barn. To the fire, to the iron, to the bowie knife, to the needle, to the cleaver, to the bow saw, to the stash of lime. While Bill spooned the colt on the dirt, held its jaw like a lover, straddled its hind legs. Smiled.

The legs.

She felt a wash of nausea, at this moment, this life. How long could they all carry on? A week last a Mountie stopped the Priest girls riding to school, inspected the brands and asked where the horses had been got.

As her insides roiled, for some strange reason, her mind called her to remember a name she'd once had, Mrs. Junk. Had anything ever been funnier? Peter Junk's fingers (still damp from rinsing his dick in the sink), coming to grips with her throat on the train, the last train. The fair. The boy. Her mind had always tried to drift off the memory, but at the oddest times a tide would rush back the child's wail, his cheeks.

Well, here it was, finally. Spoils of the animals she'd reared, roasted and devoured, were now spitting out, away. How sad, a bit of remorse that she would be upon the legs again soon.

Her expression of relief was fleeting. Outside, she heard the sound of hooves slap the earth, the cinch of rope, a cuss: "You Goddamn Goddamn . . ."

Had the stranger lost the words, or the nerve?

Her heart was a mad racehorse, dashing but to where? She stood, peeked through the cut-out waning moon, scanned the low, snow-dusted hills all around, hoping George would not rise from a coulee.

"Shuf?"

"Bill! It was you, wasn't it?"

A punch, a guttural, choking sound. "Hoah."

Bill Kinnick, her husband, was on his back, at the pig slop, wiping his mouth. They knew a man, a Swede, who'd been bit by his sow and died of a fever. Bill's hat, that old Plainsman, had landed about five feet off in the dirt.

Frank Shufletofski, her neighbour of a place eight miles south, was running to the barn. Bill Kinnick scrambled up, caught his boot, yanked him to the mud. Both men rose, to their knees and then their rage-wobbled feet.

"It's been you all along!" Shuf threw down his gloves, readied his fists. "Well I won't take it. That's my buckskin you've got runnin' there, now isn't it?"

He pointed to the range beyond, where a herd of horses that'd been stampeding for no reason came to a still behind Morning Star, the head of the herd. The buckskin ran drag, at the back. Its coat, like wet hay, glistened. It had dark socks and dark eyes that always gave it a look of fright. Even from the biffy, Belle Jane could see Morning Star's nose jerked high, ears tall. Feeling for the vibration, the smell, of danger.

The sky wanted to watch the fight too. The dark clouds and puffy white tops sailed above their ranch, threatened rain or hail or sleet. Or sun. This was Saskatchewan.

Her breath became edgy, panicky. She fumbled for her stockings, her lace underwear, her skirts. Where was Old Angus, the deuce, when shit like this was doing?

Shuf knocked Bill across the jaw, then boxed his ear. Shuf had a funny way of punching sideways, like a raccoon burrowing in the dirt.

Bill gave him a look: half glare, half grin. "I'll take you Shuf, and I'll take you again."

The button of her skirt, she couldn't get it to hook. It was dark. Her fingers were dumb and fat and shaking.

But as the men's boots and fists collided, it was sideways-punching Shuf who was getting the best of Bill.

Oh hell, she thought, forgoing the button, I better help him.

Belle Jane remembered she was in the biffy, the stash of branding irons. She let the door wince open just a hair so she could get down on her knees, wiggle loose the board, and grab the first one, a half circle.

The air was dense with possibility: it could hail, a man could lose an eye.

The hens skittered to the shadow of the sawhorse. Bill saw her coming, shot her a look of baffled terror. What was she going to do?

She stalked the backside of Shuf, who had all his blood and senses fixed right there, in the storm of the fight.

Somewhere, far but not so far, a child sang a jubilant, heartfelt tune.

If she'd thought to go for the gut, knock the wind out of him. But she didn't. She swung the iron at Shuf like a baseball bat. He ducked or stumbled, and the iron clocked Bill square between the eyes just as her skirts dropped. His face, there was no time for marvel or humiliation. His lids squeezed shut and his body tipped back like a pine log.

She dropped, her skirts dropped, Bill dropped. "Bill!"

There was dust, boots, a "Yah!" as the neighbour made south on his saddle horse. High to the hills in the west, a man she couldn't make out, crabbing up the coulee on foot. Cousin Hector?

"Get to hell off, Shuf!" she hollered. "Take your chickenshit horse too."

Her fingers reached for Bill's temple, his heart.

The clouds let off a mist of rain. The iron, how cool it felt in her hands.

STRAYED–CAME TO MY PLACE

in Basin Creek Christmas eve, bay horse; brand, a boot on left hind hip, small hump on back. Phil Carron.

1

1879

MARY CONNOLLY MCGUINNESS pinched the milk from her nipples every night, on a stool, in the dark, under a cloudless Nevada sky until her death at thirty-five in 1879.

Mary was fifteen when she wed Plain Tom, thirty-one years her senior, and since then, she'd given birth every February or March. Her "winter bairns." But Mary knew, as sure as she'd seen the face of James Patrick, his sweet double dimples, his tucked-up nose, that she was gazing at her last baby. To make it so, she let J.P. suckle until he was nearly three years old. As an extra precaution, she only let Plain Tom do what he did just before, during and after her bleeding, if it'd returned between babies. Their lovemaking in America was so different, it was not the same. Their dry, burning tongues, the trying of their sweat. The uselessness of it. How it took longer, how Plain Tom had seemed to need her more now. How all she'd wanted in the night was to have her skin to herself.

They'd come from a village in Galway County, Ireland, known in all of Europe for its October Fair, the greatest and largest anywhere. For centuries, not long after sunrise, Irish shepherds had crooked at the black legs of their flocks until the many thousands of sheep—44,000, even 99,000 once—stood like troops awaiting battle, or a ship. It was with this glimpse of the world of the Earls doing the stock buying that the men of Ballinasloe dared to dream. But it was only drunken moonlit whispers, until the men started packing ships for America.

Plain Tom McGuinness came to a mind that he would find his fortune in Nevada territory. Even though he had his wife, Mary, five children and a baby on the way, he sailed for the gold mines of America and left his family at a poor workhouse at Ballinasloe.

Also known as the "fever hospital" for the hundreds who'd perished there during the potato famine of the 1840s, the workhouse was a village of its own: it had a two-storey stone male wing, a female wing, a bakehouse, a washhouse, an infirmary, an "idiots" ward, a chapel and a dining hall, where Mary had likely been wiping cold, sticky gruel from Honoria's mouth and hushing little Mollie when she got the letter.

My Mary,

I rite these few lines with a pocket full of rocks. No gold pieces yet, but I will do. Soon.

The packet is for your passage. Mind the sharpers when you land. They're everywhere in a country such as this.

I pray God favors you and the bairns, and you are never one day sick at sea. Let me know how our James Patrick is, and wee Annie.

Remember me to all.

Ever Yours,
Plain Tom

In that year (1866) their eldest son, Josephus—their lucky boy, born on St. Patrick's Day 1855—had died of typhus at Ballinasloe, and it was in that same infirmary where she watched the Sisters of Mercy close Jos's lids that Mary had given birth to James Patrick.

In Nevada, first Virginia City and then Washoe, they'd had to send eight-year-old James Patrick out to the bars with his banjo to play for miners so his mam could buy a bit of flour and sugar and tea.

It seemed to Mary the men in America lived to want. Her husband, and, later, the husbands of her daughters, were always moving about. Towns and houses and occupations, from farming to stock-raising to tavern-keeping. And then back to farming. They could not stop, could not settle. They thirsted not just for more but the *chance* of more.

Once he'd saved enough to bring his wife and offspring over, Plain Tom'd pissed behind their shanty nearly every cent he'd ever earned. He was a pleasant drunk, though. Just one beer and he'd swing Mary 'round, singing "I love a bonnie lassie."

Mary did what women could: follow, find food, feed mouths.

When Honoria—their youngest daughter, Annie, they called her—turned thirteen and that George Corneil (pronounced Cornell) had the gall to knock on their shanty door, Mary and Plain Tom had fought wildly about it.

"She's in plaits yet!" said Mary. "Hasn't even started her monthlies." To that Plain Tom and George had winced, but Annie's face was terribly stoic for a girl. Mary still remembered the splitting, not apart but open.

George was twenty-eight, an ambitious, gold-hungry Catholic who'd been born in some forsaken place across the border called Ontario, and Annie'd liked his gifts—dolls with heads her mother hadn't sewn and that did not wear a pillow slip but a smart tartan dress; a blue-eyed kitten Annie'd called Sapphira.

Two years later, on the eighteenth day of March, 1879—and within weeks of the death of Mary Connolly McGuinness (an enlarged heart)—fifteen-year-old Annie McGuinness Corneil gave birth to a girl, a long-legged, long-foreheaded wailing purple girl they named after three of George's kin: his mother, Jane Cunningham Corneil; his sister Baby Jane, who'd died, along with her twin, John, before their first birthday; and his sister Belinda, who'd saved him from drowning in a frozen lake that'd caved at dusk.

Belinda Jane Corneil. That was the first of her names.

STRAYED

March last, one mare, nearly white, aged, branded on left shoulder; one sorrel horse, three white feet, blazed face, branded FT on left shoulder. Home range, Wolf creek. A reward of $25 will be paid for information leading to their recovery. WM Skelton, Stanford, Mont.

2

1889

BELINDA JANE SAT at her father's mahogany desk, marvelling at the cattails of light and how it felt to feel the boss.

Here she was, not on the side that waited to be told or given the what-for, but on the side with the say. Belinda Jane assumed her father's advising position sat back with fingers linked at his waist, occasionally worrying at the twists of his moustache. The bright of his glances as he listened to some miner or stock hand's plea for money. The asker, if he was not new, would be almost certain to get it from the saloonkeeper. In this way, George Corneil's shoulder was always warm with the pats of "friends" as he sauntered through the bar, through the dusty streets of Philipsburg and Granite, through almost anywhere in the state of Montana, or even this corner of the Northwest.

Sometimes the asker was family.

Belinda Jane gave a cough and imitated her father's voice: "Robby, we can't have a sheep man on that range. Chew the shit out of the grasses and what? We're putting out for feed hand over hand."

Uncle Robert was always asking her father what to do. Their families raised draft horses and feed wheat at a homestead near Dora Thorn Ridge. George also ran this tavern in Philipsburg and they stayed in a wooden one-storey on West Kearney Street—and since they were new to all of it, even Montana, there was always something the matter.

Half the time eleven-year-old Belinda Jane knew what ought to be done (sluice up the stuck calf's head with goose grease and give it a good kick; trust the horse that won't cross the creek, not the one that will) and she had no patience for Uncle Robert or any of the folks who sat at the other side of that desk. This side, one could see the door, the window. Looking down at the street, you could see the backs of skinny men in overcoats and horses going somewhere. This side, it felt like winning a footrace or giving the recitation at school: everyone saw you brighter, smarter.

"You're a good man, Rocco," she said, pretending to see off the barkeep as her father did after outing a crooked newcomer. "One in a thousand."

Rocco sometimes told Belinda Jane tales about an old man snatching him from a convent in the country and forcing him to beg in Naples, that after hearing the old man make a deal to turn nine-year-old Rocco into a cripple, he'd run away to a fishing boat and then got a place shovelling coal on a ship bound for New York. To Belinda Jane, the bar smelled more like Rocco's sea stories than the sawdust shavings that caught spit and spills, and the whiskey-sour breath of the unlucky.

The creak of the swinging door, bootsteps, then a pause. A boot sole twisting on soft, whiny wood. Beyond, the clink of tin ale mugs, the rhythm of a broom. These were the sounds of morning at The Corner Saloon above Jacky's Harness Shop, and she was privy to it most Saturdays. George'd come around to the idea that someday he'd pass everything on to his eldest daughter, Belinda Jane, and not to a son.

(Charles, Lillie's twin, was born still. During a spell in Terre Haute, five-year-old Tom-George was playing with friends on a handcar on the brewery sidetrack when the handle struck him in the head and he fell, was crushed by a barrel. In two days, he was declared recovering, then died between blinks.)

Belinda Jane had a head for numbers and horses, was fine in conversation and had no issue acting the boss, but she also exhibited surprising acts of goodwill (teaching her sisters how to "talk horse" and lending out her pet duck) and she always kept a secret. George Corneil wanted Belinda Jane to know what it was to run an outfit and often sat her here in this office. Saturday last she witnessed first a man who tried to enter the saloon without a shirt, for it had been pawned at the races; and then a gambler with double black eyes and an oversized civil war coat beg for work (he was fed warmed-over chicken pie, given a coin and sent out. When his shadow was long enough down Main Street—though she'd been warned never to take the time to watch someone walk away—George turned to Belinda Jane and said: "You got a gambler working for you, you got someone stealin' from you.") Never hire gamblers. Never hire drunks. These were among his list of "nevers." One needed "nevers" to be a figure of authority in a town like Philipsburg.

(In 1881, after two years of toiling at Hope Mill on the summit rock of Granite Mountain, there was just enough money to pay the miners one last shift. The shot was tamped, the fuse was lit and the last shot was fired. A message from the backers in St. Louis ordering a work stoppage was sent to Philipsburg, but a blizzard delayed its arrival four days; that telegram passed the one coming from the mine: "Silver!" The last shot had exposed a stick of what would become one of the world's richest silver mines. The miners unpacked their bags and all who'd worked at or near that mountain could taste dollar bills the way one knows the taste of blood. Mining camps attracted lawbreakers, adventurers, gun-toters. Fifteen years ago there were some six hundred men and only four women and four children in Philipsburg. Four. "When there were dances," an old-timer later sniggered, "we danced with each other." And when they weren't dancing, the miners played cards, raced horses and drank.)

Today was not a Saturday lesson at the saloon. Today was a Tuesday—and in her mind Belinda Jane rolled that word salty on her tongue, saying it *Chewsdee* like her teacher, Miss Lottie Pizer. All morning, Belinda Jane'd pawed at her neck and by ten o'clock she told Miss Pizer she'd like to be excused on account of quinsy, and that she'd get herself to her father so he might fetch a doctor. George took one glance at her throat, determined she did not have quinsy—an infection of the tonsils involving quite a lot of puss, common among women. She would not need to be rushed on the stage to Anaconda, or Butte, as she'd dramatized in her mind. She'd simply gone riding with wet hair again, hadn't she?

She nodded yes, she had gone out riding her mare Delilah without waiting for her hair to dry again despite her mother Annie's scraggly hollers toward the barn. Her sorry child-mother, just fifteen years older. Belinda Jane'd ridden through the white-white bedsheets still on the line, past an old woman hobbling up to the house carrying a chipped painting of a boy in blue, and, over the old branding corral, cleared by just hairs. And she'd done it riding slick—no tie stirrups. As she led Delilah to the barn to brush out the horse's glistening sweat, she could feel the arrow of damp on her own back; that cool June evening had done nothing to dry her locks. She felt the first tingle of a sore throat the moment she woke in the night.

Now Belinda Jane worried that in the nodding, she looked rather like a horse. *Horseface* was what Frank Doody called her. Jealous, Annie'd said. But Belinda Jane knew she did have a long, handsome face. Her sister Lillie (Caroline) had it too. Both girls cursed it when they got the photograph, some fake paper fireplace in back and their two young sisters, Mary-Alice and Annie May, on the settee in front. The gap in ages between the two sets of sisters was horrid; each Corneil had silently imagined where Tom-George and Charles, Lillie's twin, would've stood. Even the family dog, an all-black collie they called Fernie, splayed in front of the settee, looked sorry and ashamed, head down. *Horseface*. Well, that Doody boy just got his: last week he and Charles Sligh hopped on the tramway at the Bi-Metallic Mine to catch a free ride up the mountain and halfway, the cable stopped for the night. Some hours later, Rocco's brother—who wasn't really a brother, who tended bar at Headquarters, the other saloon—was on his way home for the night, happened by, heard their calls and got a man to hit the switch. *Horseface*. Belinda Jane wondered, did she look like the Corneil women of Omemee, Ontario, her namesakes?

And yet here was her father, his oiled black hair and doll's face so angled, so smooth. A great black moustache. His gold waist clock and his wool town suit with the latest collar. They had a stallion, Jake, who loved his filly daughter, Deborah, best. He called her over to him from wherever she was with a high-low whinny only heard with her.

"Once is unfortunate, twice is a coincidence." George emphasized his point with the rolled newspaper in his right hand. He set the paper on his desk and eyed the girl till she sat up from his chair.

"Three times, Belinda Jane, that's daftness or intention. Which is it?"

Swallowing stung, but not the truth. She wanted her father to see that she'd been out riding because she was getting to be a damned good rider (next year, she thought, she would help break the wild ones, and not by sacking out with a tarpaulin). That she had desire beyond the homely hills and the one hundred windows of the mill. Already, there'd been talk of courses at Butte Business College for her, and she *would* do it. She glanced at the hands of her father, ever smooth, ever pale, hands that she wanted to take her in, let off about the sore throat. The newspaper beneath his fingertips. She caught the nameplate: *The Pittsburgh Dispatch*.

"You got a Pittsburgh paper?"

George read at least three newspapers a day, had them sent from all corners and took any left behind by passing strangers at the hotel. George would draw a trio of lines, like a corral, next to news of note and opportunities: patents for horse boots and egg carriers, the archbishop's thoughts on prohibition (". . . it is *temperance* that we aim to teach"), mine cave-ins, "business chances," strange crimes of the upper classes. Sam Lake, a foreman at the nearby Granite mine, had just been arrested for stealing silk handkerchiefs from the Buskett store and his bedding was later found to have hidden $400 worth of stolen silver bullion bars, ladies' hose, undergarments and jewellery. How George hated thieves. "Give me an honest wrongdoer any day," he'd say.

"*Belinda*."

"I know it." She would try to spend the hours after the next washing day on a chair, book-reading or acting the teacher for Lillie and Mary-Alice and little Annie May. It killed Belinda Jane, sitting in on a rainless summer evening with a rested horse just there in the barn.

A rap on the door. Rocco's—two quick punches.

"Yes, then?"

The warped door twittered open by a shaky hand.

"Boss, there's a man's got a necktie on outside, asking for the 'proprietor.' Somethin' 'bout voting day."

"Who?"

"Wouldn't say. Won't come in to set at my bar."

My bar. George liked that, how much pride Rocco took in that plank of knotty lodgepole pine, that kingdom where all men with a five-cent piece were equal. Lord, the stories Rocco'd heard. Girls lost and diseases gained, bets lost and chances gained. Civil war stories of teenage brothers on both sides who nearly killed one another with bowie knives, who lived and stole the gold teeth of their rotting countrymen. Oh, the craze of hunting up a treasure. Rocco would bellow: "I could write a book!"

George, who'd only just sat, buttoned his coat and stood. The wool of his layers sighed as he followed after Rocco.

In the new still of the room, Belinda Jane's eyes were drawn to a tower of headlines smack in the middle of the front page:

QUEEN OF OUTLAWS.

Romantic Career of Belle Starr, the
Border Bandits' Sovereign.

A TERROR TO THE OFFICERS.

Dashing Mustang Rider, Crack Shot,
Fearless and Revengeful,

SHE ALWAYS ATTRACTED ATTENTION.

Three Times Married to Outlaw Chiefs,
She Died as She Had Lived.

Belinda Jane's blood trilled:

Belle Starr
born Myra Maybelle Shirley Reed
leader of border outlaws
dashing a bandit as any
of her three famous husbands
ran off, on horseback to marry the handsome captain
of Quantrill's cutthroat band,
Cole Younger, and for the ceremony,
John Fisher, that Texas stage robber, held her horse

locked in a closet by her father: school or seminary, girl
so she fled school on another boy's horse
with Jesse James, Frank James, Bob Younger

and Cole, who tried farming in Missouri,
tried killing the four who shot Bob, so Belle

lived with the Cherokees, married Sam Starr
(despite warnings: "She'll ruin your boys")
swore like a pirate
loved the red leaves of sumac trees, twined them in the
bridle of her favourite riding horse

slept next to a judge, disguised as a man
(hollered, in the morning, "And you can tell your wife
you spent the night with Belle Starr!")
charged with horse stealing
stole the mare of John Middleton, drowned him
in the Plateau River
sang old weepers playing guitar
robbed Old Farrell and his three sons
also dressed in buckskins
loved sour cornbread
left the trial and Fort Smith with two
double-acting revolvers that she called "her babies"
wore a cow boy's hat, feathers, Winchesters
two, four bullets in her back, shot off her mare
—it swam across the South Canadian, and home
and at her grave, Mabel Jones planted
a scrawny sumac seedling

It was as if Belinda Jane had just met a bosom friend, one you want to kiss, for all she knows of the dark corners of your life; for her darkness, her love. *Belle.*

Was it sunny out now? The dust had gained the glint of mischief.

A finger reached for the edge of the desk, its dusty jaw. She scrawled the letter *B.*

She tried it again on her tongue. *Belle.*

NOTICE

$25 reward for return of black mare,
branded JT. Four years old, white hind
feet, wire cut scar front left foot.
W.F. Fitzhenry

3

1900

SANDFLIES SWAM ABOVE the junegrass in the last of the yellowest sunlight. When Peter Junk had got the horses to a stop, to a tilt, on the side of the highway, Belle'd glanced down at the ditch, the dark and the roots just below, where the flies must've hatched alongside the nests of garter snakes and jumping mice. But the sun had fried all living things, not one other creature stirred now. So it was that every movement of Peter's—the knotting of the reins, the unknotting of his bowtie, the sliding of his trousers across the bench—scratched as if on a stage.

This is romance, she thought. The two of them, out here.

It was their third ride.

The first ride, she'd been leaving Hennessy's, the department store where she worked as a stenographer, and he'd just made his last delivery at the saloon on Mercury and Main. He'd nodded. They'd first met years ago, in Philipsburg, when he was delivering kegs to The Corner Saloon, and had since crossed paths here in Butte a time or two but hadn't spoken.

"Belle Jane Corneil, what if I take you on home?"

"Oh, I like the walk." She liked hearing her whole name—the one she'd insisted upon—called out like that. She did like walking. After a day of sitting for letters, she thought sometimes she might walk herself right to Greenwich, New York City. Be an actor star. And smoke. She could. She *could*. She'd rehearsed in her mind several times the scene: the dress of Nile green India silk, the peach lipstick, the laugh. "Isn't she charming?" they'd say. And she would feign to blush. And a man, someone named Charlie, would call over a cousin, Redcliff or Bertram, "Cousin Redcliff, come meet Miss Belle Jane of Butte, Montana—isn't she a country sweetheart?" Maybe, in her daydreaming, she was grinning; maybe that's why he patted the bench, thought she wanted to be his passenger.

"You're at Mrs. Dunmore's?"

She gave a smile, of flattery or cruelty? How did he know? Sure, Butte was not Salt Lake or Chicago, but it was not Philipsburg. There were several boarding houses for ladies, and she'd been in "the Lilac Room" at Mrs. Dunsmore's since she signed up at Butte Business College almost a year ago now. "Mrs. Lucille Dunsmore's," she said, just a hint of bitterness and boredom.

Peter's next words were barely heard. "I'm sorry, you know."

So, he'd known after all. The whole while, she'd gone to bed on that horrible metal cot imagining his rescue: his ash black horse, waiting for her in the dark just below that window in the Kootenays, the mountains across the line. He'd wrap his jacket around her nightdress, say how beautiful she looked, even more beautiful now that she was growing out, and they'd ride off, under the moon.

"I *didn't* know," she said.

"You must hate me. Do you hate me, Belle Jane?"

It was as if she were still nineteen, at that window, waiting. Sliding a hand below the sill to feel the steepness of the roof. Weighing the risks—a fall, a fall on her stomach out the window or the iron gates; a bear chasing her up a pine tree as she ran through the woods, through the Kootenays all the way to Montana; a fall, a fall on her stomach. She knew a woman in the hills who'd been kicked in the stomach by a cow when she was pregnant and the woman threw up her oats, saw a doctor, and she was fine. Belle thought she might throw up now.

"I don't hate you."

She'd tried hating him. *Peter Junk, I hate you*! Somehow, and right now, she only wanted him more.

She couldn't even remember, now, taking his hand to get in that rig, and they went slower than slow.

Two cow men on horseback sauntered past. One was chewing grass and gave a glare, the other, the one riding a black swayback with a white star above the eyes, tipped his hat, revealing the whitest forehead and a boy's smile.

Peter Junk turned his eyes to the clouds, tilted his head some and squinted, like he was making out a shape just forming. There was a shadow over the left side of his face, and on the right, he was soft, all white. You could hardly see his eyebrows and he was just a new man—not tall, not stout, not especially anything—and what did the two of them know? Couldn't they be forgiven?

"Better get you in," he said, and the team loped on.

The second time, he found her leaving Hennessy's with Fanny Sperry and offered them both a ride to the boarding house, said he knew where Belle Jane could sit, eyeing his lap, but Fanny waved her chain-handled suede bag at them and said, "Payday. Meetin' Ira at The Sherman."

The Sherman was an all-day-all-night café on West Broadway by the opera house where there was a chance you wouldn't taste the grease of the previous meal on your plate, and the flies were few. Belle wondered if Peter might ask her to a short order house like The Sherman or even the Oyster Parlor on West Park Street.

How exotic, oysters right here in Butte, and not the slippery, still-warm prairie variety cow boys choked down their throats come branding.

Ira Yates was the son of a cow man who must've been in town at the yards, the stockyards. Their folks had worked on the same ranch once and Fanny and Ira'd been kids together.

If Peter Junk had been thinking of asking Belle Jane to a meal or even pie and coffee, he didn't say. Not a word was said on the way to Mrs. Dunsmore's. What was there, was that electric, invisible tangle of their bodies: thighs, fingers, lips. Lord, if he'd just kiss her she could slap him!

There was a moment, when the team'd stopped. He looked at her, her face, wishing he could forget, see her as she was before, her lips, quivering. She looked at him, his sunburnt cheeks, his lips, thin and wanting. Mrs. Dunsmore's dog tore across the yard, barking at Peter and then jumped up to his chin. Peter, who'd been bitten in the ass by a dog when he was seven, spun around and tottered back, almost fell.

"Oh, you're a real bruiser, Doughnut," said Belle. She latched the tiny gate that kept wandering milk cows from eating Mrs. Dunsmore's scarlet nasturtiums and looked back to give her thanks, put off anything more, but Peter'd just . . . left her.

"Belle Jane?"

His voice gave a shimmer in her heart. She looked up. As his team jerried off, he remained standing and turned the wrong way around, a goofy smile on his face as he waved. The parched yellow butte waned in the distance, a nothing-something.

The third ride, he kept his team fronting north instead of turning west for Mrs. Dunsmore's.

"What if I take you just a mile on? A country stroll. Remind you of home."

In her mind, she weighed the risks: another night alone in the Lilac Room under a quilt some other sorry woman had fixed, trying to fall asleep while it's still light and her thoughts were so naggy, loud nearly as the other girls who were young women now too but acted thirteen, who were studying to be stenographers or bookkeepers, like she had, and aspired for a spot like hers, at Hennessy's, like it was the be-all.

"Must be hard, girl loves horses like you cooped up in those walls all day."

And if not a night alone with her crochet needle, a night with Peter Junk. She imagined Annie's salty rebuke: "Who told you, Belle Jane? I did. *I* told you." And yet, there was only one way that Belle'd come into being, and Annie had been a girl herself, was still growing up. Annie told Belle Jane things a mother should not tell her daughter, about men's wants, Belle Jane's own father's wants (that when Annie had nursing milk, he'd liked to suck; that with one of the babies, she was sleep crazy and it'd reminded her of the sons who'd died, and she cracked him on the head with a coal oil lamp when he'd tried to bite her nipple).

The day was yellow but for the white rush of smoke from the mill.

"Must be hard, staring at a horse's ass all day."

He raised an eyebrow at her and smiled, the way men smile over a dirty joke. She looked at him, his white-blond nothing lashes, his nothing moustache.

"Well, I got plans."

"You've got plans?"

"Once I get a partner, we're goan go in on a saloon. I already talked to Centennial 'bout a deal. Be exclusive. Mining camps, they want fellas to quit the whiskey—guys get too crazy, kicking each other in the face and whatnot—so it's a beer parlour. Beer only. Really don't have to worry about fights."

The artist of her mind drew up a picture of her father, standing next to Peter at the backroom desk, patting him on the back for such smarts. A beer parlour. She'd have all the buttons and fine French flannels, play 63 with the ladies in the parlour and they'd lunch off a cut glass celery boat. She'd stand at a pot of marigolds at the window, one of those new silk scarves, like drapery, over her shoulder, just as Peter was stepping up to the door of their brick two-storey.

"It's a bright idea, Peter. Real bright."

She didn't mind disappointing Annie, not one atom. But if she ever had to have her father look at her the way he did that morning (or, more accurately, the way he looked away from her), she'd rope a stone to her foot and jump in the Clark Fork River.

"Think so?"

"I do."

George Corneil, if he loved anything more than his daughters and his horses, it was a business chance.

It was late afternoon, maybe five, and so hot none but the driver of a brewing company would dare be out of the shade.

"Thirsty," he said and tipped a black bottle from his coat jacket. He took a swig and she reached out her hand. Whiskey, it was, and a bit watered down, she felt. But it did give her the sensation of radiance. She took another sip, boldly found his inside coat pocket and plunked the bottle back for him.

"I think my father would like you, Belle Jane."

"Oh?" She gave a tell-me-more smirk. "And your mother?"

"She doesn't like anyone." He squinted. "She likes her clocks. Shines 'em up with oil Mondays, winds 'em. Got one on every wall, just about. Two or three or more on some."

So there it was, he'd had an odd duck mother. And Peter was an only child. She thought about her own family, her three sisters and her mother's five sisters and brothers, and her father's five brothers. The cousins. A good forty of them there would be when they used to Sunday at Rock Creek, currents rushing their ankles and fly-fishing those red-streaked, black-spotted trout. Now, they were all so far away, the Corneils and the McGuinesses (who now went by McGinnis). Plain Tom, her grandfather, was still alive, old as the hills, though he'd lost his hearing and the boys of Alturas, California, often teased him.

Peter and Belle Jane had ridden far enough away from town and the nearest ranch that it was just them. Just them and the sandflies and snakes.

What do we do now?

The needing won out.

"Belle Jane, what are you . . . ?"

Button by button by button.

"Stop that. Jesus H."

But he was a well she could fill; she was a well he could draw from.

"Damn, Belle Jane," he gasped. "You feel . . ."

As their panting waned, a breeze started in, waved its arms over the day.

Glorious sweat, a softness in his trousers, the crawl-leak of stickiness.

What do we do?

"I didn't want to do that, Belle Jane." Peter glared at her.

Was that true? Hadn't he asked to give her a ride, taken her to the middle of nowhere?

"That wasn't why I—"

"Close your eyes," she told him. She set her head at his chest, the way they did after, before. She listened for his heart's beat, went soft in the going on of that glorious, sinful deed.

No, she realized, it could not be re-enacted. Everything was wrong: the buttons, the sun, the metallic smell of his chest.

What do we do now? No one alive could love Peter like Belle, and Belle like Peter. And yet, looking at the other was only a reminder.

As their fingers began to worry at their buttons and pins, righting things, one of the horses reared, kicked some and the back wheel on the ditch-side snapped. The wagon slid, beer barrels slid. Peter halted the roan mare, writhing at the bit.

"Must've been a snake."

"You got a spare wheel?"

"I do not have a spare wheel."

Didn't have the tools, either.

"I'm not a wheelwright."

Peter stood on the bench, cast his hand above his forehead to block the sun as he scanned the horizon for the nearest homestead. He slid off the wagon side slowly, fish-like, and started running.

"Stay right there," he called.

The rig was in a precarious position: the wagon perched on a hump of dirt, the horses getting shifty. If another rattler happened out. She held her breath, let her bottom grow bony on the bench. She stopped herself from laughing when she remembered a dear girlhood friend, Philippa, who renamed her old bay mare Bonyparte. Belle Jane and Philippa'd made plans to marry brothers and live in matching cabins on the same ranch, have twins (or triplets!) and their own schoolhouse, and Belle Jane would do the darning and Philippa'd wash because she liked to clean, and when all their charges were asleep, they would ride together by the setting sun doing tricks, like standing or sitting backwards. But Philippa died the day after her sixteenth birthday. TB. It was about that time Belle Jane let herself be noticed by Peter Junk.

Dad above, every second felt an hour. Belle's eyes followed the twists of a white-winged dandelion. Fly away, little seed! Fly, fly away! Finally, Peter returned with a red-faced old German who knew exactly what they'd been up to, Belle could feel it. Peter traded him, a barrel of beer for a wheel, details of which they'd somehow worked out by hand gesture, for the German didn't speak English and his sons must've abandoned him, for Peter later said he was all on his own on that homestead.

As the wagon with the new-to-the-outfit wheel kicked toward the smoke of the mining camps, and soon, town, Belle Jane and Peter held hands.

She thought to tell him

it was a boy

and he didn't even cry, and the nun, who saw newborns every day, and who was not supposed to make such comments to girls like her, almost gasped when she held up the infant, "Oh, isn't he all the light?"

But Belle Jane thought, Later. Never, maybe. Maybe he doesn't want to know. But I know. We sent a brave, beautiful boy into the world.

"I think we oughta get married, Belle Jane." Peter said it to the fields, to the auburn sweat glistening on his mare's hind.

What could you ask for, after a wrongdoing like that?

Of course, they would get married. They would find a judge. They would eat oysters.

"We'll tell your folks once we're all settled."

Why did he want it? What was all of this to him? A partnership, that parlour? Or did he love her in the thorny, sorry way she loved him?

No one else, she felt, could know the truth and want her. Besides, she could still be the "Belle Jane" of her dreams in Butte, couldn't she? Hold the crowd and their rings of smoke as she told the stories told to her by Rocco, and give the recitations as she'd always done at school? No, Butte was not New York, not even Chicago or Salt Lake, but it was not Philipsburg. Why was the face of that young woman English teacher, Miss Pansy Humphrey, who'd praised her so, coursing in her mind's eye just now? Why was the ride to the judge's fine brick house so quick? How was it still daylight? Gosh, how her world had changed these hours.

Peter turned his head to her and she was sure: if his lashes were so light and soft, his heart would be too.

Mrs. Junk.

Here she was, waiting, now, for the judge, doubts snaking at her neck like tiny sisters whispering secrets. She reminded herself of what Peter'd said to her, that first time, in the moonlight. "Belle Jane, you're full of stars."

ESTRAYED

Bay Mare, Blazed Face, with bay colt branded (tilted h with third leg) on jaw; mare branded 47 *on left hip and same as colt on right jaw. Ten dollars reward for return to Chas. Young, Gilt Edge, Mont.*

4

1900

THE PHILIPSBURG MAIL

Surprised Their Friends

A quiet wedding took place in Butte, September 5th. Miss Belle Corneil of this place and Mr. Peter Junk of Butte being the contracting parties. The young couple had intended to create a pleasant surprise to the bride's parents, and had agreed not to advise them of the marriage until their home was all furnished and they were completely located. Last week, however, the young Mrs. Junk became suddenly ill and was obliged to advise her sister Lillie to that effect. Miss Lillie went to Butte Monday and then the secret leaked out. Mrs. Junk is now at St. Paul's Hospital, gradually recovering from her illness. It is hoped by her many friends that she will visit Philipsburg and give them the opportunity to extend congratulations in person.

IT WAS THE MOST horrible hour at the hospital, late afternoon, say five, when the sun fell, dead-tired, at her window and said: *There are still so many hours left, but no more good can come of this day.* And she was alone with the racket of some lady who laughed too loud, far too loud, and another who spoke so fast and for such durations in another language—Polish?—that Belle Jane wondered if it weren't a recording.

Here she was, a pretty little withered thing, a paint-chipped ballerina standing on a half-broke windup music box. Even worse, Annie was on her way.

It was the oysters, she was sure. All the next day, she was sick until only the greenest, sourest trails of her insides were left. Mrs. Dunsmore brought her glasses of water and only nodded when Belle Jane asked if she might ring Lillie.

Belle Jane heard Lillie's sweet voice, nothing to it, and thought she might cry.

"Hello, you've got Philipsburg, how may I direct your call?" Lillie was the "hello girl" at the central telephone office, and she must've said how'do just like this, just as sweet, to a dozen people a day.

"Lillie."

"Belle Jane?"

"Lillie, I'm sick."

"What's wrong?"

"The oysters."

"Oysters?"

"After we got married."

"What now? Belle Jane, I heard you say you got married."

"I know."

"Oh dear. Oh, my board's lightin' up. These elections, got governor people calling."

"To Peter."

"Peter *Junk*?"

Oh, the way Lillie said it. A packrat could expect a warmer greeting. Belle Jane said nothing.

"Belle, I've got to go, what are you, what can I—"

"I can't think."

"I'll come. I'll get the evening train."

"Please."

It was all a bad dream, she was sure. The oysters, the judge, the wheel, the buttons. A bad dream.

Lillie'd tried to evade Annie's questions, everyone's questions: when the hello girl left, the whole town knew, even if Lillie got Edna Wyman to cover.

Lillie got to Butte just after eight, not long before Mrs. Dunsmore insisted Peter Junk—who finally called on Belle and who had to balance himself on the gate to stay upright—take Belle Jane to the hospital. Mrs. Dunsmore told Lillie to take the Victoria Room for the night ("Belle's room might put you off," she whispered, and indeed, the reek of bile lingered, for she'd only just got Belle Jane off into that cart).

Now, here was Lillie, at Belle Jane's bedside on the third floor of St. Paul's, lines of the streetcars jittering in the distance. It was not yet seven in the morning, breakfast hadn't been by. It was a dreamy place, in that same-faces seemed to float past without quite ever touching you, over and over.

"Annie said, 'Caroline, you better cross your heart three times and hope to die and sink dead if you don't call and tell me the truth.' She called me *Caroline*. Belle Jane, you've got to tell her."

"I'll get better."

"No, not that. About Peter. Do you even have a ring? Maybe it's not too late to—"

Peter appeared at the door in the same suit he'd worn three days now.

"Lillie." Peter winked at her.

"Peter."

"I got my deliveries, but I wanted to bring you these." He pushed a bouquet of flowers—blue flax, baby blue eyes, wallflowers, aspen daisies—against Belle Jane's nose and a crest of fern poked her in the eye.

"Oh!"

"Shoot."

"Well, thank you, Peter," Belle managed, eyeing Lillie to take them. "They're just lovely."

It wasn't so bad, being the clever one, the one who was loved more. Or was it? Of course he was out celebrating the good news, but the indulging in strong drink, she felt, would not do.

"You two," Peter said, looking from Belle Jane to Lillie, and back, with a wide, joyful voice of discovery, "you could be twins, couldn't you?"

Belle Jane couldn't imagine how she must look right now, an ugly forest mushroom, flat-headed and mottled and clammy. But on a good day, a very good day, she and Lillie might look alike: black-coloured eyes, dark curls, and long faces, though as Annie said, each girl wore hers well. They were broad-shouldered, big-boned girls, not at all like their ribby, titless mother. And it'd given them a kind of authority or confidence, ever since about age ten, in those years when girls get a leg up over boys in growing. Oh Lillie, Belle Jane thought, this is the end of all our exploring.

"I'm sure she'll have a ring soon, tell us apart," said Lillie.

Peter was twisting at a match, had a cigarette in his mouth, said, "Too damn hot in here to smoke."

He wiped his forehead and with stubby, bloated fingers, he stuffed the matches and the smokes back in his jacket pocket, took Belle's hand. "Yes, she'll have a ring, real pretty, won't you Belle Jane?"

It all seemed so wild last night, but now it just felt cheap. Embarrassing, really. No ring. No story. No photograph, which even her child-bride mother had had (or claimed to, for Annie surely looked a few years older than thirteen, wearing a gorgeous, tailored mohair jacket, curiously in the style of a regimental coat, embellished with braiding and buttons like ears, and she stood, without a care, as if eyeing the pasture on a Tuesday afternoon, while her father, sitting and clasping a rolled newspaper, wore a blue-black double-breasted jacket and waistcoat, from which the tail of his timepiece dangled).

Lillie knew why Belle Jane'd gone to Rossland those six months, and had suspected Peter, who'd tried giving Belle Jane rides home from Monday rehearsals when her sister was in that play, *The Man from Maine*, until Annie found out and put a stop to it. Lillie was made to stay every night during the show's run at the opera house, too. It got so Lillie knew all Mable Von Cruger's lines just as well, and one of the male character's lines came to Lillie now: "Have you taken leave of your senses? My fingers are itchin' to squeeze your windpipe."

Lillie and Peter, the gaze of both of them was making Belle Jane sick. She closed her eyes. Was she getting well, or more ill?

She was reminded that in the animal world, if a fox dog comes upon a vixen in a trap, he will kill her at the throat. If a cow becomes impaled and bellows his woes, the whole herd will rush over and gore her.

STRAYED OR STOLEN

My small bay saddle pony, branded [M] *on left thigh. Disappeared from my barn in Lewistown about two weeks ago. If strayed, may be found on the range between this place and Ubet. A suitable reward will be paid for his return or for information leading to recovery.*
Girard Smith

5

1900

LUCKY, LILLIE CAME WHEN SHE DID. A train was wrecked that morning at Tusler; heavy rains had caused the tracks to spread. The engineer had four fingers cut off, the fireman was dead and the brakeman was swollen blue but breathing. Trains wouldn't be running on the Northern Pacific Line for some time.

"Four fingers," said Lillie, repeating what she'd heard at The Sherman. "Man at the Bi-Metallic just lost a finger. Hand got caught under the damper? Chopped his middle finger right off."

"*Lillie*."

Peter chuckled, held back his joke, then went for it. "Guess he won't be givin' anyone the bird."

(*The bird*, the finger, was just becoming regular in Montana, and the cow boys, long obsessed with illustrating and imagining the form of cocks, were great fans. It's believed the middle finger came to America by way of Italian immigrants; the Romans had called the gesture *digitus impudicus*. The first known photograph of the ancient insult was captured in 1886, when the Boston Beaneaters' pitcher Charles "Old Hoss" Radbourn gave the finger to a cameraman in a team photograph, his finger just inches away from an outfielder's ear.)

"*Peter.*"

Were they both here? Could they both not tell she felt like death? There'd been a lightness, after the last time she'd gotten sick in the tin. She'd slept until the next afternoon and woke with a choking fever, searing cramps and the pick of an axe at her skull.

Doctor Treacy said: "You did come here with food poisoning, little lady, and I ought to have that place of Hum Fay's shut down, but what you've got now is something else. I don't want to alarm you and getting fussed won't matter a dime anyway," he said, and nodded at Lillie, as if bringing her on side, so as to prevent dramatics, "but you're presenting as having typhoid."

"Oh heaven and stars," Lillie said, eyeing the doctor's pursed mouth, his dark, hairy hands. "What'll we do?"

"You'll wait," Dr. Treacy said.

Now, now that they knew Belle Jane was quite ill and Annie was stayed for a few days, the three of them fell into a childish pit where nothing mattered, all was doomed, time was still.

Day three in the hospital, Lillie slid beside her sister on the cot. She had her boots off and covered her stockings with a blue wool blanket that made Belle Jane too hot. She was braiding her sister's hair, which stank of oil and sick until Lillie'd powdered it. If she was worried about catching the fever, it didn't show. Perhaps she thought they were of the tough Irish stock that had survived cholera or that Lillie might as well come down with typhoid since she was so long at the hospital and couldn't take the train back to Philipsburg yet anyway.

"Lillie, why hasn't Fanny been by?"

"She went home."

Home, the ranch where her daddy grew alfalfa for a herd of two hundred cattle and turned foreign tenderfoots into dudes.

"Why? Must be the other girls are running off their feet. She go home to help with the drive?"

The cattle drive, to bring the cows down from the mountains.

"No."

"Why, then?"

"Ira." Lillie took a breath, shook her head.

"What happened?"

"There was a cow got tangled by a rope. Ira had his knife and cut the rope and soon as it was half-free it got kicking some. First"—her voice broke—"they thought he'd come through. Just some broken ribs. But Ira died. Internal bleeding, doctor said."

Doctor said doctor said doctor said. If Belle Jane heard it one more time she'd scream. Oh, poor Fanny. She loved Fanny. Her silver-blue eyes and her candy for lunch; they could both claim having been the girl who won the most footraces at school.

"I'll send a card for you."

"Will you?"

"Sure."

"And some of my crocheting. You know what she'd love? She'd love those pieces I was working on last Christmas, the yoke and the—"

How could she remember the word for *yoke*, the delicate neckpiece, but not the matching bits that sat over the wrist. Together, they made any drab black dress elegant. One of a kind, at least.

"The cuffs?"

Belle Jane smiled.

"You'll give her that?"

Belle Jane nodded at the window. Quite beyond, the fists of mill smoke puttered up the side of the butte.

"You're a dear creature, Belle Jane." Lillie kissed her sister's forehead, clammy as it was.

"Will you put some earrings on me? These sheets, I can't stand it. I don't believe I'll say this, but I want to go home."

Home, her bedroom at the Corneil place with wicker rocker chair where she'd practised at her lacework in quiet, the tasselled canopy under which she'd made her mid-night girl wishes, the door to nowhere (for the balcony and stairs had never been built). Footsteps from Annie. She thought but did not say aloud, I want my mother.

"Lillie, you love me, don't you?"

"I love you, Belle Jane," and she nuzzled her nose to her sister's. "You're my kitty sissy," she said, harking back to the summer at the ranch when they'd pretended to be cats, even licked Mary-Alice and Annie May's cheeks, and prowled around the bunk houses until they spied One-eyed Jim flat on his back, stroking his willy with frightening swiftness. The girls giggled and Jim spat, "Little bitches." Annie put an end to the cat-acting by horse-whipping their bottoms.

But Lord, what will Annie have her do now?

$25 Reward

For information leading to a knowledge,
of any one driving my stock from their
accustomed range or pasture; or mutilating
or changing the brand of my stock.
R.C. Matterin, Forest Grove

6

1900

The Philipsburg Mail

Mrs. Geo Corneil went to Butte yesterday
to visit her daughter, Mrs. Junk, who is
quite ill.

ANNIE'S LIP TREMBLED.

"Mary and Joseph, you had a chance, Belinda Jane. Why to heck do you think we sent you away? Girl's gone six months, we all know why. But you play the part and folks play the part and things carry on. You can turn a blind eye to what's not flaunted."

Her mother was not her mother, but a wild goose gone dotty. She sat on the bed, the only place to sit in this sorry room, at the farthest corner from her daughter. Annie's gloved fingers pressed at the labyrinth of yarns of the blanket, one Annie'd made for her on going away to college. The pattern was cream white wheels, each with six diamond-shaped arms stretching over to another wheel—a field of white sunflower sisters, arms locked against the boys. That's how Belle Jane'd seen it, when she first opened the box. She was a girl, then.

"Peter Junk delivers *beer*, Belinda Jane. Beer. You know what he makes a week? Hope you like typing at Hennessy's. After we put you through *college*. We thought you'd be the one to go ahead. Well," and she paused, waved her hand over the yellow rotting feel of the room, "you're going to be workin' there a long time. Long time."

What Annie wanted for her daughter was a second chance to claim her own life, have the freedom to leave stenography once she had a husband, a *good* husband. Not some place in between and used up, like dirty dish water.

Outside, they heard horses, a mother calling for Frankie. The world was insisting on itself.

Annie glared at her shrunken daughter with bloodshot eyes, waited for Belle Jane to accept the gaze.

"He didn't even ask after you. Didn't write *one* letter."

"He's married me now. We're going to find rooms."

"You *stupid* girl." Her fist pounded the bed. "I can't hear such talk."

What Annie was thinking about then was the Connolly and McGuiness women back in Galway, seeding and plowing, doing men's work in the fields for far less pay; eating potatoes when there was some, herbs and roots when there wasn't. That Annie herself had had her hands rough as sticks in the workhouse garden; it'd taken two weeks for her hands to get clean and soft enough for the needle when she got a place doing lace work for an embroiderer at age nine, or was she ten? That Ireland had been cursed, but they'd made it to America eating soggy flitch eight weeks. That she'd pictured for Belinda Jane silk dresses and feathers in her hat, a big fat bleeding steak on her plate.

"You *slunk* around, and you lied."

The mad goose stood, boot heels clacking as she went to the room's one window and peered down at the street below, and then back at her daughter, who'd closed her eyes to it all, was imagining a goose hunt, that pearly cry as one falls to the clutch of grasses.

"Where is he now?"

The Anaconda Standard

Mrs. George Corneil, who has been
in Butte the past month attending her
daughter, Mrs. Peter Junk, during her
illness, returned Monday bringing
Mrs. Junk with her.

*

Lillie and Belle Jane were setting the table for Christmas dinner in Butte when they heard the news about the train engineer who blew out his brains the night before. Belle Jane had only been back with Peter a few weeks, on her feet a few days. She'd felt a strange rush of purpose and energy with her sister around. There they were, steam rising from pots, and Peter calling out the headlines from the settee between twirls of his second drink, an old fashioned.

That's a man, saying a thing like that before Christmas dinner.

Lillie left on the Jawbone back to Butte and then Philipsburg on the last day of December. Belle Jane took the very next train after her. Stayed three months, softened to Peter's appeals (*Belle Jane you are my wife, we swore it!*) and returned, but Belle Jane was back in Philipsburg again within days, and stayed until May, when she took the train with Annie, Annie May and Mary-Alice, who parted ways with Belle Jane in Butte, while those three ventured on to Alturas, California, to visit the McGinnis clan.

Women travelled, diseases travelled. Last names were lost. It wasn't so long ago that Honoria McGuinness had been a skinny, gazey girl in a thready dress, leaving a workhouse for a ship for America.

Men travelled, diseases travelled. Spanish flu, scarlet fever, the kind that make your loins scab and burn. Was Peter a philanderer, infecting his charming wife, whose company was much preferred at parties? Did he prefer the company of drink, its warmth, its filter over truth? Never mind the muggy, brew-rot odour of his armpits, that sometimes he'd get a smash for getting lippy. That not once but twice, after such a brawl, Belle Jane'd thought, It's his funeral.

THE BUTTE DAILY POST

ALLEGED STREET BLOCKADE

Peter Junk Got His Team All Tangled Up

PETER JUNK, a driver for the Centennial Brewing Company was arrested this way with his wagon and four horses. He was released on a bond of $20, put up by LP Best.

The point of the alleged blockade was Broadway and Main streets. Junk was driving towards Main, but just as his leaders were about to cross the line a policeman stopped the whole caravan because there was a funeral a mile and a half long passing down the street. Junk turned his horses and wagon sideways across the street car track to wait for the funeral to pass, but while waiting a street car came along. The policeman ordered him to switch around and let the car pass, but he failed to get the horses in the right position and the policeman arrested him.

Such a funeral procession was held for little Laura Murphy, the eleven-year-old daughter of ex-undersheriff J.E. Murphy. She died of scarlet fever. At the death house, the adjoining shack of the hospital where corpses were kept, the nurse who'd dressed Laura later remarked to Belle Jane what pretty nose freckles the girl had and said a silent prayer that each marked a nice memory—berrying in June, maybe, or rocking on a grandmother's lap to a lullaby. Owing to the contagiousness of the fever, on the day of the funeral, none of the mourners were permitted at the Murphy House, but all 100 carriages waited there, and proceeded down Montana Street to attend the services at the Catholic Cemetery. The coffin was cream white with sparkled brass handles, and as it was lowered into the earth, women and boys and girls tossed in flowers: grand begonias, light-as-a-kiss lilies, roses ordered special. Two of Laura's cousins dashed to tree crooks and fields for wildflowers: heathers and bear grass, pink snowberries and woodland stars. Every single young child of Butte who could walk, and some still in flannelette sheet diapers, some who'd never even known Laura, joined in. *A thousand flowers for Laura*, they'd chanted. Soft like, so the earth would not crush her, should she come to life and want to play. It was dark when the undertaker asked back Father Batens, who bawled at the sight: the moonlight, those bare feet and soiled little fingers, the petals.

The next Friday, Peter was tried and discharged, owing to the fact that city ordinances (pertaining to public morals about making way for funeral processions) failed to cover that portion of the streetcar crossing, where his four-horse team and wagon, loaded heavy with kegs, had nearly caused a tragedy, or at least quite a nuisance, in the midst of Laura Murphy's funeral. Well, the sheriffs, police chief, detective and judge in attendance did not forget it.

Peter did have one friend in the courtroom, One-eyed Jim. There'd been a bar fight, a broken bottle, and One-eyed Jim got stabbed in his good eye, and would you know, the doctor got the first bad eye working, but not the newly injured one. Blind on the left now.

*

FERGUS COUNTY ARGUS

LEWISTOWN, MONTANA

APRIL 16, 1902

Call at Once

Now is your very best opportunity to
learn embroidery, Battenburg, Honiton
and point lace, Decore, Crochet and

other different kinds of lace making, which is taught by Mrs. Junk, sister of L.C. Corneil, who resides on Fourth avenue, just above the Judith bakery. Lessons are very reasonable; fifty cents an hour. All materials necessary can be bought from Mrs. Junk.

Not half bad, she thought, reading the advertisement she'd written herself. *Mrs. Junk*, I suppose I am. But I'm Belle Jane, too, and I can make it. She *could* make it just fine if she had to.

Belle Jane folded the paper and looked across Lillie's little room for that blackberry pie brought over by the twitchy woman who lived down and back with her bearded, backward son.

Lillie Lillie eat your pie
Lillie Lillie poke you in the eye

Swallowing the buttery crust, she read the article above her own, about the horses that seemed to have "run off almost right under the eyes of the ranchers." Stolen, run toward Musselshell was the guess. Brands had been mutilated, entire bunches had been lifted. For the first time in years, Belle Jane thought about Belle Starr. Belle Jane saw flashes of imaginings of her younger self as the bandit, riding high, pistol at her hips, just daring you. What had happened?

She was married to a man on the sauce, she slept too late in a dank two-roomed apartment, just hoping for card party invitations. She was growing old. She would be the kind of woman neighbour children would remember as the lady who gave them their first orange. Or, she would lose her mind, let the ale drink her, cause disturbances in the street.

THE BUTTE MINER

SEPT. 6, 1902

Mrs. McGregor and Mrs. Hutchins gave a card party Friday afternoon. The prizes were won by Mrs. Junk, Mrs. Bennett and Mrs. Kennedy.

*

THE BUTTE MINER

SEPT. 6, 1903

Surprise Party.

A very pleasant surprise party was given on Monday evening in honor of Mr. P. J. Quelette at his residence on South Main street. The evening was spent in dancing, music and songs. The guests particularly enjoyed the mandolin solos given by Mr. V. Rooney, also a recitation by Mrs. Junk and a violin solo by Mrs. Gertie Jones. The guests present were: Mr. and Mrs. P. J. Quelette, Mr. and Mrs. G. Jones, Mr. and Mrs. J. Kowen, Mr. and Mrs. T. Crum, Mr. and Mrs. Kimball, Mrs. Tilda Carney, Mrs. Junk, Mrs. P. Telin, Misses Alice Johnson, Bella Weinstock, Alice Sweet, Louise Kenny, Lizzie Fischer, Mae Kowen, Georgine Sullivan, Bessie Vaughn, Nellie Fowler, Mollie Rooney, N.M. Morton, Miss Courtney, Miss Parker, Mr. O. Nadeau, Doc tor Keenan, O. Connell, V. Rooney, A Giles, Abe Quelette, Gridllng, William Young, T.J. Handley, Clark.

Peter and Belle Jane had been talking circles about the St. Louis Fair since they left the station at Butte. They were going. They weren't going. They were getting a divorce.

But first, Lewistown, Montana, for a stay with Annie and George above The Busy Corner, the confectionary they'd bought for Lillie. The Corneils had left it all in Philipsburg, sold out and got into cigars, candy, local view calendars and fountain pens, but already George was talking saloons and horses, a 320-acre tract he might buy from the Santa Fe Pacific.

As the Pullman edged closer, they both knew Peter couldn't run away; conversely, he knew quite well the limits of his wife's ability to quarrel in public. After "a drink to sober up on," while Belle Jane pecked at old issues (*How much* did *he lose at Little Chicago? Was he gambling now? Did he want to die a tramp?),* Peter elected to tip his hat over his eyes, nod off for a spell.

"Peter," she whisper-yelled. She held taught the thread she'd been pulling through the lace doily she was sewing. Felt for the point of the needle. "You want a divorce, don't you? You want to divorce me?"

One of the glass lights above gave a rattle as the Pullman scuttled south, a horizon shiny with edges, like the gold of Judith Mountains, wouldn't be long now, and Mrs. Junk remembered when George'd had a 32-candle power incandescent streetlamp placed over the entrance of the saloon. *The Mail* had written about it, called the bar a "resort," a "popular" one too. Hadn't George Corneil done well. What would she be known for? Her needlework? Her nagging?

"I don't think you wanted to marry me, truly." She resumed her stitching. It was like breathing, like sleeping. Going away, just a little.

Would it be different, she wondered, if they'd run off to find a judge when she was nineteen? That was six years ago, now. She pictured a son, sitting between her and Peter, telling stories about arrows in the hills or catching trout long as his arm.

And if that wasn't the worst, they hadn't been able to have a child again. They'd all bled away. She only told Peter about the first two; she'd almost written Lillie once.

It was too easy, hating one another.

Peter was almost snoring now, a wheezy snore.

"You wanted to get in my skirts and my father's business, but he didn't want to partner with you, did he? You're a drunk. And a mooch!"

Annie'd said Peter was like a poultry mite: only red and shiny because it'd gorged on the blood of the hen. It made Belle

Jane sick, tallying all he'd spent those four years in taverns, when here she was, selling off celery boats to pay for their rooms. Well, she'd packed nearly everything, she always did when she went to stay with her parents. Was it his plan all along, going to Lewistown just so he could leave her there?

"You're a joke, Peter Junk. A joke and a lazy ass. You don't have the wherewithal to open your little beer parlour, do you? It's 1904, and you're still talkin—" Her voice rose, until she was whisper-yelling, though there was only an old man who smoked so regular his hair was yellow six rows ahead in the car, and some newlyweds, she'd guessed, without a care. "All this talking. Do something!"

Peter stirred, gave a snigger. "Oh, I'm doing something." He tipped his hat upright, leaned on the seat ahead, and stood, then stooped so close to her face she thought he might kiss her, turn it all around. Say, Come on baby, let's go!

But he said, "I'm goan to that fair." He tapped the seat top twice, for effect. "Alone."

He took two steps across the aisle, and sat down in the opposite seat.

"You go to that fair without me, Peter Junk, you can go to hell too." The needle, she knew just where she'd stick it.

It wasn't just the drinking, the lying. The turning up with torn, blood-spat shirts. Nights out with no word. Days gone. Shirtless on the street, hollering. It was the perfume. Jasmine. The thought of it made her stomach turn. There was an old woman at church, back in Philipsburg, Mrs. McLanahan, who wore it too, and Belle Jane'd grown to send wayward thoughts her way during hymnals on account of the association.

In a blink, he was back at her seat, fingers clutching her throat. It was an old move of his, the choking, when he'd had too much strong drink.

"You sure do have a mouth, Mrs. Junk," he spat. His eyes were bloodshot, each vessel a wrong that had been done to him, could be blamed. "You kiss your husband, with that mouth?"

It did not occur to her, that it had wrecked him too.

If they'd just looked in each other's eyes, truly.

Bootsteps at the back of the car. Peter let his hand drop, pretended to be caressing her. Almost kissed her as she swallowed air.

"Not anymore," she muttered.

Bastard, she thought. How did he do it? Twist it all around so that even though she could suffocate him under a pillow, she still wanted him to want her?

He wouldn't leave her. Would he?

FERGUS COUNTY DEMOCRAT
LEWISTON, MONTANA
SEPT. 6, 1904

Peter Junk who with his wife visited Mrs. Junk's parents, Mr. and Mrs. Geo Corneil, of this city for a week, left the middle of the week for St. Louis for a short visit to the fair. After visiting in other points in the east he will return to his home in Butte. Mrs. Junk will remain in the city until her husband returns from the east.

part two

SHE'LL RUIN YOUR BOYS

STRAYED

ONE BAY MARE ABOUT 1,050 LBS.
A little white on forehead, foretop, and
fetlocks clipped. Newly shod, no brand.
Call Connelly Ranch, South Butte.

7

1907

IT WAS EARLY AND SHADY and Belle Jane thought her eyes must've been tricking her. There stood a woman with her head at her feet: a tulip snapped in half; clock hands at six and five. And she was perfectly still.

Two schoolteachers Belle Jane'd met on the train had warned her about Rocky Hill.

The one with the chubby nose and the grand smile had whispered, "Prostitutes."

The one with the tiny head said, "And whatnot."

But it was precisely because the teachers had told her of the ills of Rocky Hill that Belle Jane'd told the stagecoach driver it was where she wanted to go. She couldn't spend a single cent that could be saved.

"You certain?"

Belle Jane had nodded, pretended she gave those directions every day. "The lodging house."

Now it was morning, and she hadn't slept but for an hour, around four, she'd guessed, and she'd washed her face as the sun rose and stepped out of those stuffy, warped floorboard rooms of Mrs. Sparks to find the Chinese cooks cutting into alleys, a boy at the carriage maker's hammering at a wheel nut, and this woman, bent down, forehead just inches from the stone-earth. What does one do, in this situation? Belle Jane knew her conscience would nitpick at her for days if she didn't do *something*. What if she woke the woman up from a nightmare or she was inebriated? Or she had the cool blade of a butcher's knife tucked just up her sleeve until some innocent person approached? Who knows what happened in *cities*.

Keeping quite a distance, Belle Jane spoke with a gentle voice: "Are you quite all right?"

The woman opened her eyes and squinted, as if dust had just been thrown at her face. She blinked and said, "I dropped my ten-cent pieces." She feigned to study the dirt for their glint.

Belle Jane stood there, dumb as a cow, staring. The woman had lost her teeth, had grimy fingers, the brightest blue eyes. On confirming the coins could not be found, the woman glanced up, flashed an arm at Belle Jane.

"Do you have the time?"

Belle Jane took a moment before simply replying, "I think it's nearing seven."

"Oh good. Well then," she said and waddled off following the shadows of tall brick walls.

Belle Jane thought she would think about this woman all day, wonder where she hobbled off to, which dark corners would have her tonight, what she did to earn those lost coins. But she didn't. Instead, she wondered about herself in relation to that woman: how quickly could *she* be erased, uncared about? Streetwalking and nearly licking cockroaches.

She'd said to heck with Montana. Montana was what was wrong with her life.

Peter, for one. Finally got his bar, Johnson House, partnering with two others. He was charged a few months ago for selling beer to a child (seven-year-old Frankie McLellan, a good boy from South Idaho Street who'd said the beer was for his mother but had been paid a nickel by Gus Downey and his wife to have the dinner bucket filled).

Annie.

The trains carting her to the same same-people towns.

The Maude Foxes of West Copper Street who invited her to card parties, it felt, only to serve her a sliver of their lives, the silver berry bowls and orange cups, and gossip about her as they set out cloth napkins and gold spoons. In those little rooms in Butte, and her folks' in Lewistown, the air always had that charge, of *should've*.

She woke up one ugly March morning and knew she had to go. That minute. She would've taken a freight.

Well, now she was in Spokane with one silver buckled suitcase and that certificate from the business college. "It's not too late," Lillie'd said. Belle Jane had wondered, For what? Here she was, single, going on twenty-eight, starting over. It felt a lot like the first spring ride on her appaloosa on a snow-warm afternoon in April, when the mare might buck, might take you all the way to town twenty miles an hour. Lillie, she got married about a month after Peter Junk left Belle Jane in Lewistown and went to that fair. The groom was Johnnie Harvey, a shorter man with a good smile who knew how to dress. A stagecoach driver and sometimes salesman. The ceremony was not at St. Leo's but at home, Annie and George's, just the family and Reverend Pfaus. Had Lillie kept it simple because Belle Jane was on the down, bony and baggy-eyed? The wedding announcement in the paper said, "There has never been a more popular young woman in Lewistown than Miss Corneil." As Belle Jane'd looked on at her sister that night, standing by the pianoforte in her ruffles and the long lace veil Lillie'd stitched herself, she couldn't help but feel a lamenting.

Should've.

What did the air carry here, in the Peerless Employment Company office at 411½ Main? It said, *Just you try*. Cities, that's where you could make a good wage, even women. Ten dollars a week. What she wanted was a position at city hall or the state college, be an assistant, maybe even executive assistant, she'd have her own coat rack and desk far from the rest of the question-asking girls doing letters. As Belle Jane sat on a wooden bench and waited to be met, she put on her pleasant smile and pretended to read her paper, mindful not to appear a country booby looking at every little thing. Oh, if she just had that model's suit, the panama skirt and that manly jacket, in electric gray. She inhaled the tang of the office: dusty carpets, cold tea, typewriter ink, the menthol-sweet of men's aftershave. She was glad she'd purchased a paper to while the time, cast a world in which she could sit, apart from the others, distract herself from the image: Belle Jane as the dirty, toothless streetwalker.

The man across from her had tried to catch her eye once, twice already as the both of them looked up when the clerk's door opened, first to a boy with a satchel, then an old man in a brown suit. Finally, to put an end to it, she let the stranger with the slick hair smile at her. He wore the lightest blue shirt, was such a big man that she considered his history. No train man or miner or cow boy had meat like that on his bones. What was it like, being astride a man like that?

"Gale Willard," he said, with a grin, as if he'd read her mind or was confident about the answer.

"Belle Jane," she said, trying to still the blushing of her wayward thoughts.

"That's something, isn't it, 'bout that lunatic?" said Mr. Willard, pointing at the article on the backside of her pages: "Sheriff Gets Lunatic After a Long Chase." It was the half-gone finger next to his left thumb that did the pointing. He was not shy about that either, the left-handedness or the half-lost finger. Mr. Willard crossed a leg and leaned in, as if they were familiar, cousins on grandma's porch after church. "I worked there,

Medical Lake, about a month, but the boss was trying to get us to use meat gone bad and I said, 'I won't do it.' My dad was a meat cutter, in Michigan, and I know meats. Doesn't take much to smell when it's off."

She did know. Summers at the ranch, she hadn't shied the butchering pen or the cook's table for the dinners that followed: roast, steaks, ribs, stew.

(The lunatic had had quite a feast: After escaping the asylum, Frank Rou knocked on the door of farm after farm, each wife fed him while thinking him a bit peculiar, the way he put his hand to his ear and turned his head to the roof as if to hear a message better. The farmers reported it to the authorities, and the "lunatic," already six dinners in, put up quite a fight about getting into the sheriff's rig, but once he was seated, he smiled and seemed "happy with the thought of the ride ahead," possibly with the next meal in mind.)

"Meat cutter's a good trade," she said, then lost her air, and her voice went quiet. She thought of the virtue her mother always spoke of, the one thing you really wanted in a husband. *Steady*.

"It is . . ." and Mr. Willard drew out the second word, to cue his thoughts on a contrast, draw her in. "You might be surprised, cooks take a lot of pride in their work."

She knew that too. It was one of George Corneil's secrets, keeping a saloon with the best food in town. The good ones *could* cook—lamb soup, lobster salad, wild turkey, quail patties—but they'd been strange men. "Cocky about their vally," George said, always asking for more. Those cooks always had queer looks: very short and childlike in the face yet almost bald, tall and witch-nosed and pigeon-toed, handsome and big-footed. Shifty, never stayed half a year. Cooks in general had it even worse now that Typhoid Mary was in the papers.

(Mary Mallon was the Long Island house cook who'd sickened dozens and left three dead among seven of eight families she worked for. It had taken five police officers to cart off the little Irish cook ("an angry lion") to the isolation clinic at

North Brother Island. That's what they did now, quarantined the typhoid cases. Mary Mallon, asymptomatic all the while, would be there three years, until she swore she was well, and wouldn't cook again.)

"Mr. Willard, we'll have you in now."

Belle Jane smiled at the clerk, daydreamed about her running off to get married tonight, putting in her notice, remembering that lovely woman from Butte who might do to take her place.

Mr. Willard stood, gave his pant legs a shake. "You have a last name, Belle Jane?"

Shit. She'd need a last name to apply for the job. She felt for the edges of the certificate on her lap. What should she say? They'd divorced and she would wipe him and those seven years from her memory if she could, and she could, she was sure. She'd asked the judge to restore her maiden name.

"Corneil. Belle Jane Corneil."

*

He was sweating and she was sweating and the whole dance hall was athunder: knees and piano keys, elbows and lights. So packed with men and women the waxed floor could not be seen. One of the trumpets wheezed low and the song sounded out, and now it was just their hearts.

In the middle of the hall, couples began parting, making way.

A woman in a red dress and a man in a gray suit hollered out and started the dance: arms and legs outstretched wide, hands shaking; and then just barely hugging into each other, head tucked, bottoms up but still a rod between their middles; stepping back and then back-to-back arms high, like ghosts.

"What do they call this?"

"Grizzly Bear," he said, but the whoops and shrieks of the other couples, surprised but not shocked by the bawdy movements, made it hard to hear.

"The what?"

"The Grizzly Bear."

Her eyes widened: so it was, a pair of dancing bears, also, a frightened couple who'd come upon a bear. To be our wild selves, we danced like beasts.

(The Grizzly Bear, a descendant of the Turkey Trot, was said to have been designed in San Francisco and had been all the rage in the halls of Staten Island for years already, but the "abomination"—as bad, to some, as the San Francisco Glide, and which master dancers said should rightly be called "the hoochie coochie"—would soon be spoiled: mayors of New York City, Boston, St. Louis and Philadelphia would ban the Grizzly Bear from dance halls. Of course, this made its popularity only swell. Instructors were begged to teach it, but they, too, objected. It was "the swaying of the hips.")

Belle Jane spotted her teacher friends, the ones she'd met on the train into Spokane, on the other side of the bear dancers, covering their mouths. They'd run into each other at the post office that afternoon and they'd invited her to the hall, where she quickly spotted Gale. Girls were lining up to dance with him he was so good.

What fun, she thought. She liked the dance, the way you could make it what you wanted it to be. She found she liked this Gale Willard. He was joyful and he smelled good and gosh, for a big man, he could dance.

The swells of the raggy music, their hips.

*

Belle Jane sent a postcard to Lillie, of the upper falls rushing the bridge:

> *Was at a dance last night. Had a time. See what you're missing?*
>
> *Your loving sister,*
> *Belle Jane*

Mrs. Caroline Harvey's postcard (of San Diego Bay and its streets lined with terracotta roofs and palms) said:

Weather is real nice here.
In the 80's most days.
We've got a piano now. Wish you were here to play.
Had a party here Saturday last, 25 people.
Wasn't the same, without you.
We've made some dear friends.
Happy to know you have too.
You surely are 'shiny.'

Ever yours,
Lillie

And they danced. Night after night, after Gale got off work at the restaurant, until one night it was so late it was morning on her sheets and she woke to him kissing her shins, the tickle of his stubble.

"That wasn't your first time, was it?"

"Was it yours?"

His pants had been tossed on a lamp, her skirts on the lone chair by the window. Be hell to pay with the old landlady, but Belle Jane didn't care.

"That's all right, you know."

"Well, I'm glad you think so."

He held her ankles, started kissing her again.

*

They kept up the dancing a good long while. One Sunday morning, though, Belle Jane dared to linger at her looking glass—parched lips, crow's feet wrinkles—and thought, it's too much, these late nights. I'm too old.

"Thir-ty," she said aloud, each syllable enunciated with care, as if to convince an audience, or at least herself, though she was hardly twenty-nine yet. *Thirty*. The sound of it was so odd. *Thirty.*

Divorced. Single. There was something similarly short and rude in those words. Shameful. And living in this unreal world of doing the Grizzly Bear and pretending she was twenty had got her feeling low: she hadn't written Lillie in two months, there was rooster shit on her boots six days now and she just couldn't bring herself to do anything about it.

Through a friend, a brother of one of the teachers, she'd finally got a place at Weldon and Fisk, doing letters for Mr. Coffin, a lawyer who mostly dealt with estates. "Not a lot of carrying on, estate law," he'd said, as they'd strolled past the office of a colleague who was consoling a sobbing *divorced single thirty*-something woman.

Belle Jane had tried to be fun Belle Jane *and* "Miss Corneil the secretary," but one morning it took her the better part of an hour to write a simple letter to a young man asking him to call with his grandad's land title. She and Gale'd been out until two and her brain was still back on her pillow. Well, she couldn't keep it up. Gale kept going with the restaurant crowd, after getting off at ten or so, just about the time she was trying to fall asleep, hoping he wasn't doing the Texas Tommy with that sprite blonde pianist from Walla Walla.

The next week, Belle Jane was even more tired, even though she had not gone out and found she could sleep quite easily when she drifted off to images of Miss Walla Walla twisting her ankle, or Gale, that head tilted "oh come on" smile of his, slipping on the doorstep in the dark and knocking his noggin.

He did not drink. He did not flirt with the help (much). He just liked to shake a leg.

Was he what she wanted? Someone who wasn't always out getting roostered. Who did not choke her or forget her.

With his working nights and going out, sometimes it seemed days between moments when she and Gale were both at the apartment, awake, at the table, needing something from the other. He'd fix her a grilled egg and green tomato sandwich and she'd apologize about the state of the kitchen and he'd say, "That's all right." Sometimes, she'd think, if there's anything worse than a man that's mean, it's a man that's too nice. He was that way on the sheets, too. Didn't happen so much anymore but early on, when they'd gone so long he couldn't go anymore—and sometimes, when they'd only just started—Gale found another way; sometimes that involved his mouth; sometimes that involved stand-ins, objects from the kitchen, mostly. She never did ask why sometimes he just couldn't, but he was quick to show he could please her just the same.

"I'll show you what, Belle Jane," he'd say. Once, twice, it was a Lolly Pop, that new candy on a stick (named after a famous racehorse), and he'd retrieve it from the depths of her to lick it, then start again.

Lying on tousled, sweaty sheets after the radiant coming down of it all, she nagged at herself: You've had your fun. Now go find someone older, ace high. A cow man with so many acres it'd take days to ride the place, and a house with a salon and a big fat porch to see the Corneils comin' to call. He'd be a widow, with boys, a little girl. Or not, and she would raise horses, read books set by the sea of England, and crochet. Light up the place.

But after one such rendezvous, Gale stroked her bare arm and said, "Never met a woman like you, Belle Jane." He paused, rubbed his jaw stubble. Behind them, rain drizzled at the window. "Will you be my wife?"

It felt like she was a wheel in a wheel that was already going. And what if she got spat on the road?

STOLEN

BAY MARE, BLACK MANE AND tail, white star on forehead, branded MQ on right shoulder, shoes on hind feet, quarter crack on left hind foot, low built, short, heavy neck. Ten dollars reward for return to Mrs. S.G. Rand, Elkhorn stable, Lewistown.

8

1908

THE SPOKESMAN-REVIEW, MAY 23, 1908

FROM THE RECORDS

Licensed to Wed: Gale B. Willard (25) of Grand Rapids, Mich., and Belinda Carneil (24), of Lewistown, Mont.

IT WAS ALL WRONG, the way they had it. Misspellings were not uncommon, but the age? Well—on the Certificate of Marriage, where the instructions asked one to strike out the details that do not apply—Belle Jane had elected to stretch the truth on some of the "personal and statistical particulars."

Full name: Belinda Corneil
Residence: Lewistown, Mont.
Age at last birthday: 24 years

Color or race: White
Single, ~~Widowed or Divorced~~
Number of Marriage: 1st
Birthplace: Nevada
Occupation: (blank)
Name of Father: George Corneil
Birthplace of Father: Canada
Maiden Name of Mother: Anna McGinnis
Birthplace of Mother: Ireland

Little white lies, weren't they? Spokane was what, nearly 500 miles from Lewistown?

*

About one in the afternoon at Weldon and Fisk, Belle Jane felt her eyes grow heavy, her fingers slow and dumb. Her thoughts, swimming off and slipping back, like the tide. What would she get at the butcher's? What was that song Lillie used to always ask her to play, about the ship? She felt as if she were on a raft now, languid and ill and despondent. Why? She hadn't been to the dance hall now in two months. Most excitement in her life was washing Gale's socks.

The bell above the door gave a trickle and shook her awake. It was a beautiful woman dressed in black, backing in with her buggy. It was only lately Belle Jane could even bring herself to look in the direction of buggies. After all those almosts with Peter, she'd told herself a story: she was being punished and she would not ever have a baby to keep.

While the woman spoke—of a husband, farm, grandfather, Moses Lake, widow now—Belle Jane's mind swam past the events of recent weeks: her and Gale that afternoon, all afternoon. That stack of napkins in her drawer.

The baby in the pram sat up: a boy with long, curly brown hair. He slapped his tin rattle at the canopy. And she knew.

*

Little Georgie came quick: just two hours of *oh-I-can't* pangs that began after a plate of hotcakes drizzled in chocolate, Gale's special. At the speed of the delivery, the nurses were impressed, even suspicious. "First babies don't usually come so easy." Later, Gale stood in her hospital room, George swaddled in her arms, his little nose in the early spring sunlight, and said, "This is quite a thing."

Oh, to have this boy at her chest, sound asleep (for what a journey!), not a thing to fear in the world, for he can hear his mother's heartbeat.

A silent kind of crying took over. There was a chance the crying would spill up, be seen. Surely they'd all think she was being an emotional new mother, rather than one who might not deserve this second chance.

Gale kissed her forehead, then took her hand, quivering. "I'm proud of you," he said.

And they gazed at yawning Georgie: perfect skin, fat cheeks, dark hair. Fists of might. Those two hours were long, and a kind of funeral. For all her mind had been able to shut out those ten years, her body remembered. All of it crashed over her—her hair on her face and that first piercing thrust lying in the field with Peter, the ever-rocky journey through the mountains to Canada, the window she thought to leap from, the devil's grip on her womb, the eerie cool of the birthing hall after the baby was carried away. The sour breath of the tiny nun who, hours later, whispered, "A boy." Where was he now? In her waking, she never did permit herself to wonder, for that question was an old stone well; in her sleeping, she had nightmares of the baby waking up in the dark, crying and alone, and she was just outside the window so she could even feel the thrum of his lungs but the window could not be shattered, and at the door, the nuns formed a body-wall and shushed her, and she obeyed, backed away. As they waited for the stage out, Annie, her mother—who'd lost two boys, one aged five, one newly born—had passed her a yellow after-dinner mint and said:

"You look back, you'll get trapped like a kit fox. And everything else'll go on without you."

This morning, as a very tall blonde nurse with a mole at her jaw had held Belle Jane's hand, it all passed, like a procession. And Belle Jane pushed, spoke in her mind to the baby who left her, "Never goodbye," and to the one who was here now: "Please come, little one. Mama's here."

Gale, half-sat next to her on the iron hospital bed, rubbed her hand, eyes fixed on Georgie. "Who can I call?"

She was not surprised that she did not want her mother now. Maybe it was right, what Annie'd made her do. Maybe it wasn't. But Belle Jane'd felt a lightness, at letting go. The resentment, that time (though of course not the boy), it could be an autumn leaf. Annie was still her mother, but Belle Jane was a mother now too. And Annie had no idea. Belle Jane had thought to surprise them last Christmas, but a whiteout'd stayed the train, and it was just as well, Gale would've had to quit to take the time, that time of year. For as close as she and Lillie had been, Belle Jane'd had to drag all the Corneils off to the edges and the dark, like first act stage props. And yet, there was no question what they'd call this son of theirs: George, after her father, and Gale's. Mr. George Willard was somewhere in the coming-up streets of Grand Rapids, Michigan, still with the thick forearms of an old meat cutter. How excess and shifty ambition in Georgie's genes would turn out this boy, she did not ask. He was alive. He was hers.

"We'll send a postal, dear, tomorrow. We're all tired yet."

For a moment, in George's wheezy just-born breaths, they could forget they'd have to look for new rooms again in a week. Gale had been fired (again). Or he'd walked. It wasn't clear, never was. There was always some issue with the owner or the owner's kin or the menu, wasn't how he would do it. Gale could never last past the honeymoon of a new place, and it was always someone else's fault. The drift working had been somewhat tolerable, for he usually got hired at a different kitchen quick enough and she had her place with Mr. Coffin, but she was sick about how they'd make rent now.

She imagined the postal: *Dear Annie, I've married a cook who is out of work and a baby boy just arrived at our place. Will you send for us? Please never mind my age or that I was married once.*

"No, Belle, I'd like to do that for you. Let's call your folks and tell them the good news."

No, she would not do it. She wouldn't.

*

She slept with her robe open, knowing Georgie was always just breaths away from wailing. He was a chubby, blue-eyed boy now, and for the first time, he'd gone and slept in. She woke, startled, for he never slept more than an hour or two straight. The crook of drool at her jaw, the sunlight as her eyes poked open.

"What time is it?"

"Gawd, it's Monday." A day that chefs slept in.

Gale, half-asleep on his belly, whispering into his pillow. A hand reached out for her thighs, he had a finger draw from above her knee to her hip, and down.

"But Georgie."

"Let him sleep, will you? Let *us* sleep. Or fool. Remember when we used to fool?"

Belle Jane gave his hands a swat. "Didn't we then."

He turned, had his belly against her back. Now his fingers were drawing between her ribs, her breasts. They no longer throbbed, her nipples no longer bled, but God, she was tired. Gale found her nipple, circled it with a thumb. How many feedings had those nipples given George? Once the searing pain had passed and her nipples had toughened up, it astounded her: how she could hear him cry and milk would rush in; how she could even just think of him, right now, and the milk would trickle. The wonders of her body. And the boy's. Each day, he grew fatter on her milk. He *was* her, or was, at least, *of* her. She thanked God for the moments when it was good, when even if she were dead-tired, she was driven by mother-love. For wasn't it also the most terrible of times? Sleep-crazed, sweating and footsore stomp-rocking this baby who wailed for days, didn't want anyone else and not her either, and her mind had fetched frightening thoughts of how she might stop him, save herself: the biffy, the sink, the pillow. Once, she let off a spectacular scream of frustration (the baby was scarlet with crying, nothing helped), and Belle Jane could hear neighbours, outside the door, debating who should be the one to check on them. Mrs. Sutter did. But the scream'd jacked both mother and babe out of their fit, and Mrs. Sutter found them together on the rocking chair, all heartbeats and sticky tears drying.

When Belle Jane wasn't dead-tired and mind-lost, she was just bloody tired. Was it just from being a new mother, or was it also the acting at being someone she was not? She wondered, What would it be like, to be seen?

"Belle." He kissed the back of her neck. "It's been so long."

The thought of it frightened her. Their son'd had such a big head, it'd felt like she'd been beaten down there with a fencepost. Meanwhile she was suddenly cooking for herself and even for Gale, too, who'd decided to learn the trade of painting and papering walls while leaving for days here and there to cook for surveying parties. The coins and bills she'd saved in a natty white stocking, and she'd cursed herself for thinking it, but she did think, once, and now: Have I got two children now?

Georgie lifted up his chest under the table the other day, and she caught his eyes, looking at her too, and she thought: I am so in love. There was a sweetness to this boy that'd made her heart silly with joy. And yet, she worried about bringing another child into their world. Gale, "forgetting" his wallet at the butchers. Changed jobs like he changed underwear. But he would change a nappy and rock George and bake them cakes, and was a gentle, patient lover, she could say that about him. She did not consider what all of this must've been like for Gale, to be outsided, the least-needed one of three.

"Oh, Dad, let's catch a few more winks."

They called each other Mother and Dad now, and it made them feel quite the cozy family. Gale's lips paused, sighed with the gum of his sleep-breath, and he rolled over. He lay there, for she felt she could hear his eyelids blinking, and she wondered if he was wondering too how long this could all go on.

Georgie babbled in his sleeping drawer, and Belle Jane rose.

Gale muttered, "Gettin' up pretty spry for Georgie."

The soles of her feet felt for the morning cool of the dusty hardwood floors, and her eyes met her son's. It was as if seeing her made George realize how hungry he was and he started fussing, so she hushed him, drew back the robe, let his drooly mouth latch. They sat on the bed, against the cool wall. Her nipple, her milk, the suckling, her son.

*

Gale and Belle Jane stood on the doorstop of her parents' house on Hawthorne Avenue in Lewistown, with George squirming to be free on her hips. It was so cold the bones stung, breath scurried on. Here they were, at the icy steps, the shiny columns, the porch. The door. She'd been dreading this moment, all this telling, these two knocks, but now that it was here, she half wanted to cry with relief to have it all over with, or at least, to have it started. She lifted the brass knocker, let it hit the door.

Her youngest sister, May (Annie May had long dropped their mother's name), answered wearing a blue plaid housedress. What was she now, seventeen? Eighteen? She had that long face of theirs, dark hair pinned up and back, a shy smile. An innocence.

"Belle Jane?"

Belle's free hand reached for her sister, the frills at the yoke of her dress, to squeeze her, kiss her cheek. May smelled like home: lavender water, dog, quilts dried in the sun. Belinda suddenly felt sick with missing her family.

Her sister tipped her head toward the stairs, shouted: "Annie! Alice! Belle Jane is here."

May leaned in to look at Georgie, all smiles and chubby fingers pointing and squealing at the sight of the Corneil family dog, a black and white collie, tail a-wagging, just stealing to nose into the boy. Dogs know that where there are babies, there are crumbs.

Well, the Corneils could carry a grudge for all she'd done, but her family would fall in love with this baby too.

"And a young sir!" May shouted down the hall, a clatter of heels.

Soon, the parlour was a waltz of stepping in and out of embraces, half embraces, handshakes.

Where May, eighteen, and Alice, now twenty, fluttered about them like robins, their mother, Annie, strode in like an old cock (and Belle Jane thought to say: Does your face ache, making that look so long?). Her neck had wrinkles now, her hair had grayed. What did she think, when she saw her eldest here, like this? It's all wasted, on youth?

Belinda spoke first: "I'd like you all to meet Gale Willard."

Gale tipped his hat, gave the grin he gave ladies at the dance hall and even spun Alice and May. To Annie, he stretched his hand, the hand that even buttered toast with the gentlest touch.

"What a pleasure to meet you," said Gale. "This is how a guy gets related to so many beautiful women."

Belle Jane's eyes darted around the parlour, the many things Georgie would reach for: the plates, the piano keys, the silk curtains, the lace table cloth, the glass dangles on the lamp.

Georgie, finally free on the hooked rug, was tugging at the leg of a chair May held still while the dog sniffed at his pockets. They all looked at Georgie, the tuft of hair stood up. He turned back to smile, and fell on his bottom but only beamed at his audience. There hadn't been a baby boy among them in so long.

They heard the clatter of the back door, bootsteps on the hardwood. Belle Jane's father had been at the store so May had a neighbour boy run to fetch him, and put the dog out back. It was barking now at the cruelty.

Her father was older now, but still handsome: white hair, a bow tie, hardly a wrinkle. His eyes stole at the baby.

Belle Jane fetched him up, brought her son to her father. "We called him Georgie, Daddy."

Georgie went right to his grandfather and clapped at the old man's nose. A nose that nuzzled into the baby's neck, his little bow.

Dad George discreetly inhaled the delicious scent of baby, closed his eyes. Finally, he smiled.

ESTRAYED

From South Side of the Snowies, one bright sorrel horse, weighing about 850 pounds branded (like cut) on right shoulder. White strip on face. Last seen around Haystack Butte.

þà

9

1910

BELLE JANE HAD INSISTED on the lace curtains, the collie. Good Sir, she'd called him. He would nose at her to pet the loose scarf of white hair at his neck. Whenever she lifted her hand to little Georgie, Good Sir pranced over and in between them, as if to say, *That's my mother too*. Good Sir was gentle with Georgie, but sometimes, when Belle Jane had to hang the wash and just needed both of her damned hands, she tied Georgie to a picket in the earth and Good Sir seemed to tease him, dashing back and left for the boy to follow. Well, Georgie'd try to copy the dog and eventually the picket rope would trip the boy. But Georgie didn't cry, even when Good Sir got bored of him and leapt off, into the fields.

Belle Jane was sitting on a hickory rocking chair—below the Irish lace she'd strung like waterfalls above their one window—reading the paper, as Good Sir nosed at the folds and she feigned to swat him.

"Good Sir, I'd like to read just five minutes if I might. Rest my feet."

They'd only been set up on the south side of the Snowies six weeks, and it never ended: harness the horses, milk the cow, get breakfast, strain the milk, wash dishes, feed hens, start the washing. Keep Georgie from toddling off to get scalped by a bobcat or lost in a creek bed. Now, supper was a while yet, Georgie was napping in his hammock and Gale had gone to town with Cousin Hector, their hired man. Two weeks already, she'd been trying to read this paper and now that she had it, it all seemed to annoy her: the ad for the Stag Sulky Plow, looking like a metal heifer carcass. The "unshakeable unbreakable bed rail." At that, Belle Jane'd guffawed. Bed at midnight, up before the first cockcrow, at four. Winters weren't long and cold, there'd be not a baby in the state. Belle Jane had thought once they'd left her parents' house, Gale would kiss her bare neck again at the end of supper, take her waist in the kitchen over coffee. How long had it been? Was this the way it was?

She was grateful for the chair, the sun. Before Annie'd gifted her the rocking chair ("for Georgie"), Belle Jane had sat on rocks by the door, left open just now for the air and the warmth. Just two weeks ago, the worst snow storm had ended in a blizzard that overtook their shack, left the drifts knee-deep. Funny, it'd started as a warm rain. And she'd been trying to read, by candlelight, this very paper, this headline:

TO BE RECORD BREAKING SALE

Sixty thousand acres in Fergus County, going up on the block. Since the state had made the announcement, everyone had become "Montana mad." Ed Wright's two Buicks bore strangers in derby hats back and left, night and day to see properties in the Judith Basin. It was range land and probably none better: well grassed with timothy and alfalfa, well watered with cold springs, and good yellow pine for building. Branch lines to ship cattle on the hoof. The Lewistown hotels were so crowded men slept on lounge chairs and Old Sievert's "bull pen," with its eight beds of hay, Montana feathers.

There was fear that Lewistown would grow up too fast, become a Reno, once home only to the cactus and jackrabbits, and later, a few penitentiary inmates; now pulsing with divorce hunters, women in white furs and winking men at the wheel of Model 66 Pierce Arrows.

"Figgers, we just get in on a place and that land goes up," Gale'd said a few days ago. It was the last of daylight and the dust of yet another homeseeker's Buick ride had seemed to flit at them, the way a woman tries to swat a fly with a cloth.

"Sakes, Gale."

He had no mind, for the opportunity in change, that these newcomers would be daft and need something from the Willards more than the Willards would need something from them. Namely, their horses. It was a damn good thing they had Hector McDonnell. Gale'd done the plowing for feed oats all right, but he always had Hector or Belle Jane harness the horses and hitch them up, and twice she'd found him in a crook of the knoll by the creek, napping with his hat over his head, not even noon day. Maybe Gale was just tired out. But it was early days for that and not like most with their first taste of having something, having things their own way.

Gale was always finding reasons to go to town (nails, a plow clip). Lately, he'd fork the last spoonful of supper into his mouth sombrely and say, "Gotta rest my eyes." And he'd leave them, Georgie fussing, hens and stock needing to be fed or put in, and slop-in-his-moustache Hector, eyeing the pot for seconds. Was it the talk he was putting off? For the last three evenings, Belle Jane had listened for the thud of a boot, the silence of possibility before the second boot tumbled, and then its thud. Had she known Gale might not triumph at stock farming when she asked her father for the money? She only remembered wondering, was he too big to ride? Well, maybe he didn't have the sand.

Would this be the beginning of the end?

Couples just like them, with silly bright hopes, had come and gone for years already, and the Willards, too, were like captainless young mariners: they might make it. They might love it, love especially what others could never stand—the lonesomeness, the wildness and the fight every day to live. Or they, too, could drown. Or, in a year's time, take a seat on a wagon on a road to somewhere else.

The throb of crickets barely sounded the folding of the pages. Well, she thought, there might be hundreds of naive easterners out here among them soon; Lewistown might get a sparkle, but as Belle Jane read the news from counties nearby, she knew that they were still in the hills of Montana. It was '10. And so much would not change. Sons died. Men died, by lightning, by pleurisy of the lungs, by cattle gone ornery. When first sons were born, men wore smiles that wouldn't come off. And when the United States needed the accounting of its people, namely its men and sons, it sent out men: "Let the census boys give us an honest count," the paper said.

And so, when Good Sir bolted to bark at a woman in dark skirts striding up to the house, Belle Jane assumed the woman was from the camp of newcomers.

"Good Sir!"

The dog barked ever more, bounding between the woman and Belle Jane. "Good Sir, *let off*."

A wind came up and the woman held down her blue hat with one hand and braced her papers against her chest to keep them from flying.

Miss Jane C. Nash had the look of a charming goat—the low nose, the eyes, a little big and a little to the side, but there was a quiet confidence to her being. Even a prettiness.

Belle Jane, standing perfectly in front of a half-plucked chicken and her teacup, used a hand above her brows to better see the woman. Sweet mother of pearl, she thought, what will

I serve? Her mind flashed to the handmade silk underthings strung across the bedpost (might they dry and be worn, for one damned hour, without a layer of shit-dust). Georgie, he'd wake.

It was the woman's easy smile, the blue hat and its frill of crochet.

"Isn't it a day?" the woman said, smiling at Belle Jane and then raising her free hand to the sky as if to introduce it.

Horses have eyes on the sides of their heads so they can see all directions.

The two women looked up, even Good Sir with his dewy nose. Every cloud in the country had turned up, but not one could stop the sun.

"Lovely," said Belle Jane. She thumbed Good Sir's ears, mud-clotted hair on the outside, and below, so soft and warm. "Quite the change, from that blizzard."

But it's the ears, the nose, that tell a horse what he needs to know.

"Well, that's Montana."

"That's right." Belinda tried to eye the papers in the woman's hand and dreamed up stories: a mining heiress out for a drive and crashed, her fiancé's arm twisted up in the steering wheel; a silly girl from Chicago looking for trinkets of long-lost homesteading kin. Or one of those Baptists putting on a revival. "Can I help you?"

"Well, I just noticed you've got the *Fergus County* there."

"Yes," said Belle Jane.

The newspaper. So, she was a local. Those weeks, months, at her parents' stone house weren't like other times she'd lived "in town." Card parties and dinners, even if she'd been invited, she didn't think she could even lace her boots and knew she didn't have anything nice to say. "On the down," Annie'd called it. Belle Jane and Lillie could remember when it'd taken Annie, too. Baby May'd be screaming bloody murder, and Annie'd be stuck crying on the steps so Belle Jane or Lillie would hold May, let her suck a pinkie. It was only six years later that Belle Jane found herself on a cold floor, face soaked and swollen, throat rakey. How barren, her womb, where hours before, she'd felt for his fists, little kicks when she drank sugar with her tea. It was daylight, and not one knocked that day. Or the next. With Georgie, somehow it was worse: He was here, he was hers, but she wasn't good enough. Wasn't good at all. Everything about the Corneil house seemed to know it too—the photographs of aunts in their flower gardens, the quiver of the pianoforte, even the marble of the chuck roast. So, save from services at St. Leo's, Belle Jane had mostly stayed in, in Lewistown. This woman must be a First Methodist. The Methodists got two of those Croatian masons to put up a fine new stone church with a bell tower. Belle Jane's mind flashed to the hats, the holy water, the babies squirming, the Bibles. Her thrill about getting through all sixteen pages of the *Fergus County*. She thought, I'm an old lady. Be Christmas before she got that paper read through.

"I wonder if you read about the census?"

"I did."

"Well, that's why I've come. My name's Ms. Nash and that's why I've got all these papers. I'm doing the census-taking, for your district."

"On your own?" And Belle Jane stalled introducing herself, glanced at the woman's sailor-style blouse, the shine of the buttons. She stepped back her own scuffed boots, wished it were yesterday, though she'd been wearing a pair of her dad's old trousers working on saddling up Washington, a plucky quarter horse. What questions would she be asked? What answers would she give, this time?

"On my own."

"Well, aren't you ambitious?"

"Oh, it gets me out of my little place."

"In town?"

"Yes, in town."

Belle Jane thought of the days when she was staying with Lillie in Lewistown, just after Dad George had bought The Busy

Corner and after Belle Jane'd left Peter for good (again). How sweet those mornings were, to savour an entire cup of tea (or two!) just thinking on how you want to spend the day, your life. Afternoons, she taught a girl or two her crochet arts, the lacework passed to her by her mother, Annie, and Annie's mother, Mary Connelly McGuinness, who'd gone and died just weeks before Belle Jane was born and was buried in a fine crochet shawl, overworked fingers like twigs crossing her overworked heart. Funny, Grandad McGinnis, still known locally as Plain Tom, was still hollerin' at the sight of goshawks and wild burros in Alturas, California. Rather than helping Belle Jane and Gale get set up, Annie'd elected to go south for "a McGinnis visit," though she'd just been.

Belle Jane stepped toward the woman, much shorter, and peered at the hat's trill of lace. The tiniest petals and leaves within, a drape every half-inch below the swath of indigo. "I have to tell you, this is fine lacework. Is it yours?"

"Oh, that's very kind. I'm learning yet."

(In fact, at the 1909 county fair, Ms. Nash had come first place in the point lace pin cushion competition, first in the crochet hood category, and second in the crochet shawl contest. After Ms. Nash's father died in the asylum but before her mother went on a fifty-nine-day fast of morphine and water, the housegirl, Mary Susan, had taught young Jane lacing and crocheting to keep her from moping. Ms. Nash'd dreamed up the design of the frills at her hat all on her own after daydreaming in the direction of a lampshade one April afternoon.)

Belle Jane thought to say, I used to teach lacework. *Used to*. She had too many *used to*s for her taste. She held the words, gave this young woman a wink.

Ms. Nash took a breath, tried to regain Belle Jane's gaze. "We all put in quite a winter last year, didn't we?"

"Oh, didn't we."

Snowdrifts up to the window, at the Corneil house there'd been long, jubilant games of Euchre and thank God, baby Georgie telling yards of stories with almost words and pudgy fingers in the air, like Old Rocco (what'd ever happened to him?). If the boy was home. On nice afternoons Dad George liked to bundle him and take him first to The Busy Corner for a peppermint stick or a candy wafer, and then to the billiard hall. Georgie would come home reeking of cigar smoke and the musk of old men's sweaters, that languid talk. One Saturday the two Georges returned with Cousin Hector McDonnell, just off the train from Canada. A cousin she hadn't seen since the summer they were nine, the year after they'd buried Tom-George, and she'd prayed soft-talking Aunt Tinnie would drown or choke on a chicken bone at the picnic so they might have a brother again. Cousin Hector had the look of the Corneils, dark and angled. He wore a fat moustache and had a surety about him, for a man so short. That night, Belle Jane and Gale'd gone upstairs to the room that'd been Alice's, with the green curtains. Soon, Gale was wheeze-snoring and Belle Jane poked him in the arm, said: "Let's go ranch."

His eyes stayed closed. His talk was croaky and slow.

"Why'd you want to do that?"

"You want to stay here, forever? Fixing roasts for Dad George to carve? You've papered every wall."

"I thought maybe I'd try to go in on a restaurant, have my own place, for once. Be the best in steaks. One of the Ouellette brothers was telling how twenty years ago in Montana no one dared order the lamb, and if they did, even the waiter girl would sneer at him as she called out for 'a plate of sheep.'"

Belle Jane had her back to him as he lay awake now on the bed, fingers clasped at his belly. She rolled her stockings over her heels and toes.

"He cuts you the ass fat every time. Every time."

Gale drew the storefront sign in the air. "Willard's Grill."

She was under the covers now. The sheets were ice cold, but in a few hours she would wake, cloaked in sweat. Peter, Peter in his undershirt smashing a bottle at her bare feet. Or Georgie, throwing his plate of eggs and beans and Belle Jane on her knees, reaching for every bean, and there is always another. Always that sick feeling of food gone to waste.

Awake yet, Gale withdrew his fingers from the air to do that thing he sometimes did along the petals of her self. Sometimes, it changed her mind about being tired, but she swatted at his wrist yet. "Gale, I'm tryin' to talk. Anyway, folks got their own steaks now. This is Montana. You shorely know that."

It'd struck her, then, that twice she'd married the same man: hopeful, big on talk. Twice, she did not learn: romance was not love was not the ability to provide. Another Belle Jane might've been kinder, gone in for the grill idea. But this Belle Jane'd been led around. She would do the leading now.

Belle Jane could see it: Cousin Hector would be their hand, they would raise and take in horses to break. Grow their own feed like they did on the home place. Gale could cook!

In the moonlit swirls of those papered walls, she remembered the glittering words of that outlaw queen, Belle Starr: "I want to die in my boots."

Belle Jane felt it then, in bed with Gale, and she felt it now, too: time, cinching at her ribs.

Ms. Nash shifted her papers, and Belle Jane thought, If the sky won't fall just now, best to just get on with this. Her chest pattered with the dance of what to do: stretch the truth or tell it plain. She hushed herself: *Quit it now!* And with the sun and jets of dust motes hanging on their talk, it went like this.

"Your family name?" Ms. Nash coughed. "We'll start there, and will you kindly spell it for me?"

"Willard. W-i-l-l-a-r-d."

"Oh." Ms. Nash stifled a giggle. "I'm sorry. My granny had a pig called Willard."

"She did?"

"Do you know it was a sow?"

"Oh?"

"She had a big black spot on her eye. I remember stepping out in my shawl in the just-light to do my chores, and there they all were, the piglets, all tumbled on one another and she was so enormous—size of a church, seemed to me at the time; of course, I was just a girl and that was my first summer—I wondered that pig didn't roll right over and suffocate one but I guess she knew, or the piglets did. And when it was sun up and that sow just slept while they all suckled, it seemed so . . ."

Belle Jane gave a knowing half-smile.

"Well they all looked so warm and cozy, together like."

"It is a sight."

Tears welled up in Ms. Nash's eyes. They didn't look so goat-y now. Just green.

"I'm sorry. I don't know what came over me."

"Oh, not at all."

"You just, you hear so many stories."

The Willards were her seventieth residence.

"I'll bet that you do." Belle Jane noticed Ms. Nash was not reaching for a hankie, so she offered hers, ivory lace and initials stitched *BJJ* in crimson from when she was Mrs. Junk. Gale had never noticed. Ms. Nash did not notice, the initials or the lacework. Had that life even happened?

"Well now." Ms. Nash took a big breath, smiled. "What's your lucky mister's given name? Gosh, we're just getting off aren't we?"

"Gale."

"Gale*r*?"

"No, Gale. G-a-l-e."

Every word-scrawl was a lifetime. Who and why and how did she get here? With this man who knew the intimacies of cuts of beef but not the secrets or longings of his wife?

"He's the head?"

"That's what it'll have you write." Belle Jane barely tried to hide the snicker. If Cousin Hector were gone, it was Belle Jane that harnessed the horses and hitched them up. Branding their yearlings, while Hector roped the ankles and Gale wrestled the neck, it was Belle Jane that heeled in to those bony spines and thrust the orange-hot rod to the hind flesh till it smoked. Gale turned his head away, coughed at the stench each time.

"And your name?"

"Belle Jane." She'd be in for raking and threshing too. Calving.

"Do you know my first name is Jane?"

"It is?"

"Well, we must be friends."

"We must."

"Mr. Willard, what was his age at his last birthday?"

Belle Jane glanced past Ms. Nash's cheeks, to the window, the empty rock trail from the road to the house. A smile crept up. Heck, she could lie about Gale too.

"Thirty." In fact, he was twenty-seven.

"And you, what's your age please?"

The truth: Belle Jane was thirty-one. Gosh, should she feel guilty, now that she was talking to a friend?

"Thirty."

"Oh, that must make it easy, remembering."

"It would, yes."

"Yes, I suppose."

And on it went: marital status: married; years married, two; children . . .

"Children living?"

Belle Jane turned her head to Georgie, still asleep somehow, one sock fallen off, mouth so wide that in could crawl a rattler, or, a carpetbag packed with lies.

"One."

"Children born?"

The baby would be, what—thirty-one take away nineteen—gosh, twelve? And to him Belle Jane would be an utter stranger, a flighty Ms. Nash in his kitchen, asking questions to which his mother might lie too. Except Ms. Nash was proof: a woman could get on, on her own. Could Belle Jane have kept him?

Lord, if she could slap herself. Instead, Belle Jane whispered, "One."

Ms. Nash looked up from the grids of all those names, the stories, and she seemed to understand what Belle Jane was holding back. She placed her hand on Belle Jane's wrist.

They looked in each other's eyes, truly, and felt what they could not see: heartsickness, wrongdoings, wayward thoughts. Wanting, of love and answers.

Belle Jane closed her eyes and, to the boy, wherever he may be, issued a promise: *I will not forget you.*

Outside, Duke, the milking cow, was bellerin' and Good Sir was barking, probably at another party of landseekers. When Ms. Nash rose, Belle Jane felt the urge to kiss her.

Instead, she woke Georgie so he might cry and so she might feel his hot cheeks at her chest. Holding him, she patted the sweaty tendrils of hair at his forehead. She drew aside the tiers of her lace curtains at the window and watched Ms. Nash snag down the way toward the low blue hills like a feather quill.

FOUND

One two-year-old iron gray; three bays, two blacks, one light gray. Brand on left leg. Thomas Lane. Route 2. $10 reward for information

∀

10

1910

AT THE HOTEL BAR, Gale and Hector'd got caught up on some notion to watch a comet on the rooftop, but Hector'd had about eight too many shots of whiskey and nodded off on the stairs. Gale wanted his rope bed, so he carried Hector out over his shoulder, stumbling clear around the woman in a dark coat and white flowered corsage on the street, hollering, "Glory, glory, glory, get down on your knees you sinners and pray the Lord to forgive you, for this is the end of the world!"

Gale kicked the heel of the livery stable boy to wake him and chucked Hector in the back of the wagon.

Belle Jane heard the horses first, and then Cousin Hector, squealing, "Hooree, we're all goan die!"

Gale started to talk. "Oh damn, Belle Jane, somethin's doing for sure and I think—"

"Shhh," she said.

It was a dream. It was gold. All earth was light, and lighter. Midnight, could be, or two in the afternoon.

It had tails, millions of miles long, finning at the heavens. Feather plumes—pink, crimson at the crest, blue.

(Entranced by the very same sight, two heart-shocked women—an Alabama farmer's daughter and a Virginia slave's daughter on a crowded bridge over the Rappahannock—fell dead. A girl looking through a broken bottle, edge of a street fight in Little Italy, got shot in the back. Bullet shattered her spine.)

It was a golden globe towing streamers. A valley of mauve.

The clammy lips of Peter Junk, whispering to her nineteen-year-old self, "Belle Jane, you're full of stars."

It was a dream that went on for weeks, six moons.

(Just hours before King Edward died, he asked if his race horse, Witch of the Air, had won at Kempton Park (it had). Upon receiving word of the king's death in Fort Bermuda, they gave a salute of 101 guns. Not long after the echo of the last bullet at half twelve, the comet flashed scarlet in the sky. Pineapple pickers, and slaves across the Americas, refused to work.)

It was celestial doom.

("Get your soul saved now!" they shouted on the street corners, waving Bibles. The flat earth advocates wrote to the Harvard Observatory: "That comet will be the end of the earth! Why don't you tell the truth about it?")

(In fact, the story of the science was beautiful: English astronomer Edmond Halley'd urged his brilliant friend Sir Isaac Newton to publish a paper gone dusty on Newton's desk about gravitation—"the mistress of all motion in the universe." Halley thought: Comets, too, must move in accordance to that principle, travelling around the sun, just like us, on earth. He reconsidered comets on similar elliptical solar journey observed in 1531, 1607 and 1682, which he himself had seen. (In fact, astronomers now identify this 1682 comet with the one seen during the Norman Conquest of England in 1066, captured in the Bayeux Tapestry.) Halley calculated they were the same comet seen before and predicted it would be seen again—at its closest point to the sun, perihelion, in 1758 or 1759. When that comet did brush the sun in March 1759, they called it Halley, and used his science to forecast its next approach in 1835, and then 1910.)

It was a golden globe.

(Mark Twain entered our world eight weeks early, in November 1835, fourteen days after Halley's Comet reached perihelion. On April 21, 1910, just one day after Halley's Comet nearly touched the sun, Twain took his last breaths.)

It was a glorious star.

(On Friday, May 13, farmer Amos Rhoades of Pitcher, New York, witnessed his prize Dorsetshire cow give birth to not one or two but four calves; two with the unusual markings of stars on their foreheads. Rhoades's dairy maids said the comet did it.)

It was a gauzy tail, sweeping at its own head.

(A boy, who'd packed three sandwiches and a dime novel, slipped up to the school belfry to see the show. In the dark hours of the owls, he was too scared to come down. To sound the alarm that a boy was missing, the janitor, told to ring the bell, found the boy in the day's first light, quite asleep. He still had one cheese sandwich left.)

("We may die laughing when the comet comes," said frazzle-haired French astronomer Camille Flammarion. He predicted the poisoning of humanity when the oxygen of the atmosphere met the hydrogen of the comet's tail. He fear-mongered euphorically, wrote wild, wild fictions and endorsed a brand of binoculars favoured in France. Believers believed "forests and cities would flare up like matchwood." On the words of Frankish astronomers and Flammarion, dozens killed themselves (by gas). Not so his devoted wife, who cut Flammarion's hair herself and stuffed her footstools with it; nor a woman who willed Flammarion her skin to bind a book of his own works, which was said to rest at his table.)

(A sixteen-year-old sitting on an apartment skylight fell through and broke her neck. Her mother, at a packed rooftop across the street, heard the girl's scream and knew it was her daughter.)

(Roosevelt was sailing back to Oyster Bay, New York, after his eleven-month safari. For the Smithsonian Institute, the former president and half-time Montanian and an entourage of 260 porters and guides and taxidermists had killed more than 11,000 animals in Africa—among them hippos hunted from a rowboat, nine rare white rhinos killed in the Congo and elephants shot on the slopes of the Nile. "Did he leave anything?" Dad George'd asked, on reading the account. On the face of the comet, cartoonists drew up images of Roosevelt's natty moustache and squintin' eyes, his hunting cap, plunging toward Joe America while safari carcasses—lions and giraffes and monkeys—pit the sky as constellations.)

Halley's tail swam earth, and the fire in the sky drew pale and paler.

Gale fell on the bed still wearing his boots, but Belle Jane could not look away. It woke an awe, a wondering: What was beyond them? What could be known? Do we matter, at all? She stood against the corral, swallowed, let her cheeks go wet.

*

LASSEN ADVOCATE

NOV. 18, 1910

The oldest man in Superior California
voted at the recent election in Modoc
County. He is Thomas McGinnis,
Democrat, and retired farmer, aged 99.
He is in excellent health and says he
expects to vote at many more elections.

LOST

One sorrel and two gray horses, branded on left shoulder IV. One bay horse with glass eye. Two black colts. Five dollars reward per head for their return to P.J. IRISH, Lewistown

11

1911

IF IT HADN'T RAINED THAT DAY.

Inside, it was dark, it was light. Gale sat at the table drinking coffee. Behind him, fog bunched liked cattle on the mountains. It'd been a strange November. Last week, it snowed three days straight, but the air was so warm every flake melted as it fell. Kiss a death for wheat sitting unthreshed, and guess who had that?

"Gale, didn't I tell you?"

"Dammit Belle Jane, it's a wonder the doctors aren't after you for your hindsight."

"Shouldn't of let Hector go."

"No?"

"No."

And then it was a day or so before they spoke much again. Dad George came to fetch Georgie, take him to Lewistown for a few days so they could finish threshing what wasn't killed by mould. Dad George'd been talkin' cars but he turned up yet with a team, an extra blanket for Georgie. Gale'd been in the yard and came to see the boy off and Dad George said we missed a sight at church Sunday last.

"Goose flew right in over the altar."

"D'ya shoot it, grandad?" said Georgie, both hands turned pistols firing a show. Three now, and crazy about guns and hunting and horses. She'd just sent Lillie a snap of the boy in his button top and hat, making a face in the sun. On the back, Belle Jane'd written, *My cow boy.*

Dad George laughed at that, shook his head, no.

"The ladies shrieked to heaven and Father covered his head with the good book." Dad George imitated the priest, ducking to avoid being the target of pellets of green shit. "Damn goose was mad all over."

"What do you think the goose come to confess?" said Gale, both arms leaning over the corral. "Maybe we should of picked the goose, not the eagle."

America had just chosen its national bird: a bully that stole the eggs and the rotting after-kill of other birds. Belle Jane was reminded to fetch the eggs: a dozen for her folks, two for Lewistown Grocery. But she would have to wait until Gale was gone. She calculated in her mind what she'd pinched away, hidden in a metal tin under the nesting boxes. Forty-five cents here. A dollar there.

"Well, Old Curly nicked his wife's scarf and shooed it in the rump. I opened a window and the goose flew off." Dad George loved a true joke, loved church, if only for the tales and gossip on the steps outside the doors.

Georgie, those blue-blue eyes, he waved with his free hand while his other hand took the sweet from Dad George, and they'd been off.

So, here she and Gale were, no boy to talk through and just enough rain. Shadows of the hills, the edges of regrets. *Could I's* sittin' right there on the road.

Well, if they were already in it.

"The taxes?" Belle Jane asked.

Gale turned away, gazed out the window. She imagined their name among the list of delinquents.

"Robinson'll be around, settling up." Belle Jane tapped the *Fergus County* on the table.

"I don't need to read your paper. I said we'll have it, Belle Jane."

They would not have it. That's what Belle Jane's heart knew, but her silly heart also wanted to believe that he *would* take care of it, that it would turn out. Where had the money gone? She herself, and Cousin Hector, had broken and sold twenty horses already these last months. It was Belle Jane who knew each horse's little language, their whickers and whinnies: *Where's my breakfast? Where's my son?* It was Belle Jane who knew horses didn't need to be sacked and tortured under tarpaulins to be ridden; just time, faith in one's authority and clear instructions (versus shouting, for horses know the language of the body, not English). But it was Gale, who rode sat so far back his horses goose-stepped in protest, that neighbours asked for at the gate.

Did she and Gale have enough to even pay the interest on the mortgage, buy next year's seeds? The taxes, that was public. She could see it: DELINQUENT TAXES, 1911. WILLARD, $146.20.

If he didn't have it. If he didn't pay.

Divorce wasn't so unusual now. She'd just read a story about a husband filing because his wife had deserted him—on their honeymoon.

He'll pay it.

They had those hides, what would that bring? She'd see Hawkins herself. Christmas was coming and she wanted to buy her boy an iron train. Dad George'd offered, but she didn't want it like that.

Gale stood, righted his hat. "Good coffee."

It's the never knowing, she thought. The constant accounting while Gale could not care less, looked like.

He was making notes in his book, about the calves. They only had a handful of cow-calf pairs now but not for long. Great Northern was building a new line, Lewistown to Moccasin. They wouldn't be one of the lucky ones to get an allowance for passage through their land, but Belle Jane'd had a mind they could be the ones to supply the beef. Those Basques could eat T-bones twice a day, they wanted. Get a loan, get a few dozen head. Dad George'd know someone letting the contracts.

"Think I'll go to Butte. Bankers in Lewistown are all tenderfoots."

"What now?'

He was going, he was going without her, but she had a feeling there was another reason for Butte.

"I'll take the noon, get there tonight. Be back tomorrow, might do."

Belle Jane wanted to resist, for the sake of it. "I suppose I'll stay?"

"Need somebody here."

Gale'd bungle up talking to a loan man for sure. A kid could see it in Gale's face, that he'd try with all his might, smiling too, but Montana would win. Might as well bring a coffin along.

"I have connections in Butte. I might—"

"Oh, we know you've got friends, *Belle* Jane."

He looked her straight in the eye.

"What are you saying, Gale? You want to piss on my boots, do it plain."

Belle Jane had adopted the colourful talk of Cousin Hector and ranch hands in general. It suited her and she found it often saved time, making a point. Especially with men, by whom she was surrounded.

That train was coming. The tax man. Christmas. Winter. It was all heading this way, and what could they do?

Gale stood, reached for his overcoat, his gray felt town hat. Facing the door, he said: "Let's don't, Belle Jane." He took a breath, looked down. "Just want to get on the right side of this, get things going for you and Georgie."

The door creaked low and he was gone, in that between place of the house and the gray hills trying to snow.

That night, and two nights more, Belle Jane lay awake, foot-sore and heartsick. The huffs of breath being issued from her lungs were not her own. Did she even have a body? Her mind seemed a brute of its own, afire with images: the truth of a *no* settling into Gale's ever-smiling face as the banker stood to show him out the door; that half-finger and thumb waving at a bartender on Mercury; the twists of her own rope in her hands as she led Dandy, Duke and Cotton to the hands of one bearded stranger and another; walking down the road to town with Georgie, him holding his tiny fishing rod, her with a sack of her curtains and pots. All the lies like an ornery wind. Georgie, twisting out of her arms for Dad George.

She was bone cold. She did have a body. When had she last fed the fire? She weighed it out, the embers of warmth against the chill at her toes, that she'd likely need the biffy then too, and a coat and boots. *I want to die in my boots.* She elected to run, in the bed. No use, once she stopped, the heat flickered off. She remembered Gale was gone and folded over his half the blankets. How wide the bed was without him, and yet, she remained in her nook of it. Eyes open.

Could she?

*

She started the letter in her mind six times.

Dear Lillie, I woke up this morning and never knew I'd know this day.

No.

Dear Lillie, I imagine San Diego is a wonderful place to be this time of year.

She considered how winters past she'd thought, Something magical happens when it snows.

I hope you and Johnnie are having a good time of it. Georgie loves the rod you sent him. He caught two trout with Hector in September and said, Mama, you want to catch a fat trout, what you do is . . . He held a one-hour lecture on the subject while I did the washing, which is still a two-day operation, and he could've gone yet but finally I had him go slop the pigs. Maybe we'll have our teacher or preacher yet. Well, I don't know what will come of Georgie and me.

If it hadn't rained. If it hadn't snowed.

Dear Caroline, Oh Lillie, what have I done? Only you could love me now.

Her heart was not the Little Rockies. It was a volcano. Or, the dregs of the coal cart.

Gale left Tuesday for Butte, for a loan.

But she couldn't write. The telling rose in her blood and drained her dizzy. Did she even have a mind? It couldn't think, only flit.

*

The snarl of Gale's lips storming toward her in the yard, ice-dried sheets in the wind. "Mrs. *Junk*? Hellooo-oo, are you 'round, Mrs. *Junk*? Mrs. Juuu-uuunk . . . I have a message for you." She'd leapt and stumbled. No use, her boots. "From your *husband*."

Were these her fingers? She'd held them up, trembling and veiny. Pretty once. Gale's fingers coming to grips with her arms, a suck of breath, a crack against her skull.

She'd come to on the frosted ground, rocks gnawing at her spine. Good Sir's warm nose at her ear. Clouds rolling quick across a dark sky, the throb of her head. She felt for it, just a trickle of blood and her hair froze stiff. She opened one eye: the horses were still hitched to the post. Could she?

She was not a crib-whore on the Line, any man could shake his dick in her ear and swagger off with her laying splayed, scales of his sweat and drizzle. A dollar. She'd be richer then. She was not a snaky-necked cormorant, fetching up dead friends' black feathers to fix a nest. Voiceless but for burpy pleas.

Gale's good boots, turned out in a V and quite still. Was he dead? She crept closer, saw the folds of his grimy vest rise. Gale was slunk against a corral post, tears like petals. Or were they? It was snowing hard now. Fat fast flakes that said, *Catch hell.*

The dull glint of the pistol. "Everything, Belle Jane," Gale sobbed. "It's gone."

"What's gone?" The house stood. The road stood. She willed a wagon to it.

He wasn't right. His face was tinny blue. He wasn't hearing her. She was not here. The pistol, he had it pointed right at his heart.

"Man says he's the agent and attorney at the Tennessee Coal and Iron Company, you believe him. Got letters from the LaFollette National Bank. You believe him. Was the banker, Mr. Sitzler said no who told me about him. Banks only give loans you don't really need 'em. That's why I took it all. Mr. Sitzler said there might be an 'opportunity' for me yet. I remember when I met you in the employment office, Belle Jane." His lips curled in a feeble smile. He lifted his eyes to hers, pointed the pistol at her cheek. "You remember that?"

The wobble of the bone in the half-finger. Could he do it?

"I thought that was an opportunity too."

The rot of drink on his body, his teeth. Even out there. The cold wind tugged at the cut on her skull. She felt for the crust of blood, did not make a show of it.

"He's got The Johnston, Mr. Peter Junk. Friends in high places. Was Jim from Tennessee Coal and Iron said we ought to have a drink. Celebrate. He had the Indiana way of talking, like my folks. It was real good, sitting with Jim. We were set at the bar and Jim says, here's the man I ought to introduce you to. The proprietor of this fine establishment, Mr. Peter Junk."

Belle Jane remembered Peter's white-blond lashes, the smug of his face. Like a wild horse bucking on her ribs. She had a body. It stole scraps of breath. She was alive yet.

"My lucky day. An investment chance. Two new friends. Couldn't wait to tell you."

The cows just beyond gave in to the snow, bony legs kneeing down, tails down. Whites of their eyes like a mirror, like a clock.

"Come to me, Belle Jane." He waved her to come forward. "Come on."

Good Sir, nose at her shins, looked up. As she took the slightest step, pebbles gristled under her boot.

"I just want to . . . Oh . . . you mean everything to me. You and Georgie. I saw a woman on the train with a white fox coat. Matching hat and everything, and I thought, I'd like to buy one of those furs for my wife this Christmas."

Keep right still.

The half-thumb rubbed at the butt of the gun, then stopped. He lifted the pistol so slowly.

FERGUS COUNTY DEMOCRAT

DECEMBER 19, 1911

News from Our Neighbours

Gale Willard, residing five miles south of Lewistown was seriously injured Thursday by the accidental discharge of a revolver. Dr. Myrick was hastily summoned and investigations proved that the bullet, from a pistol, had entered Willard's left side just above the heart, but that it struck a rib and passed around under the arm, lodging under the shoulder blade. The injury is of a serious nature but not necessarily fatal, and the patient will be on the road to recovery within a few days unless infection or pneumonia occurs. We are unable to learn the circumstances surrounding the accident.

She fed her son stories. Strange lore she hadn't thought of in years. That on Christmas night the cocks crow, startling the evilest of spirits. That bees sing in their hives and sheep rise, at midnight, to dance for the visit of angels 1900 years ago. That cattle awake their eyes and kneel, the way those on straw did at the birth of the Saviour.

"You saw it?" Georgie asked. He thought he needed to know.

"No." She kissed the top of his head. How good it smelled, always. "You can only see it if you've never done wrong."

Her son. His lips, his lashes, his eyes.

What was, what could have been, what is. Imaginings, crashing.

"Let's hunt up their tracks in the snow. Tomorrow."

Gale lay on the hospital cot, swallowing broth and calling for his boy, while outside it snowed, and snowed more.

She told her son of Belle Starr, the lady cow boy who married Cole Younger of the Quantrill bandits. That Belle Starr rode off with Jesse James, dressed in buckskins, robbed stages, stole horses, married Cherokee brothers. *She'll ruin your boys*, loved her double revolver. She did not say: And one by one, her husbands were shot. To death. Belle Starr, too, wore her killer's bullets, *I want to die in my boots* those patched up boots etched at the shin in white starlight.

*

Georgie woke being carried by Dad George up the steps into the church for midnight mass. His eyes lifted to the dark, the earrings like fish hooks, currents of wine-soaked breath.

Her father in his dotted bowtie, and her son in that blue sweater, they lit a candle for Gale. It flickered, with the others, a good long while.

JANUARY 13, 1912

THE BUTTE MINER

TWO SEEK FREEDOM

Belinda Willard has instituted divorce proceedings against Gale Willard, to whom she was married at Spokane in 1908. She asks for custody of their one minor child. Failure to provide is the ground on which the decree is asked.

Georgie became a professional question asker. Or a mute. He wanted to go. He wanted to stay. Anything but packing and the ride ahead.

"What about our potato onions?"

She said, "Son, the garden will go on without us."

part three

HANDS TALK

STRAYED

Two gray horses, six or seven years old, weighing about 1,400, strayed from Vipond Park. No brands. Suitable reward for return or information leading to recovery.
G.W. Chapman, 740 West Park Street

12

1912

GEORGIE PLUCKED AND BRAIDED the long throats of dandelions as his Aunt Alice had taught him. "You'll be the best ropemaker around, Georgie," she'd say, and tuck the braided yellow flowers behind her ear, behind a smile that was always true because it only knew good things: the blushing gardenias out front, motion pictures at the Bijou, dried peaches by the pound since they still had The Busy Corner. Since she was always happy and happy to see him, never *shush*ing or *shoo*ing him away, and did not have dark sacks under her eyes like his mother, he thought of Aunt Alice and Aunt May as some other kind of human entirely. *Girls*. He'd only heard stories about Aunt Lil, who lived in that paradise place, San Diego. (Uncle Johnny, who ran a garage there, had become a race driver of note: January last, he and another fellow raced their Stevens-Duryea from San Diego to Phoenix, Arizona, a distance of 400 miles, and won over the nearest driver by two hours).

Aunt Alice was his favourite. She wore her eyebrows skinny and her hair short and wavy, bulbous white earrings that had the look of a mint. He reached for them, for her, every time. That winter, meningitis was on the spread and everything was closed: churches, saloon, schools.

(A woman from the Belts, Mrs. Shawhan, became locally famous for her cure of all ailments: kissing a calf right on its oily nose every morning.)

George's mother was . . . where was she? Out with that Miss Jane Nash, sometimes the much younger Cute Nichols and Tennie Horns, too. Georgie'd heard talk of tea leaves, green eyes, crystals, and his bat-eared Gran Annie: "I don't like it, Belle Jane. I don't like it one bit." When it wasn't Aunt Alice's turn to run The Busy Corner, she and Georgie spent long hours reading *The Wind in the Willows* under quilts and nibbling on toast with honey, the fruits of bees.

This is the place of my song-dream,
the place the music played to me,
whispered the Rat, as if in a trance.
Here, if any place,
here if anywhere, surely.

Once, Georgie'd fallen asleep sitting up with her and a book and he woke in the night and saw the ghost of his father papering the walls, skittering up and down the seams of the olive vines like a rat, and as dawn neared he remembered his father was alive, not dead, just gone. (Would keep his vow to never set foot in Montana again in his long life.) Soon, Georgie saw a bloom of pink at the window. It was dawn, beyond the next house and a stand of ash trees, the sun was rising. But the sky blew it out like a candle, and all was gray, all was darker even though, surely, it was morning.

That was the last time he slept with Aunt Alice. Harry Briggs with that moustache started coming for Sunday lunch. George studied the way their bodies bowed into each other, like cucumber leaves, blocking out all other things. Instead of holding his aunt's hand, Georgie was being asked to carry Harry's fishing box to Spring Creek, so the boy sawed its bottom in half and he said, "I don't know, just got broke" when he got to the creek. Aunt Alice stood from the log upon which she'd been sitting with Harry, holding hands, and saw a spotty trail of fishhooks shimmering in the cracks of Georgie's boot prints. Anyway, it was so dry a spring all the fish had land-drowned and all the dogs had done jigs on shores of rotting troutbacks, carrying the pernicious stench to town so that the newspaper editor called for an end to fishing and even picnicking. By July, everyone was in a mood (a hired man'd said: "So dry I got off my horse to take a wiss, two gophers come up with Dixie Cups"—throwaway Dixie Cups, invented in '07 to end the germ-spread of sharing dippers).

Bully good winds shoved at haystacks until the grasses lay like horse blankets over creeks, vegetable gardens, even the pews at church. Finally, on the Fourth of July, as even the nutcake frosting sat weeping, raindrops. Sweet and tiny, at first, then in gobs. In town, children and dogs ran out to let it rush their tongues, women let it wander their necks as if it were a lover, banker men nearly kissed one another. At nine o'clock, the firemen rolled their wagon up to The Busy Corner and shot off fireworks.

It was there, as Georgie sat alone under the store's awning, cross-legged in his short pants, digging for the last kernels of popped corn and licking the paper bag, that a cow boy struck up talk.

"Think you got it all, kid."

The cow boy spoke while watching a golden firework, fizzling then kicking out sparks. He had little eyes and a long nose that'd been smashed at least once.

"Yep."

Behind them, the voices of his aunts and mother swelled, went low in whispers. He'd wanted to drag them out, but he didn't want to miss it. They'd said, "Coming Georgie" three times, giggly and almost choking. *Pah, pah*! The flickers of red and blue almost made his heart sad, so fleeting and impossible were they.

"What're you doing then?"

"Bottom's where the butter is."

The firemen were arguing. Did Arvie forget a box? Could he nick a horse to go back? No, the horses were spooking with all the ruckus. Better run on foot.

The man with the horse-drawn popcorn wagon had risked it, and his roan kicked up and nearly tipped the outfit and its barrels of popped corn, and the children of Lewistown saw their dreams in a flash: raining popcorn, raining rain, raining fireworks. Two strangers swooped in to unhitch the team, ride the wild one and get them on to the livery stable.

The cow boy boot-dragged a little hill of rain-specked dust until it was flat. "I'll give you a penny, you could get more."

"That's all right. We got The Busy Corner. I get whatever candy I want."

An old, three-legged dog yapped at a gang of boys racing so fast only the tips of their toes touched the dirt road. A donkey-faced boy at the front hollered, "Beat ya!"

"You got all that candy there, why don't you have any friends? It's the fourth of *Joo-lie*."

"Not a town kid," said Georgie. In fact, he'd been staying in town more weeks than not the last six months.

"Where's your place?"

"Flats at the Little Snowies," he said, tongue wriggling at a popcorn kernel skin stuck between his two front teeth. Finally, he put his thumb to the job. "The Quay Place."

(Rancher Quay and his shepherd pup had disappeared eight years ago, all his fifteen head roaming thirsty and $300 in the log cabin just days before the arrival of letters from the old country, informing Quay he was the heir of a fortune and needed to return to Scotland at once. Never turned up, here or there. Still a mystery, what happened. Georgie, on hearing scraps of the story, had nightmares that he would come upon Quay's skeleton, gnarly finger bones pinching his wrist, pointing at the moonlit Spring Creek. Once, they'd found Good Sir gnawing at a bruisy red bone as thick as Georgie's neck and Georgie just knew it was the Scot's shepherd. He wondered, Had the dead dog howled at Good Sir to be brought up? Now, with stories of gunshots on the place, folks took not just one but two steps back from Georgie and Belle Jane.)

"Ah, I know it." The cow boy's cheeks flashed purple as a spark whizzed high. Georgie saw the man's gray, looking-away eyes. "Shit, kid."

The cow boy looked at Georgie a good long while, and Georgie looked right back. Did they see it at once, together, Georgie's little boots right beside the cow boy's as they pinned a calf's hooves?

The Corneil sisters swirled out of the store giggling and tipsy, like windswept leaves. His mother wore a smile that was as sure of itself as the stove; the bow at her chest was astray. Aunt May was first to notice the cow boy, the faint of a connection between him and her nephew.

"Georgie, aren't these fireworks fine?" said Aunt May.

Georgie nodded. The sky was fits of yellow-white stars, falling, falling.

The cow boy glanced sideways at the lot of them, three women and little Georgie with his big brown eyes. The stranger got the smile, they say, of a fox in a henhouse.

Belle Jane lifted him, though he was too old for it, and whispered with breath that was ripe and warm, "Happy Fourth of July, Georgie."

She kissed his forehead, held her lips there. "It's going to be a good summer."

In the glint of the fireworks and the perfume of rain, he could believe her.

Belle Jane felt the cow boy's gaze. It was a strange thing, an evolutionary thing, but men seemed to study her—her breasts and her hips—more when she was with her son. She liked it, she loathed it. She shot a bullet-note to his eyeballs, *Oh get hanged.* That was the whiskey.

Then their eyes caught. The light took on just one side of the cow boy's face, his lips were just apart, like he might know something, say something.

Aunt Alice reached for the cow boy's arm. "Bill? Bill Kinnick?"

He looked her way, eyes still low under his hat, gave the slightest smile.

"I'm Alice, Harry's fiancée. Harry Briggs."

"That's right. Where is that rough old dog?"

Aunt May leaned into Belle Jane and whispered "Cousins" of Harry and the cow boy.

"He was with Dad George, probably at the Elkhorn."

Dad George couldn't help himself. He'd gone and bought another saloon. Annie was not pleased, and she didn't even know that above the bar hung a portrait of two naked women—their pearl and pepper hair, their tiny bodies like woodland fairies. The frame sat just right to the head of the namesake stag and its four-foot tall antlers. Georgie'd heard the tale of a stag's antlers more than once from an old Métis trapper, who said the horns had reached the stage of being covered with fine hair and being *en velours*, in velvet.

"You comin' to the wedding?"

Wedding. The word made little Georgie's stomach roil. His aunt, his favourite aunt, was already lost to Harry Briggs and the place she was fixing up for them on 5th Avenue.

The talk went on until the firemen rang their bell in jubilation and in warning: the show was over. One of the firemen threw a Tootsie Roll at Georgie. By sheer magic, he happened to catch it with one hand.

"Ma'am," said the cow boy, tipping his hat to one sister, then another.

To Georgie, he winked, said in a low voice, "'Night, kid."

And he walked away, hands in his pockets.

In that vivid pink sky, the kiss of wet, was the promise of a story.

LOST, STRAYED OR STOLEN

Dark sorrel mare, white face, two hind feet branded 6d. $20 reward. City Dairy.

13

1912

WHILE THE OTHERS STOOD GANGLY in the parlour like April trees waiting for leaves or dogs, Belle Jane, legs flaring with a rush of whiskey nipped in the kitchen, remembered the Grizzly Bear and laughed aloud.

"What now?" said Jane Nash, eyes trying to read the mischief of her friend. Belle Jane whispered in her ear, then turned to her youngest sister.

"Alice, play us something, fast-like." For just a moment Belle Jane and May were fifteen and five again, at the piano bench in the Philipsburg house in their turquoise slippers, their cheeks as white-smooth as the keys. She kissed her sister on the lips. That was the whiskey.

"*Belle*." Jane eyed the eyes.

Lillie, up from San Diego, picked at a scruff of lint on her husband's jacket and nodded along as that odd stick Old Forrest puffed from a briar pipe and asked, as he always did, about

Tommy McGinnis, the brother of Annie's lost in the 'Frisco quake. "No word, huh?" The guests of Mr. and Mrs. Harry Briggs—mostly Alice's sisters and friends and neighbours, and Harry's brothers and brother-cousins—it wasn't they weren't in good cheer; Belle Jane felt they just didn't know how to show it. Where was a fiddler anyway? Harry Briggs could do it. He was a fine fiddler.

(A fine performer, too. At his commencement exercises and the class performance of *The Merchant of Venice* at Culver's Opera house, Harry Owen Briggs, the editor wrote, "sustained the part of Antonio in a manner which augers well for a successful stage career." Judge Cheadle, who'd granted Gale and Belle Jane's divorce, gave the graduation address, and in the play, the judge's son Barlow had played Bassanio).

With the new rules that it only took three years instead of five to make proof on a homestead, Harry had just claimed himself a section southeast of Grass Range not four miles on from his aunt, Mrs. Ida Briggs Kinnick—but Harry, with his rollicking voice and his bowties, he liked working at The Art Music Store.

"Come now. Let's dance. For brother Harry," Belle Jane pleaded, holding Alice and Jane Nash's hands, leading them like a triangle of lovers, to the pianoforte. Georgie, looking up from under the table where he played with a stick horse, saw how anyone in his mother's grip could not refuse; whatever she said was too fun, too wild to ever do on their own.

You see, Belle Jane didn't give a damn. No one in their right mind would have her now, so there was no sense play-acting. She could own her wayward story. Her flesh. Thighs, a babies-softened belly. Thoughts that good women would swallow like the cold skins of yesterday's hare stew. And what glory.

After clearing the ivy and fern that'd been ordered for the reception off the fallboard, May struck a key, *da da*, held it, then hit a tune that galloped. They were off: Belle Jane and Jane Nash circling one another, hands high, like blind bears feeling for one another in a cave, in the night.

All around—the old ladies, with their camel faces and daughter envies; the young men, with their jaw scruff and hungers setting in—talk burned low as they watched.

Belle Jane and Jane Nash fell in one another's arms, knees kicking back as they swirled and stepped apart, only their chests locked, hands still out in a fright, or to frighten.

Jane Nash accidentally kicked a boy, whose mouth was so dropped that the motion sent his tobacco spit dribbling on his collar. Others, among them Bill Kinnick with hair combed slick, shuffled in from the hallway and the kitchen, where the wedding couple was cutting cake. The room was a fug of cigar smoke and sweat, bodies trapped in the pinings of new wool and a parlour on a blazing July night.

The last keys climbed and the dancing lady bears gave a silent roar, toppling into one another, rosy-faced and laughing so hard they were not laughing at all. Belle Jane's heel slipped on a skirt pleat that'd loosened and she had to lean on both the chew spit boy with red hair and her sister, May. She ended up sat backward on the piano bench with a spray of fern on her neck.

"Comes to it, you could give dancin' lessons." This, from Bill Kinnick with a smirk.

Belle Jane heard it and she didn't. After the jobble of the dance, it felt like her very cells were restacking, whizzing blood up from her ankles to her collar, hadn't got to her mind yet. As her body swirled still, and she realized where she was—a woman, alone, half drunk and divorced, at her folks' house in Lewistown, *again*—her younger self laughed at her. *Look at you, now.* A half-dance more sober, Belle Jane glanced at Bill, saw the bulge at the left of his crotch.

Much too late, but better late than never (she believed), she said, "That your way a asking to dance, Bill Kinnick?"

He had his ear to her, but he was looking at Georgie and a neighbour girl on their knees, playing ranch with paper horses and sticks.

"Oh, I want to dance with you, you'll know it."

May squeezed her sister's shoulder: "Belle, won't you play?"

Belle Jane gave a laugh to Bill, an *oh I will then* smile to her sister. She righted her bottom into place at the piano, rolled up her lace sleeves and gave a salty smile to Bill: "Well, you couldn't keep up."

She woke in the dark, wanting Georgie. If only she had a baby to hold her. Where was he?

Oh, he didn't need her, didn't love her. How he used to want her, would punch Gale in the chest till Gale gave him over.

Tides of a dream rushed her mind's eye: Dad George, back at the old homestead, in the corral, holding a halter for her own neck. She was the mare, she would be tied while Dad George led Bill Kinnick, the stallion, in.

Her lungs let out a breath so fearful and coughy it were a dying old man's. Nasty things, dreams.

She catalogued her injuries: a bruised ass, an achy skull. Possibly she'd said *Holy Christ!* right in front of the reverend when someone told her that Fannie Sperry Steele, her old friend from Hennessy's in Butte, had just won the Lady Bucking Horse Champion of the World at the Calgary Stampede, in Canada.

God, had she ever been this thirsty in her life? Where was the pitcher?

The wind was the only other one up. It itched at the window. Said, *You might be a bitch, but I'm the Bitch of Bitches. Awaker too.*

A tired heart.

She asked herself, What are you doing now?

> *A cow and a calf, if separated, return to the place*
> *where they were last together. And wait, for days.*

The boy. Teen-aged now. She could see him: Sat hunched on a corral post, one hand holding the reins of a star-faced bay. Punches of clouds. His hat, the shade, covers his face. She can't get close enough to see his features plain, but it's in the slunk of his shoulders, the still of his dusty, nibbled boots, the looking straight on: *You left me.*

He is not happy, he is not so sad. He is alive. He's alive!

She is not happy, she is not so sad. She is alive. She's alive!

Could she?

In the kitchen, out the window, she could see the gold of sunrise in the distance.

The door creaked open, and she kicked her carpetbag under the table. It was just dark enough still.

Dad George, hair still parted just so. A little tireder, a little older.

She thanked God. Annie, her mother, would've taken one look and known right away.

"What are you doing, girl?"

"It's too hot," she yawned. "Couldn't sleep."

He shuffled toward her and the sun's light. It smelled like sugar, like afternoon, with that graveyard of sliced cakes on trays, covered in cheesecloth.

"You're dressed."

"Uh-huh." Stop now! she ordered the tears.

"Belinda." He brought her close, hugged her tight, called her the name of his sister, as he still did. What did he see in his daughter then? For he'd witnessed so many party tricks at his saloons. *Below below* the flames of laughter is a heart, radish-purple and surprising and bruised.

Her tears came. She unfolded herself from his embrace. "I'll be in the garden."

She started to tip-toe on the stone path, toward the dull sun and the musk of the tomatoes on the vine and the morning birds singing *surely you can!* when she heard her father's voice, through the screen door.

"If you lie down with dogs."

"I know, I know." You'll rise with fleas.

"You stay by," he said. But he let her go.

She imagined she was on a stage. Drums, a violin. Glossy blue tracks. She had been here so many times, never. A world was alive and waiting, just for her. The trolley conductor having a smoke, the rangy horses that will draw carts of Mama's teacups and feather beds that will fly off, the man in the new suit and hat, holding his overcoat, walking away. That bitch of a wind.

As she stepped inside, heels clacking on the station-stage floor, she rehearsed: Second-class to Spokane. A sick granny. Yes, it is a shame, leaving this time a year.

Hush-up, she nagged at herself, her clenching ribs, a wild pulse. She studied the board, again, but she couldn't read it, not whole. Memories surfaced: the last mile of the stage ride with Annie, how in her mind she'd puzzled with the latch, the possibility of tumbling out, getting wheel-stomped or being free; the gate, the slowing, the going in, her and her belly, swollen and tight, like closed petals in the night. Her long, long hair.

The ticket gate was shuttered yet, but on the other side, she could hear voices, the clatter of coins.

She felt now below her hat for hair that barely covered her ears, still curled from the wedding, the fake pearls at her chest. Funny, she thought, women cut their hair because they can, and then they grow it long because they can. She looked down, at boots that'd just danced the Grizzly Bear, and her eyes caught the back-and-forth skitter of a red-brown deer mouse, its giant ears and black eyes. You belong in the grasses, you twit. Must've snuck into a hay wagon and now what would it do?

Behind her in the line, a whiskery old man with yards of silver hair twiddled with his cane, shakin' his head, she guessed, at the land grab people. Spilling in and out, no chickens, no cows, just powdered eggs and condensed milk to live on.

Behind him, a couple spoke not so low.

"What'd I tell you?" the woman teased.

"Oh, let me kiss ya once."

The woman's voice was familiar, a bit breathy and loud, for a lady.

"*Hal.*"

"Mrs. Danzer," he said, slyly.

Oh God. Emma Knight and Hal Danzer, also wed last night (at the Presbyterian manse) and due to take a tour of the national park with Alice and Harry. Belle Jane forgot—or did she ever know—the train they were all taking? Surely they'd be leaving at some other time, on some other train.

Just then the shutters rolled up and the agent joked, "Now here's a little lady knows where she's going."

Belle Jane pointed at her throat as if to indicate a malady and whispered, "Jawbone to Spokane, please."

Jawbone, what locals affectionately called the Montana Railroad, now the Milwaukee Road. That line hadn't even been running to Lewistown ten years yet, and just in the paper yesterday there was talk of laying tracks the twenty-four miles east to Grass Range. Belle Jane remembered her scheme, to supply beef for the workers of the Moccasin-Lewistown branch line just getting the ground levelled. What she regretted was not the idea's audacity, but that she'd let it wither, like a bed of water-starved pansies.

"7:18?"

She nodded. She'd have to change trains in Harlowton and find a stage across the line from Spokane, but she'd do it.

"First class, missus?"

Belle Jane held up two fingers.

He reached for the tickets marked: SECOND-CLASS. "Now that's good and on schedule so best be ready."

Ready, that's all I've ever been, she thought. What good had it done? She'd gone too fast. But Lord, she liked to go fast.

Belle Jane stepped sideways without a word, and sideways again, and again, keeping her rump to the Danzers, probably thick-lipped from kissing all night. God, if Harry and Alice saw her now.

You're fine, she told herself, and tipped her hat just above the eyes. She scuttled past two rail workers, one in a tie and coveralls smoking a cigar, the other dark-haired and so short he looked like a child in his father's suit and boots. Was he a Basque?

She found a bench on the freight side tucked behind crates stacked on a cart.

It's fine it's fine it's fine.

She closed her eyes, saw the boy again, sitting on the corral post.

"Belle Jane?"

A voice that she knew and didn't. A man's.

"That you?"

She opened her eyes.

Bill Kinnick tipped his hat. She noticed, in the just coming up hair at the jaw and lips, the hardly there lines around his eyes, that he was young. Younger than her.

His eyes turned toward the tracks, glinting in the sunlight. She sensed his patience, his hesitation.

"Thought you'd be in your curlers yet."

"Thought you'd be licking the floor."

He grinned. "That what that sawdust taste is? Knew I shoulda turned in after the cake."

He gave a *May I?* nod to sit next to her. He wore the simplest, no frill shotgun chaps she'd ever seen and a low-brimmed Plainsman hat with three toothpicks in the band. Told her he was waiting on a saddle for two that his father had ordered special from Republic, Idaho, before riding back to the farm. For his kid sisters riding to school, to save a horse. She told him she'd come to see off an aunt who'd been in town for the wedding.

Belle Jane impressed even herself with how she kept right still. Bill spied the carpetbag at her side, eyed the distance from the freight depot to the passenger cars. Just past the hills, a train whistle echoed on.

She was too old for this, and there wasn't time, anyway. She stood, said, "You don't know what you're doing, Bill Kinnick."

"It's no trouble."

"No *trouble*?" Any warm minge will do? Oh, how vile she could be.

“I’d take care a you.”

“Ha!” If any claim could be made so falsely, surely it was that.

The steam, the steel, the cars, they were comin’ now. Felt like her toes and her knees and her collarbone were the railroad ties being rushed.

“And Georgie.”

Georgie, with his little straw hat tied ’round his neck. He’d be just waking up now, all lashes and soft, bendy limbs, wanting. Georgie!

Bill gave a far-off look, a sure look. She recognized it as one she’d seen on hired men when they were scouting cattle: couldn’t see the stock now, and yes they were bone tired but they were going the right way, they’d find them yet.

His voice was just soft enough.

Swells of men and women in hats and coats went toward the cars and back. She had just a minute.

Her ankles felt a tug to the boots of this man. Or were her feet trying to fly?

It was just windy enough.

But God, she couldn’t. Again. Could she?

FJ

$15 REWARD
for return of bay mare branded on right leg, to Ceseri Marionette, Geyser, Mont., or Little Chicago.

14

1912

CHRISTMAS DAY THEY'D GONE to the Kinnick farm. Bill had ridden out for her and Georgie the night before. Annie must've come around to the idea and carried hot rocks in a picnic blanket to keep Georgie warm on the journey, though the sun was brassy. Belle Jane searched her mother's eyes, asked with her own: *You're certain?* Annie nodded and waited, impatiently, for them to be off so she could go in with her bottles of Dad George's blood pressure pills and Sloan's, the arthritis liniment sent by some odd stick aunt in Toronto that Annie couldn't leave off longer than a half-minute. Annie would sit on her chair and boss her daughters over the fruit salad with the creamed dressing, and she would ring her sisters. Since the telephone company gave half rates on Christmas Day, the McGinnis women would spoil the looks of an hour for sure.

At the Kinnicks, the gentlemen had already filled up on Tom and Jerry and were waiting for Bill to shoot the heads off turkeys in some kind of tradition they'd started the year the Kinnick boys got their first rifle.

"Ya got your muffin here now let's shoot," said Lewis. He was married to Bill's eldest sister, Letha Mae. "Fairly growin' a beard over here."

"Have you all heard about the bearded man in the Dakotas?" said Belle Jane. Bill was uncoupling the team, and Georgie'd run off with Bill's kid sisters, Allie and Alma Melissa, and the other men were talking bullets. She was talking to no one, really, but she raised her voice yet. "He's got the world's longest beard—eleven-and-a-half feet. Says it's nothing against the chill blasts."

"How long'd that take?" said Bill, unsaddling his bays, and she followed suit, uncinching, brushing out the ice-crusted waves of sweat, and Belle Jane guessed that meant she and Georgie were staying the night. Her stomach felt a pool of unease. Was Bill going to ask?

"Thirty-six years," she said, her voice falling. She imagined what the white crinkles of the beard had seen, had faced, and bravely so. She herself was thirty-three (though that specific detail'd been kept from Bill, who was turning twenty-five in February) and what had she accomplished? She had a son, and God, he was a wonder. She'd kissed the top of his head that morning and inhaled the sun, the goodness. She had two ex-husbands who haunted her: Gale, with the revolver, papering blade or serving fork; Peter, with his drunken grip at her throat. Christmases with both, looking back, had been a disappointment. She remembered the clash between the image of what could be, laughing over champagne punch, chestnut dressing on a turkey aglow, voices singing while she played at the piano, a strand of tinsel fallen on her hair—and the image of what was, the newspaper rings strung around the tree, the fights looming like the moon, the lonely voice of hers that sang without the keys, the going to bed too early, too tired, in a room that was too quiet. Bill'd been honest about Christmastime at the Kinnicks: "We do a turkey shoot and the little folks skate on the slough and we have a bird of a feast. Probably an excess of Tom and Jerry, and smoke, but it's Christmas, ain't it?"

"Lessssssssie," Bill hollered, in a voice akin to hog-calling as he strutted over to the men and the guns and the birds, rope-tied to one another like prisoners. "Yer' goin' ta lose."

"Quit that," said Leslie. He was the eldest by two years, but he'd always acted twice his age, studying agriculture reports from other states, plucking nose hairs and shining his coins before going to town. He left the supper table as soon as it was polite enough and ate lunch standing up in the kitchen, alone. His wife, Lulu (a former candy girl at the Mercantile), had taken a train back to her folks in Beach, and Belle Jane'd heard it said her wrists were blistered yellow from burns. *Fifty days for fighting.* That was the going punishment, for wife-beating.

"How 'bout your old dad?" Mr. Kinnick had that long nose that Bill wore too. The little, can't-hurt-you eyes, the swagger of a smaller man, a second son with a big heart and little airs.

Leslie wiped his nose with a shiny white hankie. "You ain't won in ten years," he said, almost in a whisper.

"Letha Mae?" Bill held out a rifle to his sister, who'd been eyeing the guns as they stood below the slaughter hook. Did she want to take his place in the contest?

Letha Mae was twenty-two, dark-haired and freckled and said silly things like, "Why can't you ride to China?" But she was a crack rifle shot, and it was regular that she held the irons and ropes come branding. Last summer, Letha Mae and Lewis buried their first baby. Diphtheria.

Belle Jane smiled at her. "Bet you'd put them all to shame."

"A bloody mess they make," Letha Mae said. "And then a day of work for us, is what. I know I can shoot."

Alma Melissa, bored with the younger ones, had sought the company of her horse and was feigning a nap, bareback. The girl was perfectly lovely, in her coal-coloured braids and green wool sweater, breathing in and out with her bay mare. Belle Jane felt the shiver of girlhood horse love. Was Alma thirteen now? Those swollen, telltale buds of nipples. The class solos that fetch her headlines in the local and "good girl" pats from the cloth-shoed old folks. Was Alma Melissa still dreaming? The cruel one in Belle Jane thought to say, someday, none of this will matter. You will say yes when you wished you could say no. You will become a mother. And the parts of you that shimmer—that wonder and attract—will be excavated, swiftly, like the dead placenta. And none of it will matter.

Belle Jane and Letha Mae, like half-broke curios planted by a widow's window, turned their eyes from Alma Melissa to the men to the younger children, though that last perspective was painful for Letha Mae. A barrel of apples was got for them, and little Allie had about fallen in, skirts up. Georgie tugged at her overcoat and she fell back and they tumbled to the snow, a one-eared tabby cat narrowly missed getting tangled in their legs.

That night, Georgie and Allie were about rubbing their eyes as the adults drank coffee and they heard a thud on the roof.

Everyone startled, looked at the ceiling, the window, the door, which opened, slowly to a voice: "Any good little folks at this place?"

From behind the door came Santa Claus (Mr. Kinnick) and Mrs. Claus (Bill).

"Oh, our poor reindeer needed a rest," Bill said, imitating the voice of an old woman. He explained they'd let the reindeer sleep in one of the caves where the Swedes lived one winter at the grader's camp west of Glendive, and now they were on their way back to the North Pole.

"What do they eat, your reindeer?" Sensing a weight in all this, Georgie stood with his hands on his hips, ready to go fetch whatever eating he could for Santa's team. Belle Jane loved the little hero in him already.

"Oh, we just fed them up on some bunch grass and water from the Missouri," said Mr. Kinnick as Santa, not even trying to change his voice. "They like that fine."

Allie came up and hugged Mrs. Claus's leg, wrapped in a skirt of red blankets drawn with twine.

"Why're you here?"

"Oh, them jackrabbits in Montana, they're pretty wily. Pretty big too. Sometimes they trick the reindeer into playin' so I come to shoo 'em off."

"Rabbit's my favourite kind of stew," said Allie to Georgie, lips so close they might kiss.

"Mine too," said Georgie, nodding reassuringly at his new best friend.

Belle Jane smiled. Georgie'd only eaten rabbit stew once or twice. Much as he liked to cook, Gale wasn't much of a trapper. She remembered when a man in buckskins came crawling up out the snow-packed coulee armed like a battleship carrying his saddle and two neck-twisted hares. Where had he come from? Where was his horse? Was he mad? With the rifle tip in the pit of her arm, she'd called, "May I help you?" And he got close enough she saw the streams of dirt about his beard, the startling calm in his dark eyes."Nah," he said. "I'm goan surprise 'em. They're goan have ta make a decision." And he asked, "Town's five miles north?""That's about right," she said. "I could get you some water."

He shook his head no and off he walked, sure and free and determined as anyone, that saddle and the dead hares bobbing along.

Now, in that sitting room with the candles and the lingering smell of gravy and pie crusts, as Mrs. Kinnick passed each child another apple and Georgie sucked the juice with fervour, eyes locked on Mr. and Mrs. Claus, she'd thought, can we belong in all this?

The fire was stoked, a tray of figs was passed around and as the children were about to return to reading their new book, *The Shoo-fly Pie*, Mr. Kinnick as Mr. Claus pulled all three—Alice, Alma Melissa and Georgie—in for a hug.

This, this was love, family, happiness. This.

"You'll all be good and very, very good for your mothers now, till next Christmas, won't you?"

The children were a thicket of glossy hair and tiny teeth, scraggly sweaters and giggles. Belle Jane watched Bill, watching his own dad and Georgie. Bill caught her gaze and gave a kind of question-smile: *Well?*

Her heart said, *How quickly I will go to you.* Her smarts said, *You old fool.* Her fingers, in the left pocket of her skirts, felt for the stone-soft edges of a paper on which she'd written to herself (after nearing and turning away from Gale's bedside the previous Christmas Eve): *Stop getting tangled up with men who are no damned good!*

So, her body and her good sense had a little war.

STRAYED OR STOLEN

Bay gelding with star on head, bay mare
with blaze face, black Shetland pony
branded SO right leg
Call at Gilchrists.

15

1913

IN THE NIGHT, the snow and wind had mated so that in the morning, they were one. All was white, save for the shadow of the low hills to the south, and Bill, riding, to where, she didn't know. He wore his woollies, his wind-steady Plainsman, not the coonskin hat his mother had given him when—*she'll ruin your boys*—they'd left on the sly. His quarter horse, Troy II, squinted his eyes in the snow-wind yet was unafraid. It was as if Troy II were bowing to it, the queen of his new, cold country.

Above, the screech-cry of a hawk, soaring, soaring. And then, nothing.

Bill and the horse were at a stop, considering: Where did the wind want to take them?

Belle Jane—pulling on her kidskin gloves, for she would go out on her mare too—grew a soft, dazzling smile.

Not one here in Ravenscrag knew her name. This day, this country, was unfamiliar and young. So wonderfully so, that as she and her horse, Judith, trotted toward her husband, she could not control her laughter. Bill and his horse understood just as well, how grand and gleeful the world at their feet. Bill and Belle Jane chased one another, circling and circling, laughing. Hiding in that just beyond where the white was too brilliant.

They were ageless, they were no one, they were the snow-wind.

*

They had to remind themselves there was work to do. Quite a lot indeed, and nothing. For they'd turned up at the Assiniboia District south of Maple Creek in the dead of January only to find a grand, brick eighty-foot well sunk with refuse unknown and iced over, and in the cabin, a reunion of mice.

Jim Boyle, a schoolmate of Bill's who'd made work of driving prospectors to mines in the basin, had heard about the land going up in Canada, the new branch lines coming into the country with rolling hills and streams and gulches, nearly Montana and unsettled yet. That there was a beef crisis! Too many people being born and not enough cow to go around. The government was in a state about it, and looking north. Jim said Montana was crowding in and now was the time to go to Canada, especially for second sons such as them. They could raise and sell horses for all the newcomers, just like Belle Jane'd wanted to before Gale'd gone to Butte.

Jim and his family had gone first, settling in a log cabin by a spring, and they had their section of 160 acres to prove up, but that was all: the badgers'd feasted on the nipples of the tomatoes, the breasts of the hens. Their boys, with no school to attend, had wandered to the neighbours for food while Mrs. Boyle stayed in and pined for a girl, who finally came. The mother bled to her death; the baby girl lived (spoon-fed milk by a brother). Jim and his sons and their light gray team drifted back to Montana, to Butte, to the mines. Probably Bill and Jim had just missed each other somewhere along the way. Bill did not get a letter, and when he learned what'd happened from a British old-timer in spurs, that his widowed friend Jim Boyle was there and Bill was here, he turned his shoulders, his ears, to the south, as if to catch a trace of the truth, the direction of his friend. Like a horse would. And Bill's face went pale.

Later, she'd found him at their raw pine-and-nails table, striking a match on his boot. Trying, anyway, for it'd rained and weren't his boot soles soaked?

Once he got it, he took a pull of the smoke, coughed. Said, "I suppose life's a bitch and then you die." His words were wet and rotten and stringy, like the innards and seeds of a pumpkin.

Wasn't it true, out here? Wasn't it what Shakespeare had said: *As flies to wanton boys are we to the Gods—they kill us for their pleasure*?

Belle Jane wrung her hands on her apron. She was waiting for the stove to boil more snow. She did not go to him. The whorls of cigarette smoke drew a boundary. She knew what it was, to have bad news of a friend slice in half what you'd dreamed together. Hadn't her sixteen-year-old trick-riding partner Philippa died of TB? Belle Jane herself was sick thinking about the newborn Boyle girl, wrestling in her bony brothers' arms, rooting madly, like a woodpecker, for the nipple, the milk, her mother.

Bill felt for his jaw, for the stubble causing an itch. In the dimming window light, one side of his face had a shimmer, the other ashen.

Instead of bringing him cheer, she poured a two-finger glass of cognac unknowingly gifted from the Corneil collection. Belle Jane heard Old Rocco's soft, husky voice: "Nothing a stiff drink can't fix." Bill shook his head, at first, then rubbed his hands for warmth and said, "To hell."

That was the end of the honeymoon—the licking of ankles, the chair they'd broken in and broken, the resting only for bread and jam and coffee, for who cared what they ate when it was just them. Now that they knew one another's every weakness and whimper, every taste and scent, they went to work. What they could do in the snowdrifts high as the horse's belly, anyway.

Come April, she would fetch Georgie, and her son would break from practising at his roping to help her sow the onion sets, scarlet runner beans, the peas. Or maybe Georgie'd sit in front of Bill atop his horse as they checked cows and cut out strays, for they all seemed to run together and bunch at the head of Blacktail Coulee and the Farwell Creek that ran through it.

They were only just getting to know one another, and this land, but they found their bodies and their horses and their acres of snow-grasses wanted to be met, travelled, even bitten.

*

It was blue dark, but she was sure of it: A hat. Hoof steps. By the creek scrub, pointing south. She went to the bed. On his side, the blankets were fallen, flat. Where to hell was Bill? The rider was some other man. At the door, on her knees, she felt around. Just scratches of mud where his boots should've been. She looked up, and the hook became her chorus: *Where did you go?*

Her eyes rose to the window, snail slow. The horse's tail, night was sinking and she could see the arch of its long, windswept tail. Scared horses take a shit because that's five pounds gone to run all the faster. The horse's ears pricked forward, toward the ruffles of dust ahead.

Bill!

The rider's hat turned toward the house, the window, the head of hers, trembling. *Hold right still.* The rider, black and one with his horse, gave a kick and disappeared into the tall thickets along the water's edge, the eddies of dust.

STRAYED

To my ranch, small sorrel geldings
branded on left shoulder. Owner can
have same by paying expenses.
R.N. Train, Lytle.

U~U

16

1913

THE BOYLES HAD LEFT a reclining pine chair, a dusty tin of dried juniper berries. Blue-black with wood-specked eyes that said, *We're alive yet*. Was the tin left for the ghost of the mother? Or was it just overworked and underthinking boys, tasked with packing up, not knowing how precious, in winter.

Belle Jane'd been the one to suggest riding to their place, to see.

"See what?" said Bill.

"Well, I don't know, do I?"

It'd been a hell-cold but sunny February that'd caused their bunch to rub their noses raw and bloody, poking for the blue grama grass below. In the cabin, the playing cards had speckled, used up hearts, and the "newlyweds" were now annoyed by one another's breath. Then, a warm wind waltzed in, like a drunk uncle, dancing the snowflakes and milking the snowdrifts.

"Good a day as any, get out for a ride." The chatter of town, her prattling sisters, her sweet son—she was heartsick for all of it, and if she didn't leave the cabin that minute she'd scream.

"Oh, all right."

On the way, Belle Jane heard the traddle of a bird and suggested they let the horses drink. Bill got off Troy, said, "Oh, I know what this is. You tryin' to look at my behind, Belle? You tryin' to seduce me?"

She laughed. Belle Jane thought he did have a fine ass. He always said, after, that there was something about how the two of them fit. But they were not like other couples that shared a look. Bill was skinny and tough and pensive. Had that long, hook of a nose. Belle Jane had big breasts, big bones, a big voice. She was eight years older and soon, she worried, her eye skin would crack and sag like a dropped vine tomato and the truth would be told.

Peter Junk, that pale, veiny-faced crook, had just remarried. Miss Matilda Mulholland. Another "quiet wedding." Annie was in Butte when the notice was printed in the paper. They honeymooned at Rock Creek, where the Corneils, during their Philipsburg years, had camped and caught fish and played ball in the flats. Once, an aunt who was a nun had joined, and she was the best lady ball player Belle Jane'd ever seen. Got a home run, twice.

Bill walked toward her, stumbling over snow-covered rocks, took her arms and kissed her on the lips. His lips were so warm and now he had a moustache (and she found she liked that arrangement). He tasted, just a little, like coffee and milk (she was the one who had her coffee black). He stood back, and they looked into one another's eyes, wondering what the other saw: What I want you to see? Or, what is?

I could be good. I could. This could be something. He did not know she'd spent her girl nights reading Shakespeare and balancing the saloon's accounts; that she'd survived womanhood drinking—pouring half-truths and cognac. Should she ask him, now, about where he'd been in the night? The dark rider?

To the west, the sun was like a star. The world was snow-glittered.

No.

Their smiles faded as they met the trail, the cross with just one nail and the nail-scratched letters: *Mother.* Jim had planted and tied steel stakes around the cross, should time or wind tilt it.

Bill got his faraway look. He did not get off his horse. Said something about a calf in the brush. Belle Jane went in the cabin. It did not stink of manure and saddle leather and pine but of cold earth and mice shit. Everywhere, the riddles of their tails on the dirt floor.

"Go!" she said, though she could see none of the creatures' eyes. "Go!"

The mud-chinked boards wore the window light like a sash. In the murk below, she saw the pine chair near where the stove would have been. Above the light, the antlers of a buck. And on a warped little shelf, where Belle Jane imagined Mrs. Boyle doing her washing amidst the pangs of birth, sat that dented tin of juniper berries.

She stepped out, into the light of day, another universe entirely, holding the tin under her armpit the way Georgie held his rubber ball. She heard what she heard: a trigger.

Atop a ridge, she saw Bill on his horse hemming in two calves, his rifle pointed in the direction of a white-eyed cow, moaning at the separation.

He waved at Belle Jane: *Get coming!*

If he thought he was picking up a slick. "What're you doing?"

The calves were white-faced, but a few months old. The herd, sucking at yellow grasses patched with snow, raised their heads. Most out here, it seemed, raised Herefords, their red-brown stocky bodies known for turning out more calves, better beef.

"Ain't branded," said Bill.

Belle Jane raised a brow. They didn't know whose grazing land it was, whose animals.

"Oh, fellas do it all the time. Herd like this, see, it don't matter, one gets picked off."

Bill was not wrong. It was a bit like spying the flap of a fifty-dollar bill under a rock and electing to leave it. Also, like marrying a big little lie you'd have to sleep with every night of your life.

"The range cow boy'll be out and find a bellerin' cow with milk bags down the dirt," said Belle Jane. "Anyway, it's young yet. To be weaned."

Belle Jane could still recall the soreness of her nipples when Georgie was just days old, how she suddenly knew that of course her body had been given these grand breasts for this infant's sustenance alone. And then, the loss and dismay she felt, when, at six months, even in the dark, even in the morning at his most hungry, he turned his nose away. She'd imagined he did not want to *become her*.

Twins, maybe, the calves were barely higher than their mother's belly, where they suckled, steadied their legs. This spring, they would be fattened on these grasses, have their owners' brand seared to their hides, and if it were a bull calf, have their testicles snipped loose. In the fall or next spring, they would be rounded up to be driven to the new railroad, bought as beef on the hoof. Chicago, maybe. Vancouver or Montréal. Fed and fed again, then slaughtered, quartered, wrapped and served as a fine chuck roast, prime rib, rib steak or baseball top sirloin. The whole world was mad for steak. Ground beef would do.

Bill let off his rope, rode off without her. She watched the calf twist its ankle, tumble and rise, under the sun. Run for its mother.

*

Now, in their one-roomed cabin, here was Belle Jane, in lipstick and drop earrings, cutting folds of crust for a juniper berry pie.

The berries had a sharp, piney flavour so she thought they'd do nice with some canned pears given her by Annie, and given her by Aunt Mollie or Aunt Jude, in California.

"What you got there?"

Bill, in from checking the horses, strode over still in his boots, which she eyed. They were talking again.

"Don't you get in it when it's baked up. It's for the family." Belle Jane pointed west.

She'd heard they were French, the family in the cabin the other side of the creek. Wintered away somewhere and back, now. Once, twice, when she'd been near enough the creek fetching water she'd seen their figures: a short man waddling about with a pipe, a boy not much on Georgie, a woman, a girl.

"I talked to the boy."

"Oh?"

"He was carrying two pails a water. Little bugger tripped on a rock and had to go all a way back."

"They don't have a well?" said Belle Jane.

"They do," said Bill.

Belle Jane crimped the edges of the pie, brushed the egg, sprinkled the sugar. Precious sugar. Soon, it would be a gobbled, delicious mash under someone's teeth. What a simple blessing, pie.

"Got sheeped," said Bill.

As in, screwed.

(Before fences and the Great Die-Up winter, when cattle and sheep crossed paths on range land, if a band of sheep got there first, they ate the low range grass down to the roots, and cut, trampled and hoof-stunk up the rest, leaving cattle to starve and die of thirst, while the sheep forged higher; and so, a cow man would say, "Got sheeped.")

"Like ours?" Belle Jane asked.

Bill's eyes were fixed on the pie, its lattices, its crust, just browned and out of the stove. "Like ours. The boy said there were rocks and sticks, too."

Bill fed the stove. "Thaw comes," he said, a toothpick between his teeth, "we'll find out what the deuce is in there."

The sugar and spice of the pie and the wood smoke had filled their cabin. The sun's light gave the crust even more of a shimmer. A little, for all she'd cared of it, Belle Jane didn't want to let it go.

"Thank you," said Belle Jane, a breath too late. Sometimes she forgot.

Bill tipped his hat, the waiter girl, the livery boy, and as he stepped outside, called, "I'll get Judy harnessed for ya."

Well, at least with the well, Belle Jane and the French mother would have something in common, something to commiserate about, tease out possibilities, and best of all, point a finger! Which is the best you can hope for, with a stranger. If they could find the right words.

*

Her mare tip-toed across the creek rocks, the water low and ice-specked yet. Judith didn't like water, the unknown, the possibility of sinking, but she'd crossed this icy creek dozens of times now. Belle Jane remembered the story of the dead baby. A group of Lewistown boys'd been fishing, in Big Spring Creek. A stream, too, really. Ran right through Washington Street. The baby's bare skin had hastily been wrapped in sheets, raised from the silt by a boy of five, no front teeth. Drowned or buried in the water after it'd stopped breathing, Coroner Attix could not tell. The paper called it "ghastly," a "mother's crime."

What an image to carry in to another woman's home, she thought, as she tapped at the sun-grayed wooden door. What kind of mother-woman am I?

"Please, you call me Germaine," said Mrs. Arnal. Her accent was rose hips, the eyelashes of a horse, the cracks of skates on a frozen pond. She wore a plain white blouse tightened half up her neck, a dainty cross, her hair atop her head but fraying.

Below a half dozen books and a painting of a woman in a dress in a meadow, a small girl with a bowl haircut kneeled on a bench, churning butter with a frown verging tears. She begged with her eyes for her mother to see, below a lovely blue handknit sweater, how tired her arms were. Mrs. Arnal listed for her daughter, Louise, the chores that needed to be done, how each family member was doing one, and if the girl should stop her churning, could her brother stop his chopping? Should Louise like to go cold tonight without wood for the fire? Would she tell father, sorry, no butter for your bread? Mrs. Arnal told the girl she knew it was hard, but that the girl was strong and she knew she could do it. The girl nodded, came to grips with the churn again. One thumb was red and swollen and wrinkled.

Belle Jane'd understood it all simply by the language of mother talk, Germaine's pointing, and, from long-ago St. Louis Day dances in Frenchtown, the scraps of French words she could make out: *beurre, frère, froid. Forte!*

Germaine told her that she'd learned English well enough at the camp in Algérie where Mr. Arnal practically grew up (and where her job was to lead the sheep to the well at night, and in that black-dark, the gaze of lions' eyes), that she'd found work as a translator for the courts in Calgary. That she'd made dresses at first and then, on the side; had once made dresses for rich Americans in Paris alongside an aunt who died of pneumonia.

"My mother, she knew I was not for farming. I ran off at the markets with our dog. He was a Newfoundland dog and so big we were always found, but she tired of it. So, she let me off to the city with Aunt Elodie. But, she died."

It all sounded like a fairytale adventure (Belle Jane'd sworn she would have adventures!), except now the heroine was stuck on a *farm* in the throes of milk fat and crying toddlers and cruel hens (on tying her horse, Belle Jane'd watched the boy get finger-nipped by a half-moulted chicken who went on to stand on a sister and peck at its head).

Germaine beat her to the thought: "And now, I am here." She presented her backdrop—this one-windowed, one-roomed cabin on a farm at the edge of a place that only just had a name—as if on an opera house stage. Only a hint of remiss.

"This pie, it is so kind of you. Would you like to take a coffee?" Germaine rose, slid the kettle to the fire, reached at the shelf for the tin of grounds. She was an ox, she was a duck.

The girl glared at her mother as if she were a traitor, fixing coffee for the enemy.

Back to her stand of pots, wrists resting on the table, Germaine eyed the kettle, willing it on. "I have been thinking to try to come to you, but I only walk to the barn."

"It's hard, I do know . . ." said Belle Jane as the kettle wheezed. She'd meant to qualify it, but where would it end? "Well, I had those berries and I thought, I'll bake a pie."

Germaine stared out her window, at their little kingdom. The sky was the softest blue, almost white. Outside, hens pecked at elusive mites in the log poles of the cabin till Germaine kicked at them from the inside.

"Those creatures would gobble *us*," she laughed.

Germaine would make it, Belle Jane could tell. This family would have victorious photographs taken—in front of this cabin on a sunny day in a clean apron for the occasion, of the boy and a baby to come atop a pony, of harvest stacks half up to the clouds, of sofas and fur coats and anniversaries. They would last.

Belle Jane thought to ask about the curious case of the wells, but it felt, now, too private and rough a matter, after just learning one another's names.

Germaine strode to the table eyeing Belle Jane's neck, the point of her lace collar. Five tiny loops, locked, like the hands of sisters, around the mother loop. A swan, mid-flight, looking back.

"This is very fine," said Germaine, suspiciously, admiringly. "This is *le fond du mariage*, no? How do you say?"

Belle Jane had made it ten years ago, when she was Mrs. Junk. Alone in the bedroom, while the riff raff and drunkards of Butte, among them Peter, found their hats and ambled home in the reek of boiling cereals at the brewery.

Belle Jane could only nod. Yes, "The wedding *background*," she whispered. Yes, you may touch it, touch me.

Germaine traced the lace's knots the way the doctor inspects a child's spine, his breath from the back, the knees. Her hands were warm.

Belle Jane got that heady feeling one gets, being touched, fawned over, by another woman in a shop. Suddenly she missed her sisters and Jane Nash so much she felt sick and the slow, jolting knocks of the butter churn seemed to stir *her*. Was that a bite mark, at the base of the girl's thumb?

She did take a coffee, waved off the cream.

"Ahh, like a cow boy, they say?" joked Germaine.

It would only take a slight costume change for them to be ranch hands playing cards and cleaning rifles at the table. The white of fine teacups and cigarettes dangling from their moustached mouths. *Deal me in, will ya?*

Belle Jane felt the sickness glowing, and yet she'd held off the last of her coffee, hoping to prolong the visit, be offered more. Though she was not offered more. Of course, there was work to do. And yet, who should care? The cooking and washing and animal-tending would never end!

Belle Jane managed to tell that her people were from Ireland, both sides. That her father'd tried being a gold hunter then figured out he could get richer faster selling liquor and beef for the miners, and horses for the quitters.

"We're raising horses," she said.

"Ahh, yes. I see them, sometimes."

Montana, it suddenly sounded brave and beautiful. Populated by philosophers, triers. It was where Georgie was, and that was everything. The wanting for him now, it was a big soggy rag growing heavy in her heart.

"My son, he's in Montana with my folks, but he'll be here soon."

"Ah, it's good!"

Belle Jane would fetch Georgie and yes, the boys—Eugenie's Clement and Belle Jane's Georgie—would be friends. Good, very good friends. Riding and hiding and fishing.

She thought again of the dead baby, the boys—fishing.

The creek that also seemed to want to keep animals and secrets.

*

Two afternoons later, a man stood at her corral in tall riding boots with his hips cocked, one hand on his horse's bridle and reins, like he'd been waiting too long. The corral must've been fifty feet from the creek, where she was fetching water, but she could see the long moustache, the arrogance: *I've been more places, my horse is faster, I've had prettier women. Naughtier too.*

Bill, in a soiled and sweaty wool shirt and necker, his baby face, he nodded but stood his place.

Should she come up? Should she stay under cover in the creek brush, be a mouse? Belle Jane eyed her dented water pail, the dipper. She would offer the stranger some water.

The man watched Belle Jane making her way. He kept up what he was saying to Bill, pointed all about their place with his nose. An old lady who had rooms next door in Butte once told Belle Jane that flared nostrils are a sure sign one is a spendthrift.

Bill swept his hand south with enthusiasm, folded his hands in the pit of his arms. Had they met before?

It had rained hard yesterday, and the two days before that, so she tread slowly in the mud, which lapped at her skirts.

"Indade, I'll tell you why," said the man. He had a Scottish accent and mud-slicked spurs. His horse's coat was liver chestnut, its mane tousled over its eyes.

The milk cow bawled. His horse gave a whicker. The wind. Their words dropped off.

"Damn right," said Bill.

The man tapped the gloves at his bridle. "He did try."

The Russian. They say he wore rags on his feet, tried roasting a rattlesnake. A rattler tail'd been nailed above the door.

Bill gave Belle Jane a smile. After a breakfast of sow belly and bread, they'd fooled. Twice. She swore she could still smell his spice on her hands. She worried, had it been too soon since her monthlies? Sunday last she'd laid her head on his chest, nose to a rib and the trickle of his heart, and he'd whispered, "Might be nice, having a little girl around to help you some."

His voice was taller now: "Mr. McDonald, my wife."

"Mrs. Kinnick," he said, his face straight.

He'd be the type, she thought, to stay sat and shove a whore's head down.

She held out the dipper, the pail. "Are you thirsty, Mr. McDonald?"

"Thank you." He drank and they watched his whisker ends soak and darken, blond-white to iron gray. He took a navy silk hankie from his pocket and wiped his mouth.

"Well," he said to Bill, "you see that mare, you might hold on to her for me? If you can fetch her."

"I will."

Belle Jane studied the branding job on horse's hind, the fat welts where irons had seared the gelding's hide. Solo range rustlers carry irons so skinny they can be hidden in a boot.

"You've got the half-circle AP?" she said.

The man's eyes darted to the barn, and back to Belle Jane. "Cattle is bar AP. A with an arrow, is horses."

He spoke again: "She'll be foaling soon. I got a mind someone knew that."

"Couldn't of got far then," said Bill.

"We'll keep an eye," said Belle Jane.

They all three looked south, to the short forest of creek shrub that wound wide and skinny, the two willows. Strays and the branded ones seemed to bunch there, by the water and the crooks of places where the wind does not blow. Come April, maybe May, once the snow was behind them for sure, the horses would be rounded up, sorted out. The Kinnicks'd hoped at least a few—a buckskin, a blood bay, a red roan—would go unclaimed.

Mr. McDonald mounted his horse. "You need anything, anything a'tall, you call on us. Neighbour in need is a neighbour indade."

He looked back, gave a wink.

STRAYED

Buckskin mare, wire cut on hind leg,
branded on left thigh; $10 reward.
Nick Olson, Kevin, Mont.

17

1913

CURRENTS OF SNOW SWAM THE FLATS, threatened to go on, like little beasts, forever, or at least all the way to Montana. The sun was nowhere, but was out, still. Things'd thawed enough, they thought they'd try the well. Bill had an old civil war shovel given him by his grandfather, Calvin Briggs. Better as a garden hoe, but it was all they had.

Belle Jane, in her shawl and cow boy hat, stood by, took turns with a pail for the softer snow at the top. Snow has layers, lives. It prefers to be left.

"Damn packed tighter 'n hogs."

"Think it's frozen yet?" Belle Jane had learned the woman's art of asking. Sometimes she even practised it.

"Be my guess."

Bill's fingers were turning pink, and he reached for the gloves in his rear pocket. He began to stab the snow-ice with the pick end of the shovel.

"Grandpa Briggs, thought he was the big shot."

All Belle Jane'd heard of Bill's mother's father was that he'd been some kind of war hero, that he'd lived in Illinois, that he'd been hard on his sons and his wife. He'd only been dead a year.

"One winter, Ma thinks we ought to go to stay with the old man. Les stayed back and I went and Letha Mae went and soon Ma was about goan to burst with Alma Melissa. So big she wouldn't leave the house. Even for some big talk at the opera house. A caucus. I remember that, didn't have Les to joke about it with. *Cockus*."

A shovel, when you can't stand on its shoulder and thrust forth its tip, is merely a spoon. A fish.

"So they called this town caucus because the women of Homeburg thought they should have one of their own on the school board."

"They sure as hell weren't going for that," said Belle Jane. The snow had wet her boots, and her toes were ice cold.

"Nope." Bill took a break, rested a boot on the rock rim of the well. He didn't mind, her cursing. He didn't try to change her. She didn't try to change him (much). She liked his stories, when they came.

Belle Jane looked down. Still snow, but below, something else, another texture, another kind of white.

"They brought in old Briggs, with his half arm and his cough. Fifteen years ago already. He'd got into politicking after the war. So he stood and spoke on why a woman shouldn't intrude, should stay home. Must've been hundreds of folks in that opera house and not a word. Thought he'd closed the case! He sat down, put the lid right back on his fountain pen. Letha and I were sitting on a bench by the curtains. He winked at us. Then this woman stood and oh Lord his eyes went wide. His whiskers fairly tried to run. This woman, she said," and Bill's voice pitched high: "'That's all right, Mr. Briggs—You can't make me sit down, Mr. Chairman, you nor any of you politicians. You're a fine man to talk about schools, Mr. Briggs.' There someone tried to call some order on her. 'No, I won't stop. You know a lot about children, don't you, coming up here with tobacco juice all over your shirt front; and why don't you pay some taxes before you get up here and tell how to run a town? All right, chairman, I'm done.'"

Belle Jane'd laughed aloud more than once. It was the very sort of thing she liked to think she herself would do.

Bill switched back to his regular voice. "Grandpa Briggs dared not look down at his shirt, but she was right. He kicked the wheel of his buggy when we were leaving. Broke a toe."

(Ms. Emma Madigan, a "town character," went on to attack the editor of the paper, who'd attempted to reverse the disgraceful attack by a woman on a beloved citizen, and even though the chairman called to order, she stood and said: "You're the biggest coward of 'em all. If you thought you'd have to lose the school printing, you'd vote for the devil for president of the school board.")

Belle Jane'd taken the shovel, turned it upside down to poke and whittle at what was left of the snow-ice till she hit something that cracked. She saw flashes of the black gates, the purple-black placenta in the pan.

"Bill, Bill there's something in there."

Wells too low to the ground, sometimes calves fall in, but this well, built by some Russian who got a tumour near his ear, was raised.

They both looked down and saw what they saw: bones ochre-gray at the edge. Legs, ribs, the head. Hooves. Dumped there to be hidden, not so long ago. In the coming days, as a "Manyberries chinook" rolled through and the warm air dripped the snow away, they knew. The well was socked with cattle bones.

Belle Jane's mind drew a scene: the shadows of men, the hog-tied hooves of cattle, the saws.

She thought about the stories Old Rocco'd told her, about the Montana gangs of civil war misfits who stole horses and cattle, took them to secret hideouts in gulches and the Badlands by the Missouri River, blotted brands and even scorched horses' foreheads with hot baked potatoes to give them "stars" before smuggling the animals off to Canada, the Dakotas, Wyoming. Until the Deer Lodge ranchers'd had enough. Caught the rustlers and took them to the trees. Bandits got lynched and their foreheads wore the words: *Horse thief.*

Strange, Belle Jane's memory fixed not the lariat that hung them, in the end, but the ones in the mid-night chase, the hide-outs. As a girl she'd had a dream of being in it, rolling down a coulee, the prick of brush thorns, wads of dust in her mouth.

Two wells stuffed with bones.

Just days ago, she'd watched a pair of antelope leap toward the creek brush, the sage and box elder and cottonwoods, and disappear their antlers, even their white tails and bellies, entirely. The perfect underworld for a boy to explore. Or, an outlaw. What and who had that brush hidden? Now that the Kinnicks were here, was it gone?

Presses of steam, how exquisite, on her skin, the cow boy's shower with a cloth and a pot, when she wonders: Why didn't McDonald ask why she was getting water from the creek and not the well?

*

She woke in a sweat, empty. Drained of everything. She was afraid of becoming that well, socked with bones, other lives. Dry.

She wanted to swim with her son Georgie. She wanted to hear the boy's wild and meandering stories—of triumphant footraces and falling stars and even Annie's potato suppers. She wanted to watch his arms fly-loop the lariat, his brown eyes squealing, "Ma, d'ya see that?"

She left Judith with a heather-white crocus flower, soft as moth wings; and Bill, with a note.

The sun rose at her side like the ghost of a man. Outstretched arms, a slicker, a hat. The sun said: *I'm coming for you.*

No mind, thought Belle Jane. You come right along. Wouldn't be a day of my life, didn't have a man trying to get in my way.

"East," she taunted at the sun-ghost. She would know her way. She was heading north and a little west, to Maple Creek, to the trains.

The April snow at her horse's feet was dust, young and tired. But that could change, if the wind felt ornery. Would it? She looked to the purple-gray sky above, a cut of light.

She imagined Bill coming in to the darkened kitchen for his coffee and bread. Was the note in his fingers? She imagined him hot and stone-faced on counting one horse missing from the corral, the hand on his chest as he read her note.

She didn't want to leave Judith at Simpkin's livery stable, fine a man as he was, so she'd saddled a dapple gray old gelding she hadn't noticed before. A horse that wouldn't be missed, she thought. Carol, she'd called him, as they crawled into the last of the dark and rode past the Arnals' barn.

Carol fought her. He writhed at the bit, he would plod, but he would not trot nor gallop. His stride was so short and the journey so bumpy she imagined her buttocks bruising blue. Before a long train journey!

The sun was in the sky now, unknowable. Belle Jane's ass was also growing sore from giving the kick as Carol slowed, and slowed more. *'Bout as fast as a turtle in shit*, Cousin Hector would've said.

The horse should've been rested and eager for the journey. Wasn't even packed. Dresses and whatnot, there were still trunks at her folks' place. The saddlebag held just her silk crepe lace pretties, a ruby shawl and a rubbed, leatherback copy of *Evalina; or a Young Lady's Entrance into the World.* Belle Jane had only thumbed the gilt letters of the title yet, and now she would have miles alone with her book. This seemed to her nearly as good a reason to get gone. If she got the train at all.

"Cursin' you," she muttered, at the sun-ghost. She would stop, water Carol at Bear Creek, east of town.

Barbed wire cut right through the creek, and she was thankful she'd seen the posts between the scrubby aspen and sagebrush. Water flowed just enough there were riddles of currents at his feet. Carol kept his head down as he drank, seemed to know he ought to be ashamed. Or should he? Now that it was day light—and she stood across from him, boots perched on a fallen maple log—she saw scuffs near his ankles the width of rope.

The only sound was a fat tongue on cool water, hooves on lonely rocks, for there were so many.

Had he been hobbled? Tied in a waiting place?

Only a few miles of rocks and snow-dipped spear grass separated them from the edge of town, where young maple trees lifted their arms like jubilant toddlers and wind-crazed women, but she did look south, to the sea of Prairie wool and a young hawk with mottled brown wings hunting up a crittered breakfast. What had she written anyway? Would Bill know she meant nothing by it, that she wanted to save him the trip, that her mother-need to be with Georgie had suddenly sunk her body at the bottom of a red dirt ditch.

That this was something she did: ran away, ran. But always, came back.

Carol stopped drinking but kept his head down, then jolted high. Belle Jane looked to the horizon, listened, past the skitter of a wind just waking. Carol turned his head and ears in the direction they had come, his tail lifted. The wind blew his mane across his neck. Something held his attention.

It was a horseback rider and a pack horse besides. She felt for her hips, loose and free without a belt of bullets. She had no rifle today. No mind, she thought. I think I know who it is.

The low Plainsman hat, the skinny, knowing shoulders reaching, already, to save her. Bill. Reins loose. The fast, steady gait, almost gliding on the hills, the nose that knew the way, to her. Troy.

She gave a wave.

"Belle Jane?"

And soon they were a pack of bodies, shy and unsure and out of breath. Sniffing, for danger.

Bill smiled, like one splashed up from the bottom of a lake. "That was one hell of a ride."

"I'm sorry."

Bill tied the young bay to a branch.

"No . . . I come because that gelding, he's no good," he said, already undoing the saddle girth at Carol's belly. He was not trying to stop her or take over. "You took the wrong horse."

Troy stood beside Carol as if on watch, but the horse, eyes fixed on the promise of the creek, gray ears back and low, said: *Go away.*

She felt what she felt the day after Alice's wedding, at the station, the tender prick of wonder and love.

Quickly, she wiped a tear.

"I wasn't sure, if you would know."

Carol stepped back toward the creek water to drink again, become a shadow. Looking down, Belle Jane noticed his unshod hooves, chipped and craggy.

"Know what?"

It was all silly, the stories she'd invented. He'd understood her note plain: she was going for Georgie; she would be back. They'd talked about it now and then, it'd just been a matter of when. A man would do the same without a thought.

"Judith, she likes you to hold her feed bucket for her. Water, too."

"I know. I'll do that for ya." He took off his gloves, tipped her chin to his to kiss her.

His lips were salty. She felt a bit dizzy and yet righted. Against his chest, her nipples rose.

And the suspicions, like the black of matchsticks.

NOTICE

$10 REWARD will be paid for information leading to recovery of a buckskin horse, white face, branded HY on right shoulder, age coming four years. $10 will be paid for information leading to the conviction of said person illegally holding the above horse. –Tenaille

18

1913

GEORGIE'S FINGERS rolled over the gilt letters of the title: *THE TALE OF PIGLING BLAND.*

"Now, Mama? Now will you read it?"

He'd been asking since they got to the station. For a Tuesday, the place was like a beehive. She'd meant to stay at least another week, but she couldn't do it. The eyes, the dusty, fly-shit stale air, she'd started nipping brandy again. Alice and Harry were living in Shelby, and the baby was due to come in June. Her sister May'd married Alfred Anderson, and he worked at the rail office in Helena. (No babies for Aunt Lillie; she spent most days rocking the criers at an orphanage run by the church.) So it was that Georgie'd had his grandparents and the house to himself these few months.

Now they were sat in their seats and the red Lewistown brick of the depot grew smaller as they blew past the sun-got yellow flats of the Judith Basin. Belle Jane could already feel the waves of nausea, taste the bile, trying to read as their car rocked through the low green hills, but how could she refuse her son?

In her absence, he'd lost a tooth, had started parting his thick, dark hair in the middle, which he liked to comb himself standing next to Dad George in the toilet room. And he liked to read following along with a finger, the way Annie did—who'd struggled to read as a girl but persevered and now had an affinity for reading histories and Bible stories.

"Mama?"

"All right, then."

She looked at the pig on the cover, dressed in a blue collared shirt and brown coat. One hand carried a red sack, the other, a cane. The pig was stood upright, walking down a country road.

"What do you suppose is up for this pig, Georgie?"

"Well I think he's going somewhere."

Georgie, who'd been acting the stranger, tucked into her. His head rest on her chest. She hoped the wool would not be too scratchy, that he would stay there, forever.

"Ah." She leaned down, kissed his hair. "Just like us. *We* are going somewhere."

Dad George had fought her on it: "What about his schooling? Have you even got a pot for him to piss in?"

At that she'd laughed. No, no they hadn't. Men and boys pissed into the wind, though she used a biffy she was hoping to fix up some. For the ways they'd coddled Georgie (cutting his steak and tying his laces), she'd hissed, "He might as well be in nappies!"

Dad George had been right, though. Her son should not go unschooled. He'd just turned four (celebrated over slices of *torta savoia*, a layered cake of chocolate, hazelnut and sponge, glazed in chocolate and rum, baked by the Mr. Sconfienza in Helena yet). What came of the spat was an idea that she would teach school at the house for Georgie and a few of the neighbour kids once the big house was built. Give her a little pin money too.

Belle Jane smoothed the boy's hair. Her tall, thoughtful, well-read boy could easily be mistaken for six. "You'll have friends and horses."

It only just occurred to Belle Jane that Georgie was nearing the age of her long-dead brother Tom-George, that black-eyed boy with a cowlick who pocketed dinner scraps for the street dogs and resisted shoes and captaining baseball games because he didn't like to hurt any boy's feelings as they stood in a line, hands back, waiting to be picked.

"A horse?"

Georgie was church friends with a little girl, Susannah Barney, whose saddle pony was just shot in the breast in an act of spite against her father after a race in which the pony'd taken first money. Mr. Barney'd gone and offered a reward of $100 for information, more than the dead pony was probably worth. She thought Georgie might mention Susannah's pony, which he'd ridden too, but he didn't.

"Why yes, a horse," she said. "And a dog."

"A dog?"

She nodded. If a boy needed anything, surely it was a dog. She would ask around in Maple Creek.

"We don't want a dog like Sassy."

Sassy, the yappy runt terrier that belonged to Mrs. Raffy and barked with all its piercing might when even a baby blinked near it.

Georgie's eyes widened.

"No, we want a nice big Good Sir kind of dog, don't we?"

He gave a sad but hopeful nod.

"That's right."

The night of the gun, Good Sir had stayed by Gale, licking at the dribbles of blood until the dog's jowls stained crimson. After the farm'd been sold for the debts, Good Sir came to the Corneil house, but he was not a town dog. Good Sir laughed at fences and ran away. Gale ran away too. To Michigan, and had lately married a Helen Nellie Wilkinson.

A round, gray-haired woman in thick flat boots, men's boots, walked the aisle, resting a hand on each seat edge and pausing a moment. She smiled a fat-cheek smile as she neared Belle Jane and Georgie, took a breath and reached for the next seatback.

A mother, a boy, a book. Outside, a sky of clouds shaped like hobo hogs and flying feather ticks. The *whizz-glit-pah* of the tracks. *We are going somewhere.*

Georgie had fallen asleep, lips wide, sighing now and then in his bunched up little suit, and as she tried to reach for the copy of *The Maple Creek News* tucked behind Georgie's back, *The Pigling Bland* thudded on the floor and woke him. She'd known that was a possibility, here the paper had gone unread all this time since she'd left town, but she'd grown desperately bored. Along the way, over the last two days, she'd met a teacher, a preacher, a widow. This last stretch, though, it'd been just the two of them and beyond the window, a horizon of thirsty grasses, cows laid low and the *tip-top* of the raindrops.

Georgie's eyes popped open. "Pigling!"

"Oh, it's fine."

She reached over her knees for the cloth-bound hardcover that now bore a trail of silt, a soggy spine top. It'd rained sideways yesterday, but everyone agreed: *Good for the crops!* Belle Jane brushed the soiled bits off with her gloves.

"Grandad got me that."

"He did."

Inside was the inscription: *For little Georgie, our adventurer. Love, Grandad Corneil.* Even though The Busy Corner had once had a circulating library and those cloth-spined books had been everywhere in the parlour and the girls' rooms, Dad George happily bought new books, new everything, from the boy at Power Mercantile. So much so the child turned his nose at the trousers and overcoat given to him by Mrs. Blink from church when her son Charles'd grown out of them. "I don't like handy downs." Georgie refused it when she said the phrase was "hand-me-downs." Well, thought Belle Jane, wouldn't they just see about that?

As the boy flipped the pages to study the illustrations, finally, she would read the paper: Mrs. Kearns was hiring a girl, there wasn't a single Cypress tree in the Cypress Hills (just white spruce, Scotch pine and lodgepole pine), and a Cree woman pled guilty in Regina to having more than one husband. Then the notices: *ESTRAYED* . . .

Georgie tugged at her neck, "Aren't we there yet?"

In the warmth of the afternoon and their breath, the windows fogged. Georgie stood, snatched the paper and used it to rub a patch of the glass dry.

"I was reading that, Georgie."

"Well," he said, passing her the damp, ruffled pages, and then, "Holy smokes!"

"What, Georgie?"

The train approached the stockyard, a sea of sheep. Worse, their rank and bleating now filled the car.

"Must be a hunerd!"

"Hun*dred*. And more than that." Several hundred, maybe even a thousand, unsheared, heads down, licking their own shit off their brothers' hooves.

Georgie insisted on marvelling at them when they got off the train while she looked out for Bill and saw to their trunks. She'd taken it upon herself to pick up a few things: a dandy set of forks and knives, quinine for head colds, nails, coconut, kerosene for sore throats, onion seeds, a mackinaw coat for Bill, a new copy of *The Wife's Secret*, three bolts of wool and linen (each), and three bottles of Smybert's Rye. Time to time she poked her head around the agent or crates to make sure she could see Georgie, but now that all was stacked neat, she called out and the boy neither came nor could be seen.

"Georgie!" she called, a little louder than she'd meant. Her boots clacked on the boardwalk to the yards but who could hear anything and who would want to try to respond with all that bleating, that shit-dust on your tongue?

Was he with the horses? Outside the livery stable, a two-horse team was tied to a post and a man without an overcoat or hat, nearly bald on top, was stacking crates and trunks to a wagon.

"Pardon me?" said Belle Jane.

He looked up but did not pause. The hair he did have was dark and curly, wet, like his trouser hems.

"Have you seen a boy?"

The main pointed, past the brooms and shovels resting against the side of the livery, the broken window.

She gave the man a thank you smile and called out. "*Geor-gie.*"

It was no use: the sheep, the train, the horses, the men.

She looked back at the station. No Georgie. She tip-toed in the mud to the back of the barn, one hand along its faded walls for balance. As she neared that smashed window, she heard voices and thought, oh dear, some poor soul is on the receiving end of her son's questions.

"I wouldn't," said a man, sounding like he had a pinch of chewing tobacco in his mouth.

"No?" said another man, louder, younger, some kind of accent. The tang of manure was sharp in the cold and rain.

"Nope," said the first man.

"But McDonald has all the horses always." The accent, it was French.

A horse kicked its stall. For a moment, no words were said.

That man, Angus McDonald, his strange way at their corral had made her chest alight, both a warning and a kind of drawing in. Should something be bad for us, we might like it all the more.

The French man said: "And he gives all the beef for the Studers."

The Studers, the family, along with the Garmans, that had the contract to build the railway bed for the section of the Weyburn-Lethbridge branch line that would run through Ravenscrag, nine miles south of the Kinnick ranch. The line would slip alongside the Frenchman River, just back enough from the water and the white coulees and brush. The Studers, and most of the others—the barn boss and the plow man and the dump wagon boss and the mule skinner and the cooks—came up from the States, where their families had done this work every summer since most could remember.

(The Leaches and the Shipmans—a respected black family from Omaha—would not be there: on returning from Montana in a democrat pulled by mules, they didn't realize heavy rains had caused the Frenchman to flood. Mules walked right in to the river and tipped the democrat; the men drowned—one in the moment, one later, with a torrent of water in his lungs. For Mr. Leach, they'd had to fetch the man with the barge and hook.)

A gang of the rail workers had just returned and locals, like Mr. Arnal, who blacksmithed, had got day work, many tasked with shovelling earth to level the track, which was quite a job in these parts. From a great distance, you could see the white tents, the smoke of feeding fifty men.

Belle Jane's heart fluttered. That had been one of her schemes, to supply beef to gangs of railway workers.

She heard the drag of a rake, the men's voices growing wider apart under the livery roof.

"And how's he got all that cow, is what we're all wonderin'. Y'ever see him dickerin' and tradin'? Y'ever see him here with the same horse more 'n twice?"

"That black bay."

"Well, might be. Might be he tries not to be in our company much for a reason. Anyways, I'll say this once: you buy them horses, might be trouble."

The slat of wood she was standing on, above the mud, slid out. She looked down to make her next move and nearly stepped on a rat with its face smashed in, still in the motion of running with those tiny paws.

"Oh Lord!" she cried, peering at it. Was that its bulbous tongue out? *Fuck right off Peter Junk.*

"Mama?" Georgie came running her way from the alley. "Why you—?"

She waved at her son to be quiet and give over his hand to help balance her, get back to the wood sidewalk. She thought to lay down the pages of that paper, but Georgie towed over an old two-by-four.

"I found Bill," said Georgie, turning his neck to see two livery men in muddy overalls and ties stroll out the back door to see about the commotion.

Belle Jane gave them a wave and a smile. Livery men, you want to be on good terms with them.

"You're to call him Dad, Georgie."

"You call granny 'Annie.'"

"Well." Sometimes, it was no use. Adults made no sense. The world made no sense.

The boy let his mother hold his hand, and as they walked west to the station, they fell in to the shadows of the setting sun, its strokes of gray and rose and gold.

That night, she closed her eyes and her mind told her still-rollicking body she was riding the horse, the wagon, the train yet and plunged her *down down down.* Her heart dashed, her legs jerked and her arms flared to stop the fall. She woke. It happened twice, three times. Until enough minutes passed she was more awake than asleep, and her bladder knew it. Oh, even on a spring night, the biffy. How she wished she were a girl, not needing to go in the night, or a dog that could lift its leg, or a man that could turn his arse.

Under their feather tick (one she'd shared with two other husbands in two other lifetimes), her fingers felt for Bill. His side was not just barren but cold. She sat up, lit a candle. There was Georgie, upside down on his pallet, arms tall, as if he were on a hill watching the clouds with a friend, not a care. He'd go to heaven right off.

No sign of Bill. Well, she thought, and found her boots and shawl.

She closed the door slowly. Outside, an animal leapt from a basket, retreated to a post below her washing table, then turned back to stare at her. Glassy-lit eyes. Ears. A tail? Belle Jane fell against the door and braced her chest. *Oh stars*. She realized: It was Mary-Mary, the tuxedo cat with a three-quarter tail they'd brought from town. (It'd fled a barn fire.) Georgie'd insisted on calling her after the queen not once but twice, to differentiate from the other children's cats.

"Mary-Mary! You frighten me like that, you'll get the wrong end a my rifle."

Cats, she thought, the lives they led at night. The animal stood in the limbo of the moonlight, waiting, for what she didn't know.

Belle Jane walked the other direction, to the biffy. She thought she heard a tapping sound. Like water, like a mean teacher's fingers on a desk.

Tap, tap.

Nothing.

Tap.

The biffy door was swung open, a pair of boots splayed in the dirt, tips down.

"Bill?"

He jumped back and out of the biffy until he was sat on his ass on the earth. She saw the glint of the hammer.

"What're you doing?"

"Scared the shit out of me."

"Out of *you*? I come around the corner and see boots." She was careful not to shout in the direction of her candle, but it fluttered.

Bill brought his knees up, rested his arms on them.

In the beyond, they heard a crack. A branch cracking.

"What was that now?" said Belle Jane. "What in to hell is happening tonight?"

Bill glanced over his shoulder. "Prob'ly just a buck. Or that bull moose."

It was mating season, and they'd been warned about the ornery moose that liked to wander out of the Cypress Hills and down the Blacktail Coulee. Six feet tall and 1,400 pounds. Rack the size of a hog. Take a half-minute for a bull moose to gore you.

"Lord. So?"

"I was getting the seat right, so Georgie won't fall in."

It did happen, on farms. Folks are busy and far off. Little ones going alone, their bottoms are so small. They can only stand in that sluice so long. Bill'd known a boy, a twin, who went that way.

"You don't want to do a thing like that in the light a day?"

Bill stood slowly, let the hammer hang loose. "Couldn't wind down. Think I was just so glad to have you both here. And then the Shaw boy come to mind. I was terrified Georgie'd get up in the night to go . . . and we wouldn't hear him."

Bill had that kind of heart. He would be a better mother than she would, she was sure. When they were leaving Maple Creek, two little girls—one in a dotted dress, pinafore and straw hat, the other in a white cloth bonnet that matched her pinafore—were reunited outside that fine new post office, on the weedy grasses by the steps. Couldn't have been more than three, four. And they were so thrilled that straw hat girl held bonnet girl by the neck and kissed her on the lips, eyes open, smiling yet. It'd made Belle Jane ache not for a girl of her own, but for her sister Lillie. Or Jane Nash, or Fanny, or even Philippa. Bill'd watched the kiss with a shy smile, and when they were passed, gave Belle Jane a look.

Now, under the stars, she hugged him, let her nose run along his neck, the linger of a day—nails, horses, oats. His fingers, rough and strong and wanting, held her neck, her spine. She could split in two: head and body. Or, east and west.

STRAYED

to my ranch. One sorrel mare, three white feet and strip. E.H. Fox, Truly

19

1913

SHE BELIEVED IN BEAUTY. That in the tiny, delicate petals and whorls and ropes of the lace she made, it whispered, *Life*. Why? Was it the perfect geometry? The edging toward a centre, a heart? Or the way every point spilled into another, and another yet? Like our very cells.

She hadn't the time for it, but she insisted on her lace and crochet work—Battenberg collars, sashes of roses, coasters of starfish. Bill'd learned to darn his own socks. "I'll take that trade," he'd say, for the fine underthings he could wonder at across his lover's body in the night, in the barn.

They'd meant to marry officially. They left Georgie with the Arnals and took the train to Medicine Hat: bought rings, found a judge who would meet them in the morning, but that night, their hotel burned down to ashes and as they stood in their stockings in the snow, holding hands and boots, they took it as a sign. Belle Jane believed in the beauty of church—the gold cups and blue robes in the stained-glass windows, the legions of candles, the vibration of voices singing in unison, but she suspected God did not believe in wayward women like her, *Mrs. Kinnick.*

Wallpaper was a lot like needlepoint: fleshy yellow peonies, hummingbirds drinking nectar; the seeds and leaves and vines that connected them. Over and over. Life.

So it was that Belle Jane found herself on her way to paper the walls of the biffy. The wind blew steady and light, bowling the grasses. The sky was the bluest blue, its clouds like crumb cakes set out at every lady's place, just so.

She passed the hens shooing off a wren, then Judith in the corral. She stopped to stroke her horse's face, the darker cream hair along the nose. How striking, her dark eyes and lashes.

"I'll be back," she said, and Judith, cream belly muddied, nosed at her side. Belle Jane stood a moment against the corral and took in the new house: the porch with four columns and her blue pansy boxes, the windows. It was a two-storey and when you opened the door, you faced a staircase smack in the middle of the house (almost every home around was a one or two-roomed cabin, if that, and the houses in town, if there were stairs, stood politely and sparingly at the left; though there was a new French man, Gallot, a carpenter by trade whose wife was prairie mad and drank while he stood up a two-storey with a roof that curved like a derby hat and a perfectly round hay shack, not to mention the apple trees and cherries he tended after the wheat, the hogs, the horses). From her own bedroom on the second floor, at night Belle Jane swore she could see the tiniest candle flicker in the Gallot house. She'd heard it said he wrote letters accounting of his prosperity to cousins and brothers who never came. He did have a flock of children; at least three, including their George, would be coming to the house for "school" after harvest.

She thought of the little ones as they were picking the spot for the big house. The cabin had been close to a road allowance and the Arnals, just at the flats above Blacktail Coulee. Every time they laid down the rock to mark the spot, Bill'd look in each direction and say, "Back some."

Those afternoons were so hot not a thing stirred but the parties of flies in the cow patties. For all the quiet, it'd felt like all eyes were on them in a card game.

"Don't want to make it too easy," he'd said.

"Well, no," she said, and then; "Come again?"

He gave her a look, like she ought to know. The hobos twisting their ears at the door for a meal and picking off a calf on their way out, maybe. Neighbours, calling for this tool or a hand with that load. *A neighbour in need is a neighbour indeed.*

"Windy as the deuce up here, not?" At the cabin, coulee shrubs and the low hills broke the wind on three sides. Here, on the high flats, there was nothing around. Nothing around.

"Need a spot that's good and flat." He'd kick the rock another yard, and there it'd sit for a day.

Belle Jane'd worried he was stalling because he didn't really want to have the house built, and yet, he'd been the one to hand over the bills he'd tucked away, row by row, in a sack hidden in her fern planter in the parlour. Had they made so much from the few dozen cattle they'd sold to Rumpley, and the horses they'd broke? She was in such a rush to live in a fine house with walls (and stairs!), that she didn't dare ask. Also, when he'd heard they were making a go of it and planned to stay, Dad George had sent her a package containing one new edition of *The Wonderful Wizard of Oz*, and starting at page forty-six, a twenty dollar bill every twenty pages. Must be there were a lot of thirsty folks still patronizing the Elk Horn, and a desire for only Belle Jane to find those greenbacks. Flashes of all those books they'd always had at home and at The Busy Corner. Belle Jane wondered, Had they always been his bank?

The bucks in Bill's breast pocket, they'd hauled the timber not from the Hills but from Harlem, Montana. They got the men from all around to raise the roof, and you could tell, the looks they gave, wondering at the spot. A good mile from the creek, two from the Arnals and the road to come, and high enough they had a clear view of any little thing in every direction.

"See a prairie dog takin' a wiss," Bill would say.

Mostly, though, what they saw was the wind bending the necks of the spear grass, copper-eyed sharpie hawks swooping from the barn to hunt up mice, antelope bouncing toward their mothers, the water, the cover of Blacktail Coulee, which seemed to swallow them whole.

Belle Jane walked in the other direction, north, on the well-worn trail to the biffy, carrying a small box stuffed with tools: stay pins, scissors, cutter blades, seam roller, brush. That was one silver lining to marrying that Gale, the tools. He didn't have enough of a pair to come back for them (although she'd heard he was now a father again. He would go on to have so many children they'd run out of names and call a boy George). In the way that papering walls occupied her mind entire afternoons and in the way that those patterns of swallows and buds and going up vines let her soul reach for something (what?), she couldn't stop. Bill would either yell or laugh, her papering the biffy, but he was gone now. Branding at Drury's.

Belle Jane set her tools on the dirt and knotted a kerchief above her nose. She stuck a sprig of dried lavender that'd been in the Bible between the kerchief and her ear. For the rank. Then, she propped the biffy door open with a rock. They were everywhere and the size of flour sacks. They seemed to romp and birth quints in the night. Poor Georgie would never finish his rock-picking.

Georgie, of course he was the other silver lining to marrying Gale. That boy was so good about slopping the pig, fetching eggs, feeding the horses. Between chores, he spent hours at that creek. At first, she fretted some and would call him every so often. That spring, a little boy who lived on a farm about where the Farwell meets the Frenchman River was too excited to start the day and ran out in his sleeping gown while his mother was fixing breakfast, and a sister going out to milk happened upon the boy, so frightened he hadn't yelled, his scalp in the clutches of a bobcat. Sat right on his head. The girl punched the bobcat in the neck. There was a scuffle, blood, cat cries of terror. The sister would show their scars with a little glee.

Inside the biffy, Belle Jane's fingers felt for the knots and ridges of the lumber. Not flat at all. A little like these odd rolling hills stumbling toward water.

And it was at the creek where the three Georges found those hides. Three, ice-stiff in the shade of a thicket. Tossed like a wretched sock. It looked like the edges had tried to crawl back, to the blood stain that marked the heart. The boys'd come running up, breathless. Bill rode down to see the brand. Said one of the lines looked fresh. Telegraph wire, Bill figured. We didn't know the original or the botched brand. Louis Arnal thought the steer had come from Small's, one of the big outfits over by Fish Creek. Four thousand cattle. Easy picking.

Plenty of nights, cattle haunted her. She'd close her eyes and see their maggot-pecked legs in that well, the knees, the tips of the hooves, as if they'd try to fly out hoof-first.

The rustling, would there be more of it? That spring, there had been a sense of the possibility of abundance. The bed had been laid for the railroad, there was talk of a branch north from Ravenscrag to Murraydale, about five miles west, and of a branch line south to Kealey Springs, just above the Arnals. The May rains had been steady, would give the fields a good start, the heads of crops and the hinds of cattle would be fat, and fatter.

Hadn't they all been so brave and worked so hard? Wouldn't they be rewarded now?

A strange feeling came over her, standing there in the biffy with the door wide open. Taking her time too. The biffy was a place where you rushed in and out (save for those drawn-out holy awful moments of movement that plagued her), and but for the cut-out moon, you were in the shadows, saw little. Why then, did she want to paper the walls? Why did she feel a newcomer in this place she visited so often?

She bundled the stack of newspapers and catalogues beside the seat, glanced at the faces of cheery models and the ominous headlines. Stories, of how to be and how not to be. The families with girls, all the catalogue ladies would be cut out for paper dolls, and some old women tore out certain pages to avert certain wandering eyes. Belle Jane left it. She liked to look herself.

Freshly stripped in half from one of the boys was that paper she'd tried to read all that trip back with Georgie. Her eye caught on the STRAYED AND STOLEN section. Tennaille again, with his thirteen horse brands and a reward for information to be received confidentially about one defacing those brands. Below Tennaille's notice was this:

STRAYED

From the premises of G.W. Henn,
2 miles north of Fish Creek.
1 gray mare, 8 years old, weight, 1300
Has bone spavin on hind leg.
1 bright bay gelding, 2 years old, weight 800
White strip on face, 2 glass eyes.
1 buckskin gelding, 4 years old, black mane and tail,
black legs, 2 lumps on neck close to ears.
Last seen May 17. $10 for information
leading to recovery of same.

The gray. Her chest tightened. It was forever ago, that she'd ridden out before dawn to get a train to get her son, and Bill'd dashed after her to give her the better horse. When she'd returned the gray was gone. "Sold it," Bill said, and in its place was a chestnut yearling filly to break and two buckskin mares. Well, there were plenty of grays. Did Carol have knuckly, arthritic hocks? In the blue of dawn and in her haste, and even at the creek, she hadn't noticed. That gray did drag its toes. She remembered how thirsty it was, how tired too.

Oh catch hell, she thought. She'd forgotten the water, for the papering. Well, she should get her pieces cut first, maybe call Georgie for a bucket if he was in the yard. He'd been sulking because the Gallot's terrier had had puppies, but Bill had said no. Georgie said he'd tell his grandad how mean they were. Belle Jane offered the paper to write a letter. Georgie yanked it and ran to the creek. Belle Jane had almost had him reading and writing his letters, and wondered if he just might do it.

She worked top down. A pin, a cut. A pin, a cut. The sheets were long and she wasn't going to be too particular about the biffy job. *Any job worth doing*, she heard Dad George say. But she couldn't stand tight against the wall, with the seat and all, and her boot kept kicking at the stand of wood below the seat. A slab fell down once, twice.

Lord, she thought, she would have to get right down and nail the damn thing.

And then something rolled out, hit her toe.

It was a branding iron, a flathead. Rusty and ash-caked. She stared at it, thought to walk away, but instead, she held her breath, got square down with the ground so the boards pressed her breasts and she peered past the fallen board. What she saw was a small graveyard of irons: half circle, a U, an R, a 2. She could smell their metal, the flesh they'd seared. Hidden, here.

Her body staggered, her breath staggered. Not thinking, she reached for the seat.

In the door's cut-out moon of sunlight, her eyes leapt from the irons to the Blacktail Coulee to the images in her mind's eye: Bill nailing the biffy seat that night, the hides Georgie found, the relief on Bill's face when he found her with the gray, the rope burns that horse wore. McDonald, sniffing around like he knew the place. The livery stable men talking rough about him. How he fed the railroad gangs but somehow'd hardly raised a steer. No to the dog. The well stuffed with bones. The fucking bones.

*

She caught the two of them with their hats off, in the barn. She'd smelled the smoke again, grabbed a pitcher and ran. The full moon rising straight above the spires. Yellow-pink, like altar candles. The midnight-world of drifting owls and criminal mice. The beating hearts of beasts.

But the fire was man made, contained in a pit of dirt and rocks.

And there was Bill and Angus McDonald, eyes oily with smoke and the job at hand. And a sorry horse, a white-tailed chestnut. Its eyes, exasperated. The rope at its feet, trying to kick out. A blade. A bloodied, collared shirt in its mouth.

She'd known it in the biffy that morning, she'd known it all along, maybe, and she knew it now. Bill was a rustler. Old Angus was a rustler. They were rustling together. Cattle. Horses. Four legs and could run, they weren't fussy. This ranch was the rest, re-brand and slaughter stand, even before the Kinnicks' time.

She watched from a hair crack at the barn doors, but then a bat or an owl swooped and spilled cool night air at her neck, so she let out a *whah!* as she fell back and the door handle clattered.

Old Angus, in suspenders and a soiled undershirt, was the one who strutted over. His eyes twinkled. He was fascinated rather than annoyed or surprised. He let the left side of his lips draw up in a smile.

Belle Jane did not gasp or pant or cry. The slick of danger rushed her veins, but she wore it like a tailored kidskin glove.

Bill spit a knife to the dirt and said: "Get to hell out of the barn, Belle Jane."

She gave a wry laugh.

"Tell you what, Mr. McDonald. Tell you what, Mr. Kinnick." She could feel the grit of dirt on her lips, so she wiped it. And smiled. "You two are like some young buck 'bout to kill a man for a girl you hardly know."

Old Angus stood like it was noon lunch and he was waiting for a turn with the dipper, gloves in his back pockets, cock up.

His moustache was a shabby white. Their place was up above the Cypress Hills, near the headwaters of Sucker Creek. He was a widow, had three daughters as well as the son. She'd heard about one girl, little Ruby-Anne, and she'd met Joe, a pleasant young man whose eyes lingered at her chest longer than was polite. Joe came around time to time asking for help with letters, even though his father, Angus McDonald, claimed to have read the law so voraciously neighbours sought his legal advice. Where were his other daughters?

Bill, the way the smouldering coal fire lit the one side of his face, he looked a bit like he had that night at the Fourth of July fireworks in Lewistown: the gorgeous possibility within a bright amber bottle of cognac. Could go one way, or the other.

"What you have going, it's getting sloppy," said Belle Jane. "Boys finding those hides."

Could anyone blame a thief, wanting a little something of their own? Stealing what the big outfits wouldn't miss just to fill their bellies a few nights?

"Getting greedy, seems like."

(In fact, that job'd been done by some amateur, but both Bill and Old Angus knew it was best to keep their traps shut).

Old Angus glared at Bill, who'd let the rods rest and was rolling a smoke. "You let your wife talk to you like that?"

Belle Jane recalled that night on the train, when a rye-drunk Peter Junk had sputtered, "You kiss your husband with that mouth?" How Peter took the first train to the St. Louis Fair the next day.

Bill grinned. "I am partial to that line of talk."

She was a Plains grizzly. She was a ruby-throated hummingbird.

"No." She'd meant to think it, but there it was. Needs must when the devil drives. She strolled over to the irons, flipped the pages of a ledger resting on a shelf. She might as well have been a dog, pissing on its shrubs.

She was a snowy owl. She was a bobcat.

Which moment was it, that terrified them both and made clear her intentions?

"Pardon here?" sneered Old Angus. "Now you'll get a cut, same as you been, but I won't have a *woman*—"

She could feel him cataloguing ticks against her: unwed mother, divorces (two), songs she'd wanted to play at parties in Chicago, closer now, to being an old lady with dark hair at her lips than the marvellous young woman she once was at the piano. Belle Jane didn't know what he knew about her, and he knew that too.

"No," she said again, this time, in a wistful voice. The one she used when she was reading stories to Georgie ("*What did the mouse say? I can't watch*!").

Female owls defecate on their eggs to mask the smell of the nest.

The voice she would use while she taught the children to read in her parlour by day and by night, this.

"No."

$10 REWARD

For information leading to recovery of
one bay gelding, 5 years old, branded V̲
on left shoulder, had rawhide halter on.
–Apply to John Clamdike, Big Stick

20

1915

SHE KISSED THE CHILDREN. Probably she ought not to have, and it was not so often (save for Fridays). But sometimes the delighted eyes of Ruby-Anne McDonald glittered so wonderfully, or the regretful gaze of Mottie Gallot flickered so shabbily. Sometimes it felt her lips were a needle in yarn dangling by their little hearts, called up when one was in need of patching or celebrating.

She would cup the child's face with her hand, lean down (had she ever felt so tall, so much a witch?) and peck the child's cheek. She tried not to mind the perfume of farm children: wisps of blood in cracked lips, rotting slags of beef in their baby teeth, scabs of chicken dung at their elbows. That Maryetta, who sucked her hair and chapped her mouth red, though, that made Belle Jane want to slap her.

Another teacher, a *real* teacher, could never do it, the kissing. But she was Mrs. Kinnick. Georgie's Ma. The lady who papered her biffy and played piano on her porch (she had a second now:

a German had fled this country after his wife and daughter were killed by a truck, driven by a man who'd taken the same ship across the Atlantic).

Did she appear in their dreams, or their dinner tables, sputtering "Missus" when they meant to say "Ma"? Did they notice the new flits of accidental branding iron scars above her wrist when she raised her arms to make the sky? The Kinnick place had so many irons now they practically had a store of them in the woodshed.

Teacher Belle Jane had vowed while the children were in her charge, she would *see* them. Growing up, she felt, Annie and Dad George had not seen her, not passionately and truly. Wasn't she Mrs. Kinnick, the teacher who listened to every word of the stories of kittens with frostbitten ears and hunted black kit foxes?

The children sat in the middle of the parlour at a hand-carved maple table dressed in lace or on a matching hand-carved settee and chair (covered in a horse blanket) with a tea cart pulled up and slates laid flat. Their first order of business every morning was to sing *Turkey in the Straw* while Belle played, and the wash of their voices rid their hearts of any grudges begot in the yard, and now they could start their studies as a pack.

At first, their mothers had combed their hair; at first, their eyes followed her around the parlour with enchantment and anguish, but they'd heard all her best tales now and they'd drank from her china cups. Now, they daydreamed at the rosebuds on the cherry papered walls, the shivers of the arms of the wall clock, the three tall windows through which the sun seemed to say: *Come! Come and play with my toads and streams!*

The maths would help these boys and girls account for their stock and their feed. The grammar and handwriting, when they grew up and moved away, to tell the mothers of their lives (the crops! the toothaches!). The book-reading (lately, *Peter and Wendy*), well, those stories would be the real sustenance.

Fridays after lunch, they each got a cup of tea and one of Georgie's picture books or chapter books, and for a half hour, they read while she caught forty winks sitting perfectly upright in the kitchen, back to the parlour. When the time was up, each child shared a passage.

Today, Ruby-Anne, with her knife-cut hair and spoils of lace at her neck and a hat that'd been her mother's, said, "Oh all right. I have it."

Everyone cast their eyes on the book's green cloth cover, the gold-etched rabbit boys and fairies and swallows twirling off the vines while Peter, sat atop a tree stump held up by boys and a vile croc, sat listlessly, playing his flute.

"You do?"

Ruby-Anne nodded. What a horrid sight, this girl with frightening white-blue eyes now nearly bald. Motherless, sisters shipped off to Ontario to nanny and keep house.

Two of the boys—Clement and George G.—said something snarly in a hushed voice. Ugly as a what?

What had happened to her hair? Place was lousy, must be. But hadn't Old Angus and Joe ridden in the back side, the east side, last night with those shorthorns? Resting in the barn yet. She'd gone out about four, when the night world was still shadows—hats and horse tails, leaving strange; shrub wood arms jutted up for dew. In the barn, she saw the bunch were yearlings, mavericks with fat tongues and slow, wandering eyes. They leapt to their feet, ready to run. "Oh, now. Hold tight, you ninnies." They had water, feed, their own filth and warmth. She swore it was a glare given her by Judith, her hind a perfect bed for that tail-burned cat, Mary-Mary. The damn horse knew. The cat yawned, leapt off Judith and Belle Jane held the feed bucket for her mare. Said, "I know very well. But do you like your breakfast, Judith? And your blanket and this barn?" The war, the prohibition in Montana, there was nothing coming from Dad George now. For the teaching, the families had yet to give her anything more than butter and cream and lamb pies. Judith feasted with one eye fixed on Belle. She sensed it, the exhaustion of it all, the task ahead with the virgin dozen: the iron, not the knife and needle.

If Ruby-Anne let herself be last at the porch, which was rare, Belle would give her a kiss. If Ruby-Anne would let her.

"Well, the Darling children are alone in the nursey and Nana's been put outside."

Beside her, little Louise nodded fervently, as if she were the author and approved of Ruby-Anne's summary. Those two sat like sister kittens, limbs and feet and breath entwined.

Without raising his hand, Pete Shufletofski, just five, spoke: "Our dog Zeus used to bark when we got too near the water. He got real cross. Had to tie him to the picket if we wanted to swim." The child was so young yet that when his legs tired on the walk to the Kinnick ranch, his sister and brother took turns piggy-backing him. Belle Jane'd wanted to offer a riding pony, men knew how to make saddles for two or three children (Bill's kid sisters'd used a double), but Bill'd turned her off the idea: charity. He had a saying: "Cold as charity, if not colder."

"*We* don't need nannies," said George Gallot. "We don't even need our Papa. Sometimes he takes Mama to town for two days and we must stay. Like the boys." The lost boys.

Her own George said nothing, just let his eyes follow the lines of his page. The house, his life, had once been so quiet. Here he sat, by the curtain and the fern and the chrysanthemum lamp, slouched a little, transfixed by *Treasure Island*, was it? Fantasizing, already, about leaving home. Belle caught herself, often, gazing not at her son but at the photograph of him hung by the shelf with the plates. He'd sat for that lady photographer Geraldine Moodie on a rainy Saturday they'd come in to Maple Creek for supplies. It was supposed to be a family photo, a surprise (she'd packed a second collar and tie for her husband), but Bill was fairly spitting. She'd never seen him so irate. Was it something so small as not having the means to pay the fee himself? Was it something so big as the child she hadn't given him? He left them in the gray-blue of midday and the mud outside Mrs. Moodie's studio, the wicker chairs and pine love seats upon which babies from all around had crawled. Belle Jane and Georgie went inside, calling Mr. Kinnick shy today. So, it was Georgie in his wool cap and his tie, a rifle for pheasant hunting in his hands that'd belonged to one of the Moodie boys (not the one that'd broken his neck horse-riding, she'd hoped), an almost smile. Georgie never asked about his father.

Ruby-Anne shifted her tiny feet, and the book collapsed itself. "Oh dammit," the girl said.

"Ruby-Anne," Belle Jane scolded.

The children giggled or went wide-eyed. You could always tell, whose fathers (or mothers) cursed.

"Pardon, ma'am."

"Mrs. Kinnick."

"Pardon, Mrs. Kinnick."

"Now then."

"Well, I know it anyway."

"All right then."

"Peter Pan was about to teach them how to fly, to take them to Neverland and Wendy was asking so many damn questions."

"Ruby-Anne."

The girl gave an exasperated sigh that flew up strands of her hair, asked to be pardoned and carried on: "Peter Pan said: 'I'll teach you how to jump on the wind's back, and away we go.'"

Little Louise's eyes shimmered. What would her enchanting friend do now? Louise had that kind of face, she could be a pretty boy or a handsome girl. At noon lunch when the children climbed to the roof of the barn or raced horses, she was the one you could never tell who she was.

"Ah."

Ruby-Anne stood, rose into one of those birds, those Neverland fairies born of a baby's laughter. She went to the window, beyond it, the porch, the corral, the coulee, where a band of about thirty horses drank and ran.

"I bet flying's just like riding. But horses are faster than the wind." Her voice went very soft, a whisper. This child could be the teacher, the stallion. "And the horse always knows the way you want to go."

Here was this audacious girl who had the gift, of talking horse, she was sure. What would happen to her, if Old Angus were finally taken in? Two ranchers'd had him tried, one on colt stealing, one on stealing a cow-calf pair. No proof. Really, you had to get caught red-handed. Did the girl know what her father and brother did in the night hours? What she, her teacher, did?

Last night, Belle Jane had left the light on: *Yes, come.* I am only in the middle of it, she told herself. But that was a lie. The middle was the worst of it. It was nothing, shooting dogs between the ears and picking off strays in the dark, escorting animals who begged to be led along the river under the light of the moon. Her part was criminal, ancient: searing cowhides with the symbols of families ("Who are we tonight, Joe?" she would joke, as she coddled the fire that would turn the irons white hot). They preferred the yearlings with virgin hides, straight to the irons. If the poor beast already had a brand, she "worked it" with fresh irons. The P, for example, could easily become their registered WR brand. Then, after a few days of healing, it got led by that pearl of a moon to the shipping point in Montana or the market. Occasionally cattle got the slaughtering hook straight off. Bones to the well, beef to some fool's table.

If it were a horse already had a brand couldn't be worked, her part was cruel: a knife, a skinning (nearly eight inches of hide where the old letters sat), a pan for the blood, a going away in the mind while the ankle-hobbled filly howled in pain, a needle at the white of the muscle, and then, a stitching together of the raw skin, *wide wide* to *narrow narrow*, so the scar resembled a perfect evergreen.

Had her mother's mother, and *her* mother's mother, back in Ballinasloe, learned to work needles for *this*?

A passage from *Peter and Wendy* came to mind:

> *Tink was not all bad: or, rather, she was all bad just now, but, on the other hand, sometimes she was all good. Fairies have to be one thing or the other, because being so small they unfortunately have room for one feeling only at a time.*

What would happen to Georgie?

Oh, but wasn't she the teacher? Wasn't she Mrs. Kinnick, who, on Friday afternoons, let them all out with a kiss on their cheeks—the coral imprint of her lips sailing across the Prairies, like promises, or the butts of tumbleweeds?

A warm hand tapped her shoulder. She turned from the piano keys that had been the backdrop of her own daydreaming to find Louise Arnal, eyebrows pinched, working herself up to say something.

"Forgot my rock."

"Oh, yes." Belle Jane stood and showed her where she'd left the stone—mottled gray with eyes of white stars, not special at all, not really—bathing in Good Sir's old water tin on the porch, put out for the dogs of guests.

The sky was paint strokes of silver and white. The sun was golden pink, cutting a horizon of mauve. The fat heads of wheat still standing bent in the wind. They'd had such a spectacular season of rain and sun and rain that the farmers slept only for an hour or two at night and shat among the birds in the field if they had to. Children played games of what could be found in father's beard (A pickle? A tart? A colony of ants?), and *war* was still a strange word.

The girl lifted the rock from the water, set it on her skirt and rolled it dry.

"One needs a good rock . . . to think on," said Belle Jane.

The child had seen her half naked last summer. It was one of those 104-degree days, when the air was waves of heat and birds fell from the sky. Her breasts were sweat-soaked and she'd had a fight with Bill about him shaving off his moustache and her legs stormed the trail to the creek, where she stripped down to her underwear and sat there in an eddy of cool ripples and the shade of scrubby aspen and sagebrush. Her body, learning, as water drifted in to the folds of her flesh, to let go. Little Louise turned up pink-cheeked and humming in just her shift, poking with a stick at the bed of rocks. Belle Jane, all nipples and knees, might've asked Louise in but the poor girl gasped and ran, toward the sun.

Now the girl said: "Finding a good rock is the hardest thing you can do."

Her teeth were bucking, and she spoke little. Never while looking you in the eye.

Belle Jane gave the girl's arm a squeeze. You have to have something to fix on when you're young. "Well, isn't that the truth, Louise?"

Belle Jane thought about children's obsession with the superlative: the heaviest, the farthest, the fastest, the smelliest, the ugliest, the meanest (Lucille, the Arnals' all-black, green-eyed barn cat, for it shin-rubbed and purred one moment, then lunged and claw struck with both front paws the next). Children wanted to name the worst, and get on with it.

The worst would be: They're coming for you.

$200 REWARD

The above reward will be paid to any person giving information leading to the conviction of any person or persons found defacing any of my horses. Such information will be treated confidentially in every case. – Tennaille

21

1922

SHE LOVED TO WATCH the horses running wild. Nine, galloping with the wind across the range as if there were a chase, a ritual, they must feign. The glory of the muscles, the tumbles of dust, the thunder of hooves. *Pah-pah pah-pah, pah-pah pah-pah*. It ached her heart, how the entire herd halted to mirror Morning Star, ears twitched back to gauge a new energy on the horizon: good or bad? How a mare would sniff at her son if one had gotten through the fence as if to say, where have you been, my child?

Colts always found their mothers.

Where was her baby? The boy could be a father.

Here it was, spring, the time that winter-born creatures stepped out into the sun. In March, the earth had turned up the snow-dusted, tender purple petals of the prairie crocus. Now, shocks of yellow buffalo beans in the fields, and at the skirts of the creek, white fairy bells and fuchsia-flowered avens with petals like sticky girl's hair. How she envied their wildflower tenacity, just to be.

She'd stopped to watch the horses in the adjoining section they leased from Legwin for pasture. One stretch they called the bull pasture, but it was mostly horses that ran there now. Kinnick's horses and others, too, for there were breaks in fences, there was the creek, there were heartsick colts and mothers.

Georgie was growing up. She was supposed to call him George now, and usually she remembered. Since that summer of the Fourth of July in Lewistown, he'd kept a reedy eagle feather in the hat Bill had given him. The feather, the way Georgie had leaned his little hips and boots out and scowled at other kids, said: *My dad's tougher than your dad.* Georgie had called Bill that for a while but had also made an odd fight about staying a Willard. "Because that's my name, Ma! You can't *change* your name." She supposed he was right, most members of the other gender didn't have the opportunity or need to change family names. Here, Belle Jane'd almost become champ of that sport. Well, she would forget the Willard she'd married and think only of the sweet one she'd birthed. Georgie, his sweet dark blue eyes, the McGinnis curls coming in. He liked to whistle when he was doing his barn chores and did not lament that there was no brother or sister to share in the endless putting up feed and buckets of water, fresh hay for the stalls. Shovelling shit and milking, as his skinny knees, over the summers, reached higher and higher toward his throat as he sat on the stool. Milking was when he sang his cow boy ballads, of daintily dressed girls frozen in snowstorms and lonely cow punchers.

And I'm scared that I'll be a stray yearling,
A maverick, unbranded on high,
And get out in the bunch with the "rustler,"
When the Boss of the Riders goes by.

He had a fine singing voice, but he tried not to let anyone know it.

If you came upon him, though, it was as if the critters—starlings, spiders, kittens, even pocket gophers—had turned out to lean their ears closer.

There's b-lood on the saddle,
There's b-lood all around.
And a great big puddle
Of blood on the ground.

George liked what he knew. He did not like out of the ordinary (save for having dinner at the Chinese restaurant in town, where he could eat two whole plates of pork chow mien, fried rice and sweet and sour spare ribs, grinning all the while). He did not like making decisions. On a Sunday ride, she'd say, "Well, which way, Georgie? You pick." He'd look at the grasses, his reins. "Nah, I don't mind." He devoured the books Dad George sent him: *Tarzan of the Apes*, *Riders of the Purple Sage*, *The Call of the Wild*. Upon unwrapping the brown paper package, Belle Jane had grabbed for herself *The Emerald City of Oz*, which'd arrived with ten twenty-dollar bills on page 281. Belle Jane remembered the first *Oz* book, *The Wonderful Wizard of Oz*, how she'd commiserated with ruby-footed Dorothy: wasn't the world a confusing place when you looked to the grown-ups to show you the way? No one had the answers; we maybe knew less as we got older. Wasn't everything against you once you came up with a bit of sparkle? Should she have listened to the butterfly-flit of her heart, when it'd tried to tug her to the train and her son that morning?

Belle Jane left the book feeling strange for days, and she noticed that George, too, became his books for a while. A saying or twang in his voice, an idea about how to do something because that's how so-and-so did it, an obsession with learning more on a subject. He remembered every word within, was in love with the stories about the stars, and if it weren't for the clouds of flies and mosquitoes and needing to wake up at four, he would've spent every summer night sleeping up on the hill to have more time with the constellations. When Belle Jane met him in the kitchen one morning after sleeping in the stall with a buckskin mare that'd birthed a cremello filly, not white but cream and so rare and beautiful it stole your breath, Belle Jane said she was going to call it Luna. George's face reddened with indignance, his glare said, *You don't know anything.* "You know why they call it *luna*tic, Ma? Loony? It means crazy, full moon crazy because *luna* is Latin for *moon*. Jeez, Ma." Belle Jane, who had recalled the connection (to the moon, not the lunacy) didn't hear much after her son said *lunatic*. She was thinking about that article—"Sheriff Gets Lunatic After a Long Chase"—that first got her and Gale Willard talking in the employment office in Spokane, and she laughed. Hollered, "Fine, I'll call her Dixie then." George stormed upstairs almost in tears about it: how could his own mother be so ignorant about languages and Gods and stars?

George Willard did his learning now at the new one-roomed schoolhouse near the head of Blacktail Coulee. Like Bill and the herds he drove in the dark from butte to butte, George could ride to school following Farwell Creek—the wooded otherworld of Blacktail Coulee that dripped into the Frenchman River that eventually fed the Missouri—but instead George rode the way of the creek on high just a mile and tied his horse to the post outside the schoolhouse. In the photo that'd been taken there on the first week last spring (how proud they all were!), George and Clement Arnal were the two "tall boys" in the back row. George wore overalls, Clement wore hair that enlarged his head three sizes. The hair alone said, *I'm too old for this place.* Indeed, they were going on thirteen and about three heads taller than most of their barefooted classmates, who hadn't known or cared to look at the camera. Those boys were almost getting too old for those Saturday hikes with friends—to Marble Hill to restock their supply of sling shot marbles; to follow the river up and down, bounding up to Twin Buttes and Castle Hill and into Wise Coulee, to the shady other-land of trees and rocky outcroppings just waiting to be made into caves accessible only by their very own drawbridges. Just young enough that they could not go to war, though that was over years now and the truth was out: if you went, you were killed, and if you lived—chlorine gas, a visit to the artificial limb factory in Calgary, a mind back in battle every time the dog barked or you closed your eyes. Farmers weren't made to go, but so many saps had put up their hands anyway. There was a farmer in the hills who got the gas so bad he couldn't go outside. A dryland wheat farmer, had to keep out of the sun. Got boils on his tailbone, riding a bumpy tractor hours on end in the dark.

War was something, but what they'd feared more was the flu the boys had brought home. There was Mrs. Black being driven around on the new gravel roads with her onion mustard plasters to fry the flu off your chest. There were the Mankey boys being carted off to the orphanage-turned-hospital to deliver trays to the dying. There was Bert Wilcox who homesteaded and barbered and drove the horse-driven hearse, depending on the day. Depending on the day, all three. The town, Ravenscrag, had come up enough there was a cemetery, a church, a post office and the station, where children soaped the windows at Halloween and adults danced polkas come harvest. There were young-old women now who let their breasts hang low like sows.

War was something, and the flu was something, but they'd outlasted the weather, too: The summer of '15 had been so wet that water rushed the coulees, men carried slickers over their plows and the creek beds were so boggy that one rancher got stuck with his team and democrat. By the time he was back with help, the horses and the cart had sunk out of sight. The drought years, the armies of grasshoppers that devoured the only green bits left on the new Marquis wheat and clacked like the flaps of tires that'd been abandoned when the price of gas (and meat and groceries) went sky high. And when the hoppers'd stuffed themselves, and the scorching heat and the bully winds and the hell-cold had left any crops standing, the cutworms surfaced, crawled to the kernels and ate their way—stem, leaves, roots—back to the earth.

Now, at the thickets, she spied the purple petals of a virgin's bower, dainty and low hung over its face, like the flaps of bonnets old women used to wear. She got off her horse, bent to her knees and inhaled the blossoms: Oh! She thought to finger-dig for its roots, rest it first in her pocket and then soil in a jar on the table where she rolled dough. But no, here the butterflies would drink, flutter on their bodies.

She smiled. Weren't there good times too?

They'd had their share of parties. She played the piano, Frank Shufletofski, that magpie, the violin. They danced the hambo or a polka. Always a hot whist game in the kitchen. At those parties, they discovered who could dance (Buck Drury, the champ bronc rider) and who wished they could sing (Art Chick), who had two glasses of sherry and aired their bedroom secrets at the cribbage table (Germaine Arnal), who had to be kept from the whiskey or they'd want to arm wrestle or race horses at sunrise (all the men, and Belle Jane), who knew dirty tunes (Campling), who had the Frenchmen jokes: How do you get a Frenchman out of a bath tub? Throw in a bar of soap! (Bill Kinnick, and would you know, there were Briggs in his line that were French Canadian?) And who had dirty dreams (all of them). As the dawn sun brightened the fields and folks wandered home with sleeping toddlers in their arms, they would all sing "There's a Long Long Trail a Winding," and their voices sounded through the grasses and reeds, all the way across the line, maybe.

There's a long, long trail a winding
Into a land of my dreams,
Where the nightingales are singing
And a white moon beams:

There's a long, long night of waiting
Until my dreams all come true;
Till the day when I'll be going down
That long, long trail with you.

If she sung out now, who would hear? Who would care?

Bill'd gone for a spell. Again. Not south, driving a herd. He knew every river and creek and coulee and hill, where to back-trail a mile to see if any riders were following. Those strong low winds came, Belle Jane knew in her bones how far and how close they were, if the cattle were bedded down or feeding, or watered with the rising sun. But not now. Bill was somewhere else. Maple Creek, maybe. Medicine Hat. Regina. Or farther. He would be back, wearing a greasy shirt and eyes bloated with exhaustion and sorry and fret—or, eyes jacked boyishly wide on what to do with a fleeting turn of luck. Then, to avoid the scenes, he'd snap out with a herd to their squatter near the boundary, he'd visit the home place at Grass Range for weeks instead of days. Well, it was good, Bill was gone. The others stayed off when she was alone.

Last summer, she caught George trying to follow Bill on the first leg of a midnight run. There she was, eleven o'clock at night, tucking bread and beans and coffee into the saddlebag of the packhorse. There was George, squatting by the trough with his saddle. The stars, the bloody blankets and woodsmoke, the strange colts. His eyes, startled and accusing and furious.

Was that when he started dreaming of California? Where Aunt Lillie and race car driver Uncle Johnny still lived. Or even Great Falls, with Aunt Alice and Uncle Harry? They had four children now: Harry Jr., June, and the twins, Joe and Joleen. That was another reason she'd been so careful: twins ran in the family and wouldn't that be her luck, middle of nowhere trying to birth twins on her own? Maybe she should've had another, a girl. George would leave her, had left her already.

She glanced north, past the yellow-green grasses and back toward the house. Was it a loved house? Did it hear the moaning from the barn, the rattle of bones in the well? From low over here, you could hardly see the gulches that let one enter the ranch north or east entirely undetected.

The Kinnicks needed their cut more than ever now. Couldn't sell a steer for ten a head. No givings for running a school. In '19 the first meeting about a school was held in their parlour; she was secretary, Bill volunteered to be a trustee. She'd never seen so much beautiful handwriting as when they let the ad for a teacher. Yes, she had snickered imagining Ms. Velma Johnson walking off the train in her smart hat and bright collars and thought, God help you.

Might she have been kinder regular, had she been near a woman instead of criminal men and beasts?

What broke her and Bill was that afternoon in the corral. She'd come back early from a visit to the Falls to help Alice with the twins. Bill'd already been at it for a while, she could tell by the beads of sweat at his forehead, the pleading of Judith's eyes, the gnash of Troy's teeth at her neck when the mare finally submitted. "No!" Belle Jane'd hollered, drop her trunks and ran. Judith was too old, too precious. He'd get his young stallion colt but Judith, it would be the end of her. He'd always promised he wouldn't. There were chest punches, spitting, and while Bill pinned her wrists, the act. The spectacular killing dick. In the end, Belle Jane'd called Sam Campling over to dope her beloved horse.

The wind, there it was.

Rising from the tip of one of those ravines, she noticed a dark billowing figure. A bear?

(The elusive Plains Grizzly, thought eradicated from this corner of Saskatchewan by '05, scuttled out of dens and, every ten years or so, got its face shot off.)

She slapped her chest, the rifle, then the belt of bullets at her waist. She clamoured to the saddle pack for the cold metal wings of her field glasses. It was a man in an overcoat on foot. He wore no hat, dragged a leg as if it were a pole. Wondering prickled her heart. Who in hell?

ESTRAY

On 16-14-27, one strawberry roan mare with halter on, branded 31 on left hip and RJ connected on left thigh. One bay stallion 2 years old. One bay mare 2 years old white face and white hind feet. Owner can have same by paying expenses.

JD Collins, Golden Prairie

22

1922

"DAMMIT, COUSIN HECTOR," she said. "I damned well told you."

There was just enough light behind the house, and a mosquito revival.

Bill'd elected to go with George to bring in the cows, check the salt licks. He hadn't been happy, with the cold supper of canned ham and beets and tough bread. But she hadn't known he would be back, that Cousin Hector would also turn up like a stray. There they were, family, chewing the longest bites, while Cousin Hector, that old second-cousin who'd split after he drew twenty days for hat-stealing, told rude jokes ("The fella says to me, he says, 'I'm in the Iron and Steel business. Wife does the ire-nin', I do the stealin'! Ha!") and ribbed her about her cooking.

While she held the kettle and the door, he stuffed his pipe, grinning like an idiot. Like he just couldn't wait to share his expertise on a subject. Dared you to say, *Good day.*

There was the pungent sweetness in the air, of grasses at dusk. Crickets trilled as she scolded Cousin Hector. "Thought I told you, didn't I?"

"What now?"

"That was it." She knew it. Bill was out there, breaking the news to George. Sharing some lame kind of wisdom. "That's it now."

"What was it?"

She imitated his prairie twang as he'd spoken at the table: "*You should know, Cousin Belinda, you're olt'r 'n me. How olt are we now, forty-three? Four?*"

She'd laughed it off. "Ahh-ha-ha-ha." It'd been a lie so long she'd believed it. She was shaken by the truth now too. She was eight years older than Bill, not two or three, depending on the time of year. She'd been born March 18, 1879 to a teen-aged mother addled with grief; Hector on the nineteenth to a young-old mother who'd prayed her seventh would be a girl to live. Growing up, their family'd joked they were the other kind of Irish twins. At the table, at Hector's reminding of it all, she felt the blood draw away from her face, swim to her belly. Readying for battle.

Bill'd asked for the salt, she felt, to insult her cooking. George's eyebrows were question marks, incredulous: *You, my mother, have an age? A life?*

But even George had a life of his own. Secrets. For a whole week he kept from her that he'd tried to save a whooping crane with a broken wing. The crane had stood there by the barn in the near dark, the white-white feathers of the broken wing dragging in the dirt, and its yellow-black eyes pleading. The bird knew it, the needleworker's son would wipe the beads of blood with devotion. George fixed it a nest in the hay loft, and the enormous bird let itself be carried, stick-and-string casted, adored. For days, the crane let the wing not even quiver, and then, a kind of bow after being hand-fed slivers of brook trout. A few days more, the crane stood, poked its long, pointy beak about the loft, the boy's arms. The night George let it off in the field, the sun was at the edge of the world, lighting it a gold-pink runway, and the clouds promised no rain.

"See Belinda," Cousin Hector'd said. "You went to coll-itch. You're the teacher. We were born in eighteen and seventy-nine, right? So what's that now?"

Then, and now on the porch, she thought to club her cousin with the kettle. The fantastic glare she gave him said it finally.

"Shoot the duck! He don't know how old you are?"

"No, he doesn't know!" A woman's got to . . .

sow seeds, scarlet runner beans and cucumbers
be sown
toss piss at the garden's edge to keep out the coons
pluck ripe, knuckly cukes before the hoarfrost
let the cool, wet cucumber face pool the lids, crow's feet
wrinkles, the valleys of lies
gotta lie, lie down,
sow seeds, sew hides
be sown

"You sure?" With three fingers he drew a fork of lines around his eyes.

Well, she'd slap him now. Right across the jaw.

He flinched, blocked her with the elbow.

In fact, it was sparkles of silver in the hair near Cousin Hector's ears and the thick, unruly lines at his eyes that told her: *Oh no, we are getting old.*

"Does now."

"Yes, he damn does." Maybe Bill'd guessed. Maybe he'd just thought she'd become another bloody tire farm wife, too many hours in the sun and the wind. Once, when they crossed the border at Coutts, she'd said to his twenty-seven she was thirty, when her age, that day, was thirty-four. She kept lies labelled neat on a shelf in her mind the way other women stored dusty jars of saskatoon berries and green beans in root cellars where garter snakes gave birth, grew nests, returned as mothers to lift a tail and lay eggs in a sticky pile. Memories.

Down by the poplars, Bill and George'd come upon two newborn calves in the buckbrush. Even as the calves wobbled from their grass nest to standing, her men hung back and watched. New mama range cows would just as soon kick your skull. The five of those beings—George and Bill on their horses, on their last ride together; the mama and her brockle-faced twins rooting for milk—they shared a moment, an awareness. *Life.*

"Why d'you come here anyway?" said Belle Jane. "Be a burr in my boot."

"That so? And the hay?"

"Oh that feed hay. I'm so sick of the hay." If Bill'd married someone younger, would've been two left feet.

"Well, your horses are fairly starving."

"I know it. They're asking about Justin Arnal's colt." She pointed northeast, to the section above Louis and Germaine Arnal's. They were cousins. "Why would I steal another man's colt right now, can't even feed my own? Charity, letting it run on my range." As if she were stupid and small-timey. But they *did* all thieve from one another a little, had made sport of it. *That there's just the chuck wheel/wagon wrench/berrying pail I need.* You didn't pinch something, you had too much or you weren't staying, and not one of them could say that. They'd become monkeys without scruples or power of will. Most folks had at least a bit of spite for the spectacular "have" families (the Gilchrist Brothers, the Nicholsons, the Fauqiers, the Smalls) with their thousands of acres and hundreds of stock they wouldn't even recognize. Had the war done it? Were they all alley dogs now? This bay colt of Justin Arnal's, well that was just horses running wild with their mamas by the Farwell. The bay had been foaled by LillyBee, Judith's daughter, and sold off. Once, one of the Arnal dogs had bit the whole ass off a Kinnick hen and George had to knock the hen down to stop it writhing, the torrent of blood. Did she go whining to the Mounties? No. This was farm life.

"Aren't you full of good graces."

"I'm about fresh out."

Bill rode flank. The field could've been an ocean, those waves in the grasses. He stopped, to count or dissuade a deserter. Even from here, she could see the lines edging his eyes too. Hadn't they both once been fruit flesh?

"Uh-huh."

The cousins looked at one another, though it was nearly dark. The bell of the lead milk cow tinkled as she ambled out of the creek, toward the barn.

Sakes, what'd Hector heard? He'd been in stripes, to the tables of a few neighbours on his way. She couldn't shove him off. Bill was leaving. She could feel it the way April brought the haunting pressure of rain.

Bill forgot, what a night wanderer she'd become. That she didn't know time, had such well-tuned ears that, laying under her feather tick, she could hear a shrew take a shit in the kitchen. Should she rise? Was he really leaving? If she asked, would it make it so? He'd even stepped off the porch in his socks, carrying his boots and a blanket. The bedroom window was already half open, the cuts of stars like the teeth of chorus ladies, echoing her.

"Don't you dare, William Robert Kinnick."

He pretended not to hear or see.

Until she said, "What'll I tell George?"

He stopped. Ever so slowly turned around. Even took off his hat. "You want the truth?"

All she could do was breathe, not act the mother, begging. Once, on walking into the barn in shiny kidskin dancing boots after a month-long runaway with half her pillow stash of bills and two of the new irons, he'd said, "Belle? What can I do to get things right?" She replied, "You can start by *fucking off*."

Now, up there, as she took in her moonlit land from the window, the grasses and the animals and the wildflowers, splayed and preening and sucking the dew of Mother Earth, it came to her that she'd been doing it all alone all along.

"I won't be back."

"Go," she whisper-yelled. With the meadow of glittering stars just above the roof, she flicked her hand. *Go.*

Closer, and she would've scythed his toes.

*

The red-gray squirrel darted back and forth across her kitchen table, daring her, just daring her to try again. She was reaching for something . . . salt? Cakes? She couldn't see it, but she must have it. Now.

The squirrel gave her a mocking look, sucked crumbs of the thing she was after. Her beating mulberry heart in a tin? Her dough-flecked hands wrapped in wax? She felt the rush of anger in her blood, until it trilled her fingers. Swiftly, she caught the squirrel in her hand and knew what she must do.

Her thumb pinned its throat—the fur, the bone, the vein piping air to its pink rodent lips. She choked it until its eyes turned yellow-white. For a moment, she reconsidered, lifted her thumb just a hair. Could she let it live? Her skin grazed its whiskers, its tiny nails, flailing faintly. No. The squirrel must die.

When she woke, her thumb remembered the squirrel's throat, the strangling. How easy it was.

*

The white linen hankie shivered on a poplar branch by the creek. The blue initials she'd stitched, BK, beating like a heart. The wind, pinning it there, in the crooked fingers of the tree. Taunting her.

$200 REWARD.

The above reward will be paid to any person giving information leading to the conviction of any persons found defacing any of my horses. Such information will be treated confidentially in every case.
– Tennaille

23

1923

SHE WOKE WITH two fingers splayed like scissors over her nipple, a lick of drool at her chin. She swallowed, felt for her throat. She was warm. A fever?

She opened one eye, then the other. The sun on her windows, her skin. She'd slept in!

Oh! Oh oh oh. The milk cows, the laying eggs, the coffee. Dough sat out overnight. George's wondering eyes.

Belle Jane snatched a green housedress from the chair Bill used to sit in to do his boots, and her fingers hefted and knotted knots till she was decent enough and stepping on the last stair.

The cut of fresh-ground coffee beans held the air, and she heard voices in the kitchen, George and Cousin Hector.

"How much you wanna bet those buggers'll be back?"

"Third time's the charm."

She sailed into the kitchen as if she'd been up for hours rushing chores. The buggers? She'd ask George about it later.

George was stood by the sink, pouring a coffee for Cousin Hector. The side of her eye, she caught her boy giving Cousin Hector a look.

Cousin Hector received the cup with a nod. As she hit the washstand, she heard the traddle of something rolling on the table and turned her head.

Cousin Hector fixed a pencil at his ear. "Get your beauty sleep?"

"Oh, someone get the hook." She hadn't slept in since she was fifteen. Would Napoleon sleep in?

As she fussed with pots and the stove, she could feel Cousin Hector's eyes on her legs, naked and dark-hairy. An image came to her mind of the two of them, still here in twenty years, shrunken and snail slow and Cousin Hector stood right there while he brushed and braided her hair.

George was still stood by the coffee, the window. Why were her lace curtains drawn and why wasn't he sat? Probably it was half nine and he'd been on his feet since five. But he'd said "Mama" like "Good morning" and every time she had to *tsk* him aside, he gave her his true smile and she felt her heart tingle.

Once she got the stove going she'd go out to the biffy and the barn and the garden and on and on. She had to alleviate herself so bad she could almost taste it.

"*George*," she said, nosing the chair. She hated men getting in her kitchen.

He kept his coffee cup at his lips as he shuffled over and the window was bare and what he was trying to cover up was revealed: a hatted man riding out with some horses. Three and two colts?

Belle Jane's eyes tore to her cousin. He waved his hand. What could he do?

She gripped the sink, heaved herself entirely over it until her nose nearly brushed the pane. Was that the red dun of Shuf's?

That tall hat, the reach at his pocket for pipe smoke, it was Pete Carlsen, a sometimes hand at Shuf's. Worked on threshing crews and bunked with his brother, Nels, who'd also worked for Shuf until Nels had enough to buy the section northeast of Shuf. Now he was married and had a boy, Harvey, who got spoiled by Pete with candy and toys.

Now why wasn't Pete riding south, back to Shuf's? Why was he riding east?

She looked back again at Cousin Hector, then George, who shrugged. He waved his hand too. All this damn waving, could've caught a ride to California.

The colts. The red dun of Shuf's (bought from Kinnicks, who owned its mama), the brassy bay colt foaled by LillyBee and sold to Justin Arnal, another bay they'd traded to Chaleur. The horses had been rounded up with the other mavericks and were hours away from the irons.

"Well," she said, and huffing too. Now, as if to explain the trail of the sold-off mama-sick colts, she waved her own fingers—the break in the fence that led to Shuf's, the unfenced Blacktail Coulee, water in the creek. Everyone knew. There was nothing doing about it. And yet, she felt her blood percolate. Here was a hand come to fetch the estrayed for not just one or two but three spineless men.

A blackbird crashed at the window. Cousin Hector cried "Ahh!" and Belle Jane held her grip at the sink.

$10 REWARD

For information leading to recovery of 2 year old light red roan horse colt with white on face and legs, branded UL left shoulder Apply Box 425, PO Maple Creek

24

1924

THERE WAS SOMETHING more unsettling about the days when all was fine, when the mad sky queen of this country danced her skirts of gold and wind-tickled the wings of white-throated sparrows, and the garden was an opera of greens, and the animals blinked off the flies. Because that was just an afternoon, just a day. What was just beyond her sunshine and quiet was a switch: thunder, hail, floods, blizzards, the wild things the sky queen let off to feast on collies and calves.

That day, that spring, started out *fine*: a blue sky and crickets and a marvellous warmth at your back.

Joe McDonald was up at the Kinnick place with "the ten": nine bays and a blue roan that'd been picked last August on the federal range land in the hills. Nine of the ten had arrived at Kinnicks wearing the brand of the Small ranch. Old Angus McDonald had come along today in hopes of swaying Charest to buy the horses. Charest was a farmer from Quebec who used to live above Arnals, sold to Justin and now had a section at Dollard. Of course, those asses would fix to show at half eleven so she'd have to feed them. What, was she running a café now too?

George'd been doing chores with her since four in the morning and after a second breakfast of doughnuts and fried ham, he asked about river fishing before it got too hot. They were eating right in the kitchen and she'd glanced at the hen's throat, hung on the nail. The blood had stopped dripping in the pan. George could be plucking, it would be their supper. Always thinking two meals ahead. But heck, shouldn't a young man have some time for pleasure and solitude? George smiled, knowing already his mother would say yes. And she sent him off with a can of beans, a water canteen and a box of matches.

Still in the kitchen now, Belle Jane warmed a chuck roast she would carve and serve on fresh rolls with gravy and green beans, a few slices of peppered green tomatoes. Out the window, she watched as Old Angus, leaning on a post of the big corral, pointed at the roan with his hat, revealing a forehead that was hardly white because his cheeks were hardly pink, considering it was June.

Then, the gravel dust and *pug-pug-plitz* of a car. Charest at the wheel with his moustache and who was sat beside him? A boy in the back, was it Alf? The last year of teaching school at the house, Alf and his sisters, Jean and Alice, had come for a few weeks, until it got so cold the mercury in the thermometer stopped. Yes, as they all sauntered over to the corral, she could see it was Alf, with that pussed-up scab at his mouth. He had that boy habit of biting his lip when he was reading aloud or talking to a girl or thinking what to do. One day a few years back, Bill, who'd been a lip-biter himself, gave Alf a toothpick plucked from the band of his own hat. Bill didn't say a word, just took one for his own mouth and chewed at the wood. *There, chew on that.*

Belle Jane covered the buns with a cloth to stay the flies, untied her apron, painted with dough and blood and drippings, and went outside holding it in her hand, no sense soiling a fresh one when she got to that hen. What she'd do, she ever had enough, would be to hire a cook like Dad George had at the saloons. Lot of the big outfits had Chinese cooks and that would suit her fine. Or even a girl to fix these noonday meals, carry out a tray of lemonade in the afternoon. No, she reminded herself, a girl would catch on and tell her brother. Girls had the urge to get things off their chest. Boys got quiet, went inward, fed their injustices to a fire until it got white hot.

"Gentlemen," she said, with a fun-loving smile.

She could see plain now that the other rider in the car was that short, big-footed rancher with the bunk eye, Chaleur. His place was low south, by the new school. His beautiful, dark-haired children—David, Armand and Antoinette—had also been among her pupils once, until he came back from serving in the French cavalry only to earn a bad eye (a mare at his own ranch reared her head, knocked his rifle up the socket). Chaleur's son Armand was old enough he was working out for Shufletofski. There was talk that hands like Armand were put to dragging stolen steers to the killing place behind Shuf's house. Chaleur's girls were still young and he was sweet with them, holding hands and swinging them high, like they were victors. Chaleur had always kept his distance from Belle Jane, even in the tiny parlours where school board meetings were held, and only came around if Bill were here, which was not often.

Now, as Chaleur neared behind the glass and whorls of dust, he tipped his hat.

Old Angus turned and did the same. "Now there's a riddle."

"Don't I know," she joked and rested her fingers on the bony shoulders of Alf. "Well, this one anyway."

"Mornin', Mrs. Kinnick," said Alf. His voice had changed, was at once bubbly but low, threatening to crack at the edge of either spectrum. Alf searched beyond her, at the barn and the coulee. "George around?"

"He's off fishing in the Frenchman. You could take a horse, try to catch up?"

Charest, his father, shook his head, breathed out the gap of a missing front tooth. He always wore a smile of surprise, and bruises. Belle Jane'd heard it said the wife did the beating at that house. Whenever Charest journeyed back to Quebec, he took the children that could walk with him.

Alf bit at his lip and caught himself as he looked at Belle Jane. "Ah," he said. "I'll stay by."

The men'd resumed their talk, and there they were at the edges of the corral, the four men, a boy, a woman, and the ten horses.

"Well, I've a roast in for noonday luncheon and plenty enough." She fixed her eyes on Chaleur and Alf, glancing at Old Charest, who only spoke French. The McDonalds were already in.

Alf translated. The men, after glancing back in the direction of their fields, their wives and handmade tables already dressed in cloth, stood in their hungry bellies and the neighbourly obligations in front of them, and nodded. Belle Jane hoped, as did the McDonalds, to have the deal made by then. If not, Belle Jane understood, by the watered-down shots poured by Old Rocco at The Corner Saloon, that if you gave something, even a nothing-something, the receiver would feel obligated to give in return. And that's what she lived on now, owings.

Old Angus took a long pull of his cigarette, let the smoke out of his mouth like a sad, slow ballad. "Right, then."

Alf took a few steps toward Belle Jane with both hands in a pocket, and asked, in such a soft voice, "Will Mr. Kinnick be up for luncheon?"

Belle Jane could only look at the boy, his scabby lip. She saw Bill's face, that morning at the station. In her mind, she'd cut his throat, left him on the parched plains for coyotes. But no, he'd left her under those brilliant young stars.

As if the boy saw the story she was playing out, his face became one of regret and pity.

Belle Jane turned for the house, the hen that needed plucking. Flies weren't so bad, she'd do it at the chopping block on the shady side of the house. Let her keep an eye on things.

Chaleur righted his dusty boots so they were square to Old Angus. "These horses broke?"

Joe, who'd been a little giddy, a little too smiley, piped up. "You bet. Broke 'em over winter."

Holding the cigarette not between two fingers, but at the side, between thumb and pointer, Old Angus nodded. "I helped some but Joe's an old hat."

Belle Jane stepped back outside carrying the cleaver, the limp-necked chicken, the pot. The hen, yellow eyes frozen, seemed to be staring at her, or beyond. Belle Jane stole a glance at the sky, all blue but for a cloud that was like a cloak, save for a hole in the chest, swimming their way.

"Broke to wagon?" said Charest. He knew enough English, just detested it.

"That's why we're asking the seventy-five, a head," said Joe, "because they *are* well broke."

Chaleur said just a few soft words in French to Charest. Joe, as if to prove the point, went to the corral and knickered at the horses, calling them to come. But they kept their hinds to the posts. The yearling with the "glass eye"—perfectly and strangely blue—held the men's gaze. Back at the Small ranch, among 300 head on 7,000 acres, it'd been picked out and called "the little glass eye colt." Or was this a Nicholson horse nicked out on the federal range? Since Bill left, her mind felt like a nearly dead candle, those sideways and tiny flames, flickering yet. Belle Jane couldn't keep it all straight and Joe lied half the time, but she ought to know. Lately it's been her new half-circle *TU* brand gets used, if one does.

Charest wandered over to the bunch, hands in his pockets, and the horses stepped sideways, afraid of this stranger, and, it seemed, of the strangers they knew.

The hen had gone willingly. Belle Jane'd reached into the coop in the last moments of light last night. Sleeping hens were like pillows. This girl, who'd gone and moulted her ass right before a cold snap had survived forty-belows with horse blankets stuffed up the door, only to come back to laying this spring and get a taste for yolk. Belle Jane'd caught her twice with yellow drool dangling from her beak and only chips of shell in her nesting box. Belle Jane felt so angry she could've slapped it to death. Instead, she glared at the hen, which she could pick out for its feathers had returned with a strange arrow of black at the neck, and said, "Do it again and I'll make a meal a you." Would you know, the hen stopped eating her unborn chicks?

Charest and Chaleur exchanged words.

Chaleur pointed at his countryman and said, "He need to know they're good and broke."

"Oh, they're just a little shy," said Joe, who reached into a pocket for traces of oats. "Ain't that good? Don't want 'em too friendly, do you?"

Eventually, one of the bays trotted over and sniffed his hand for the oats, bared its teeth, let the white strip at the bridge of the nose be pet.

Belle Jane tried to make out the talk of the French farmers. She'd never let on that she knew enough French from her days with Blanche and Flora at the hotel in Frenchtown, the annual trips from Philipsburg, to take in the dance on St. Louis Day. Ha! How they'd all been ripe and rosy-cheeked and soft, once. Here she was, lines about her mouth like a marionette, cunt gone rusty, the queen of irons. And lies, and cleavers. Some that'd come to this country took out chickens by stomping a broom post at the throat, but that seemed like a cruel, boyish approach to her. Belle Jane preferred to hug the hen, clutch its head, tug out the neck until the spine dislocated. *Glewck.*

Charest rested an armpit on a corral post the other side of Chaleur. He was a farmer, really, and was as stupid about horse-dickering as he was the poetry of English.

"Aren't they gentle?" said Old Angus, slicker than owl shit. "They're good horses."

The sleepy hen had so easily given in to all of it, her kidnapping, her killing, that in her last breaths, Belle Jane felt a rage. Why don't you fight? Peck me, dammitt!

Chaleur's face was tight. The horses were familiar or queer to him. Both, could be.

As she plucked away, feather after feather, she wondered: Had Chaleur been the one, in the cavalry, to help save the wounded horses? The knife, the flesh, the blood, the string. The stitching up in the shape of an evergreen tree. The whispers of the one who held the horse's head, spoke to it as if it were a virgin.

A few yards past the breaking corral, a runty, sharp-shinned hawk rushed the grasses.

In the starry voice of a radio man, Joe said to Chaleur, "You should make Charest buy these horses because they'll be good horses."

I've had no part in the thefts, Belle Jane told herself. And that was true.

Belle Jane could feel Chaleur's eyes on her, her land. She looked up, at their moustaches, the sweat on the horses' necks, the sun. The sun held like paintings of the Bethlehem star.

"'Bout time for luncheon," Belle Jane called, topping a bucket over the hen while she fetched the horses more water.

Chaleur and Charest spoke in low voices, eyes fixed on the shiny backs and blowing manes of the band. One of the bays stood shoulder out, I'll fight you. Another horse, the cow-hocked and splay-footed one, glanced at them with longing eyes: What'll you do with us?

Alf and Joe took the pails Belle Jane'd brought over to pour fresh water into the trough. To Joe, she said, "Aren't you chivalrous today?"

She'd heard Joe'd been in Maple Creek the night Bill passed out behind the hotel, drooped in the snowbank like roadkill. Walked right on by. Told Hector he couldn't be seen by the

Mounties in town that night. Joe'd been about to go against the judges in Swift Current for a charge of perjury, getting two boys to lie about his whereabouts after crossing the Chinese laundryman's wagon lines and causing a ruckus that left both the laundryman and one horse with a broken leg. Now Joe was running with Buck Drury, a good boy from Murraydale.

Belle Jane tried to keep a smile, a conversation, but it was glaring: the swoop of a P, the Small brand, could still be seen above the hip of the mares and geldings. That night, when Old Angus spat at her for not going deep enough, she thought about putting the bowie to his saggy-sour neck.

Chaleur, with his good eye, winked at Belle Jane. She felt the lightning strike of his thoughts: *Bitch thinks she knows how to own a place.*

Belle Jane knew he was fishing about *his* colts, those escape artists, and Justin Arnal's; the colts that'd been caught running wild on her range land and rounded up, then roped home by Pete Carlsen.

She gave a smirk, took a step his way and said low: "How's Armand?"

Was Chaleur right? Was she grasping at the sands of a broken hourglass? She was getting the age she was too old for this. But hell if she was going to take another man's name, lick another man's ballocks.

"Oh, fine. See him Sundays. Eats for a giant."

"I bet he does." And then, to remind him we're all thieves and accomplices here, she said: "I hear they eat pretty well at Shuf's. Real well."

Chaleur gave her a look that said, *Go to hell.*

On the walk up to the verandah for that warmed-over chuck roast on a bun, Old Angus hung back and caught Chaleur's arm. "These horses are well broke. Charest can make a good buy with them and I can make good with you."

There was a pause in their bootsteps, the talk. Belle Jane would not look back. She would lift her skirts, take the steps, smile as she chewed the roast, heart thudding.

Old Angus's gone dippy! How it stunk, desperation. Then he did one better. She heard him say: "I need the money."

There was hardly a spit of gravy on anyone's plates. Sorry Piggy Ruth! The sow would not be the best fed among the beasts today. Belle Jane shifted her head away from the steam of the hot water, decided to let it soak a while so she didn't miss the last words outside. The French men must've thought she was the type to do her dishes right off, for as she left the kitchen, she heard the spoil of her name, *Kinnick*. Like she was not just a weasel, but a *mama* weasel.

Belle Jane let her boots be heard, saw a rider leading two horses just above the Blacktail. "Heck, we're about Grand Central today."

Charest, that goofy, just-woke smile, wiped at flecks of gravy in his moustache yet, said, "That Carlsen?"

"It's Carlsen," said Chaleur. "Got some horses for Charest."

Belle Jane felt the sting of treason, here in her very kingdom. "Does he now?"

Joe rolled all this in his head and said, "Be right on by" as he ambled toward the biffy.

Pete Carlsen took in the odd gang about the yard—Belle Jane in her apron, Chaleur limping down the steps, Alf by the car, Joe and Old Angus at the corral with long, sorry faces of bucking horse riders heading home without first money.

Alf all but ran to greet Pete and get the rope and saddle out of the car. Charest came out and gave a wave, started to make his way. Chaleur explained about the delivery to Mrs. Kinnick and the McDonald boys.

Once Charest had turned the motor of his car and Alf was saddled and riding off, Old Angus met Pete at the post where his horse was at a strung-up bucket of oats and said: "What'd you get for 'em?"

"Fifty."

"Funny you sell him horses. I cannot sell him mine."

Horses take sides. Men take sides. And then one tells a story.

"No?"

"Nah." He pointed over the wind-bent grasses, to the corral. "I got well broke horses for sale. You come look."

Pete Carlsen peered at the bunch, buckled at the south posts of the corral. Wound-scabbing and skittish. Those sorry eyes. Just seven bootsteps in, Pete stopped. He looked back at the slick moustache of Old Angus and the brow-wiping of cocky Joe.

Jesus wept, thought Belle Jane, what had Pete seen? What did he know now? About a week after Bill left her for good, but not, they believed, the gang, he sent a telegram:

HOLD 'EM.
W.R. KINNICK

She imagined Pete riding by her lease pasture after a steamy rain, the blue roan and the copper red bays by the fence, and on those horse's thighs and shoulders, the scarlet of cuts so raw legions of flies were enroute. Would he tell? No. But if someone asked? Oh, the possibilities swung across Belle Jane's stomach like the slaughter hook. Hell.

Pete followed Old Angus to the corral. "What're you askin'?"

Joe wandered back from the biffy with a snake in his walk. Was it a boner from the catalogue women that he was walking off? Belle Jane remembered how George started acting strange first thing in the morning the summer he turned twelve. Dashing around the hall and down the stairs in the dark, straight out to the barn, always with his back to her.

"Seventy-five a head."

Pete looked back at the rumbling-off car, Chaleur's glance. Pete was savvy to all of this. There it was, the hook. The sinking. And the rising, his indignance. Would you know a confidence man had swindled Pete's father, who, in the terror of desperation, drank gopher poison to die?

"What d'you call that brand?" asked Pete.

Old Angus, stone-faced, said, "Sheepshear brand, that."

"Looks about like torn out wire fence," said Pete.

Was that the tip of a smile at Pete's mouth? He was playing the dummy. Probably thought if it were fences caused the scars, the horses would have done a neater job of it.

Wasn't so long ago, this country was open range. The first horses to know barbed wire had gored themselves half to death. Twenty years ago, you couldn't convince a saddlehorse to ride between two posts, even with a carrot all the way. Now, the fear of the fence was in their noses, their blood, and colts knew, from birth, to stay away.

Old Angus let his head low and blinked, like a horse going against a spray of dust.

Joe was a hound panting at the point man on a cattle drive: *Which way?*

$5 REWARD

For one black mare, 3 years old, branded
Z on left shoulder, strayed from Forres
James P Mitchell, Forres

25

1924

ANOTHER WOMAN WOULD'VE stayed home, but Belle Jane remembered what her father used to say: "There's only one thing worse than being talked about, and that's not being talked about." So here she was, still wearing her ring, still answering to "Mrs. Kinnick" at the Murraydale Stampede, itching to get a nip of gin in her lukewarm lemonade, betting with herself, which bones could Harold Perrin break, riding that steer? Every man and every woman's arms tensed as the beast bucked the boy. He still had his hat too. His own hat.

Next to Christmas, the Murraydale Stampede was the best day of the year for folks in this country. In anticipation, on a town trip and if the money was there, men bought new hats and sons wore the old-new ones to the grounds.

Jack Redhead, in his polka-dot shirt, was the caller: "Will he stick it, folks? Will it be pay day for this hard-working Perrin boy?"

Belle Jane's arms were still sore from dragging the barrel of limestone and pots to the well. The shock of it by day, by time: bones cobbled and flecked with minty dust. The immovable layers, like cement. She remembered the first time, believing it would destroy the knob of every knee, every knuckle. But no.

What a good boy, George'd brought her the lemonade. Popcorn too, but she didn't want to chew like a camel in public. The gin!

The bull, a Charolais from the Gilchrist Brothers' place, nearly nosed the dirt. The Perrin boy thrust above the bull's head, his boot scratching the beast's cut-up ear. The boy hung on by two fingers.

With all eyes fixed on the spectacle, Belle Jane reached into her boot, poured quickly and indiscriminately, and took a sip of her gin lemonade. She craved the burn as much as ever. She feigned to study the rodeo ring: the boy's back knocking at the steer's, the starfish spread and flop of Harry's body, the mad animal, charging so they were one, both off the ground by a good foot.

Belle Jane let her eyes wander to her unsuspecting countrymen and women.

There was Mrs. Drury with a white kerchief over her hair, fairly biting a finger. Last time Belle Jane saw her, the kids had shined up the Murraydale school barn for a banquet for the soldiers. The returning soldiers—Ted Jefferson, Fred Paxton, Frank Bowles and George Ambrose—got rings. The gone soldiers—Ward Nicholson and Norman Drury—their mothers were given eight-by-ten photographs of their sons in fresh-pressed uniforms, buttons like spits of gold, smiles like there was any chance the sea and the enemy would have mercy. Cruel thing was, Norman, eldest of nine, died of the flu, in England, just before the end. When her name was called, Mrs. Drury stood, shaking yet, but she could not walk up. She couldn't do it.

The gin, what a delight to Belle Jane's veins, her thinking. Like indigo-winged starlings riding the wind.

"George, where's Buck?"

Buck, the third eldest Drury son. He was riding the big shows now.

As the Perrin boy's crotch crashed back against the bull's spine, all the men bellowed. George, too, winced.

Jack Redhead gasped: "That does *not* tickle. This horse, Dark Sue—brought across the line from our friends in Harlem, Montana—is making our Harry work for it."

"George?"

"What, ma?"

"I said where's Buck."

A little barefooted girl holding a bald doll—was it the youngest Drury girl, Belgium?—said, "Buck's at Wembley! He's going to meet the *queen*."

"Isn't that a thing?" said Belle Jane. Buck, that's right, he was riding at some exhibition in England, with the big guns, Calgary's bucking horse champion Pete Vandemere and Maple Creek's Alex La Frambeau, just as that killer heat wave was about to strike Europe.

"We saw him off at the train and a tramp hollered, 'Rope yourself a redhead'! But Buck's got a girl, a teacher. She's from Big Stick Lake? Told me they're getting married when he gets back. Mother's making my dress. I feel my sister Myrtle has the prettier dress."

"How so?"

Belgium felt for the buttons at her waist, the ruffles of cotton. She pushed down at her hips as if she were a young woman in a corset, about to step into the new dress. She shrugged. It was inconsequential or she didn't know. A dark brown crumb spread when she smiled, looking beyond Belle Jane to find someone amidst the horses and carts and tall men's legs.

"Will the dress twirl? That's the main idea. If a dress can twirl—"

"Oh, I think it will." She spun now, as if to prove she had twirling skills, and Belle Jane recoiled, remembering the itch of stockings in summer. The girl quickly grew bored, said, "Myself, I'd rather have a new riding skirt or a cage for my butterflies. I know a lot about butterflies. Caterpillars too, of course. You wanna know something about butterflies, you ask me."

"Well, I just might," said Belle Jane, grateful for the talk. Whenever she met a girl with that kind of pluck, it pinched at her heart.

An older woman in a pale dress with broadly spaced thin black stripes limped into view.

"GG!" Save for the combs of white-blonde hair frayed out of the braids, Belgium had the same stunned, sweet look of the doll. "There you are. I been starvin'."

"Should we go have a sandwich?"

Belgium nodded and they turned without a wave.

Butterflies and dresses and weddings. Yes, the Drurys were doing fine. They had cattle and grew hay and feed, and hauled water from a good well on the O'Hare place, sold it in town for twenty-five cents a barrel. Buck liked to rodeo, had taken to other games of chance and chancing his life, and had lately been almost inseparable from Joe McDonald. Word was those two had been breaking a few horses to saddle on the side. Belle Jane had one guess about how those colts had been got, and it was not the lawful route.

George said, "Joe got a letter from Buck, from New York City."

"Oh?" said Belle Jane. She could tell by George's voice that it wasn't a how-do postcard.

Now, were those two here, Joe and Old Angus? Their families mostly acted strangers at kitchen-sweat dances and Christmas concerts and the Murraydale Stampede. Belle Jane scanned from the "home stretch" of wagons and buggies toward the crowd: chubby Grandpa Chadwick on his spring seat, the young women by the crock of lemonade, wearing their short-short hair with that new Marcelle wave. Cousin Hector, in a clean shirt, taking another stroll past them toward the tank of spring water.

"Look at all the cars this year, George."

His face was twisted at the mess of dust and limbs. The bull'd finally got the boy, or Perrin jumped, she hadn't seen. There were corrals now. Last year, a bronc and his rider hit top speed at the homestretch just as the first car was coming around the corner, also at top speed. The horse climbed right on to the hood of the baby Rolls Royce and kicked through the drop hood; narrowly missing the pink freckled neck of Mr. Hubbard. Used to be at least once in the day a boy'd ride a wild steer right into the crowd, barely missing the women and children. Joked they were on the way to the iced cream.

Oh, there was old Mr. Boardman, at his hand-turned freezer. "Iced cream for the ladies, oranges for the babies!".

She could go for some iced cream but she better not, not with this burning riot of fizz in her belly. She figured she'd poured at least two fingers.

George returned to his mother's talk, counted the cars. "Seven in a row, right there."

He wanted to race cars like Uncle Johnny, Lillie's husband. They were out in Yuma now. This sweet boy, he'd stayed at her side here at the rodeo and he'd stayed at the ranch, but he was itching for adventure. Boys go crazy, that age, if they don't leave home and decide on their own, to come back to the farm. She had a pillowcase stitched *GW* with sixty dollars ready for him. Used to have two hundred.

Belle Jane recognized Old Angus's white hat, his stance: one boot half up, one hand twittering like a string puppet as he talked off something to, who was that? The fool had a law certificate now, or so he claimed, and wasn't afraid at all of being solicited for advice. That ass had been the one to give advice to the German by Kealey Springs who didn't like the neighbour's new fence and marched over with an axe and a revolver, started chopping, and left the place with a bullet in his shoulder. War and farming out here had turned some of them into saints, rocking sobbing orphans or plating out bowls of stew for strangers; others had become nasty squirrels who'd huck rocks at your eye socket you so much as glanced in the direction of his den. The soldiers, they'd left as boys, come back trembling henchmen gagging in the mirror. Her sister Alice's husband Harry'd served three years and was now a skinny, one-legged spectre they couldn't drag away from the tight smoke of opium parlours. May's husband Alfred had died in the mud at Passchendaele. Alice envied May, her altar of medals and the crumbly last cigarette left in a case at the barracks. Night came, May pretended to smoke that rollie, felt a communion with Alfred's lips.

A few hats down from Old Angus was Eldridge, tallest of them all. An Englishman who'd served in the Boer War and had stepped forward here in his new country too. Made it back and got the place as forest ranger at the Birch Creek range, the federal reserve most called the Hudson's Bay land. His youngest, Jack, proof of Eldridge's happy return, was pulling at the coat of one of the two much older boys, Eddie or Dick, who'd adopted the rodeo-watching stance of men in starched jeans, hands in a pocket, hearts high below the cool sliver of a pocketknife, thinking: I could ride better 'n that. Or, I like my ballocks just fine, thanks. Eldridge, who'd always been polite but curt with Bill hadn't looked her way once, but she had caught the gaze of some other dude with dark blue eyes and a white kerchief taking shifts in the ring as pickup man. He was riding one of Charlie Smith's quarter horses. Must be a new hand. Must be he gets those dark curls from his ma.

Belle Jane took her eyes away from the forks of men. She could tell her son wished to be among them and the man talk. "George, you go on."

"You sure?"

She nodded. The chords of grief struck always in crowds, always when she admitted what her heart and her eyes were praying for. The boy. Did he wear a beard now? Did he smoke? Was he the one cinching ropes at the chute, or was he an arms-flailing rider who loved full moons and crazy horses?

George put his arm on his mother's back. "I'll look for you at the race."

Rodeo boys crossed lines all the time. Would a rodeo boy be ashamed of his criminal mother?

"Hell you will," she joked and covered her mouth. She wasn't used to minding about children anymore.

Soon as George walked away, fears let off like the snaky wild cows in the corral. Who knew? Who knew what? What would they tell?

Belle Jane had also been in the gin three nights ago when Old Angus turned up in his car in the dark, waved at her to come out and said: "Eldridge saw Joe with the ten."

"Pardon?" she said. Couldn't be. They only rode at night. Was he screwing with her? "Probably some hand right off the boat doesn't know his letters."

Old Angus'd pulled at his moustache. "Forehead tall as Saskatchewan. It was Eldridge."

And he drove off, waving the "round for the house" signal they'd never had to use before: *Get rid of everything.*

Her lips'd been numb when she thought to ask, what brand? She couldn't remember, what brand they'd used after they'd elected to put irons over the stitched up "sheepshear brand," if they had at all.

Now, her mind, like wisps and spirals of candle smoke.

No mind, no mind. We weren't the ones.

Old Angus looked up at her and she looked away.

Those marionette lines felt like a ball and chain about her mouth. She forced a soft smile at the dust stage.

Before the big races: the wagon race and the magnificent bareback ride of the Nekaneet women, the half-mile foot races and the 100-yard dash. There was a race for the boys and girls. A fat man's race. A woman's race. She remembered all those footraces at school and church picnics as girl. The slap at her lungs at the end, the peels of breath, the glorious wink of the hatted man at the end, shouting: "First!"

Why not?

She wiggled her toes, swayed her hips.

Jack Redhead, now the footrace caller, told the crowds how Joe Carson was giving five cents to every racer, ten cents to every winner.

She bent her knees, said, "Legs, what do you think?"

The children dashed faster than fire. There they were, dozens of the whitest skinniest toes. A trio of girls'd elected to hold hands the whole way and tumbled, laughing yet. A blond boy with big ears and toothpick legs was holding up his dime like he were king, king of Murray.

Belle Jane unlaced a boot.

Behind her, she smelled Cousin Hector coming on, all that pomade. Greasy as a butcher's prick.

"Belle Jane? Your boot?"

She shot him a look. The breeze took her hair across her eyes. She giggled, in all seriousness.

The other boot, unlaced, tossed.

"You're goan race, you goat?"

Shit, she thought, the bottle. Well, better Hector has some fun with it.

"You don't want to save your moves for the dance?"

The heat of the dirt, the prickles of dead grass. The eyes. She passed her pearl-drop earrings to a little girl sitting cross-legged in the shade of a wagon. Belle Jane plain hip checked Shuf, that buzzard neighbour of hers, fixing to bronc ride Tom Kenny's mail horse. As she passed Shuf, she whispered: "Step on a nail."

Now, who was she up against?

Immie Morris, the teacher who couldn't ride and was always getting lost. Flossie and Florence, the twins. Josephine Able, a pin-waisted Basque. Good fifteen years Belle Jane had on them, depending on her age today.

Kinnick. Folks said her name as she passed. No mind. She had her lipstick, her legs. Her breasts were terrific yet. Made her back ache like a sonofagun. If anything would get in her way, they'd do it.

Cha-pa, cha-pa, went her heart. No, she told her mind, so it could tell the heart. Isn't this beautiful? The fat baby toes and the pleats of sunshine and the quilts laid out by the boiled egg sandwiches. The wild horses and the tall hills that'd lately disappeared a crazy granny, shoe by shoe, and then her shawl. How riotous the owls and the coyotes, the night everyone went looking for her.

"Ladies," Jack Redhead called, and pointed to his pistol. "On the shot."

Cha-pa, cha-pa.

Two boys hung their sweaty faces on a corral post. One said, "How much you got?" The other said, "Five cents." First boy said, "Well I got fifteen and if I give you five, we'll both of us have dimes."

Redhead turned to the crowd, waved his arms high to get them to cheer, then turned back to the women, a true smile. "One, two . . ."

Pawp. The shot.

She was a girl, she was Belinda Jane, she was the balls of her salty feet. Ha! The legs! She'd give it all up. Sell what's left, give it to George. Ride Dixie across creeks and mesas and moonlit nights toward the boy. See Jesus.

Shoot! If she wasn't neck and neck with one of the twins. The poplar-drawn line in the dirt.

Let them all remember her like this. A grayling fish, glistening . . .

Oh! A glorious pain at her heel: the heel of the other twin, who took down her sister. Belle Jane's legs threatened to kick-wobble. Not today! She steadied herself by elbowing one of the sisters in the ribs.

. . . an elusive fish that fought, even when hooked, leaping clear out of the water.

The far-off jeers, the beautiful folks.

The finger, at *her* heart. "First!"

It was when she was almost at a stop, gawping at her own victory, that she felt a stone under her big toe. Her body needled sideways, fell so slowly it wasn't real at all—her bones were back there, about to claim the dime—and then the topple, the slide of dust on her gums. The warmth of the strange hand's hand that reached for hers, his eyes like star sapphires. The gin-shimmer of their fingers, connecting.

Under the moonstone and lamplight, Cousin Hector lay in the dirt with his jeans at his knees and his ass-white willie twitching as he dreamed. Was it hooked?

"Oh hell," said Belle Jane. "I am not helping this fool to bed."

The drunk were like wet blankets: floppy and heavy and, most of all, ungrateful.

Cousin Hector's bandana was still knotted neat at his neck. She'd noticed, at the stampede, what care he'd taken to trim his moustache and scrub clean the thorns of soil at his ears. Forty-five and still thought the ranch hand could take a wife. Dummy. Maybe it was true, the joking she'd overheard, maybe Cousin Hector did have a hook dink.

Her boots set off toward the woodshed—she'd woke in the night and remembered what Old Angus had said—and then the balls of her feet halted. Her conscience reminded her: Now how many times did Cousin Hector help you to bed?

It was true, she'd sat like a fool on her chair on the porch swearing he was going to come riding up in the dark like there'd never been a lie and she'd draw her big toe up his shin to his crotch and her eyes, young as ever, would say, take me now. But instead, night after night, moonrise and sandflies were her only guests and she fell dead asleep, eyes sore from hunting up his shadow, body sore from all the doings of the day. And it was Cousin Hector who took her, by the arm, in the door, up the groaning stairs and he'd leave her strange at the landing, like she had to make that last bit in her sacred space on her own.

Belle Jane looked up to her window and then the moon, hardly higher than the band of scrub at the creek.

"Hector, Hector, Hector." He'd been passed out drunk the night of Halley's Comet, when all the sky was a giant crimson-gold fish tail: *Never never catch me!* Something must've bit his lip or his willie or who knows what but now, just like then, Cousin Hector shot up and declared, "Well this ain't my damned bunk!"

"Not just a pretty face, are you?" said Belle Jane.

As the facts must've stacked in his mind, he flopped over and languidly dressed himself lying face down, ass to the sky.

"Frig, I've seen enough. Get your damn pants on."

"Tryin'," he said. "You were goan leave me out here like this, weren't you?"

"I was just thinkin' how to help without . . . touchin' you, I'll have you know."

"Belle Jane."

"Yes. That's me. You're a right scholar, this hour. We oughtta start your shifts at two of the morning."

"Belle Jane," he declared, his voice soft and sleepy. "I gotta tell you something."

"Oh?" She thought to tell him to wait until morning, the real morning, and coffee. But he might forget or might not tell then.

"See, I was with Pete by chutes."

She thought she'd spied his hat and pipe over there, after the marvellous races of the Nekaneet women.

"Drank my gin, didn't you?"

"Didn't leave much," he said. "Didn't matter. I was goan to stay sober as a judge. There were some teacher skirts, see, from Robsart." A finger rose, pointed south, then east. "And Eastend."

"Uh-huh."

"Guy can't hardly find a girl. Should be you live here, you get first crack, right?"

"First crack?" Like they were livestock. Weren't they? Slaving and breeding, slaving and breeding. Cows and horses had it better, might be. Got a break for calving and foaling.

"But somehows, there's a bottle of rye-whiskey and those dudes from Montana fightin' about who's better, at steer wrestling?"

"Hector, what is it then?"

His breath was whiskey sour, and what he said next was: "Pete gets on about Shuf and says, 'You want to hear a story?' I screwed up all chance a dancing on air so I says all right. Pete says, 'I suppose Shuf and Armand was on their way to a dance at Garrison's when Shuf started riding slow, said he wanted to take a look at some stock out on the Gilchrist place. A yearling red and a two-year-old white-faced. Next morning, before feeding chores, Shuf said he was going to get a steer to butcher.'"

Shuf raised horses, grew and ground feed for his neighbours, but he himself only had a milk cow and three steers.

"Well, what does Armand see standing dumb in the corral but the white-faced steer with the bar X brand on its right hip? So he says to Armand, he says: 'Get the double trees and chains.' So Armand goes to hitch the team, Shuf knocks the steer down, then Armand drags it over the snow to the killing place. Shuf doesn't even lie 'bout nicking it from Gilchrists. He goes and takes an axe to the cut-out brand until that piece a hide was just strips."

Belle Jane could see the scrap of hide, like jaggy severed blades of October leaves.

"And Shuf tosses them all about the place, like they was hen seed. Rest of the hide got rolled up. Couple days later they was goan to Ravenscrag, Shuf throws it over a snowbank."

Thrown, Belle Jane imagined, into the jaws of Blacktail Coulee. Within weeks or even just days, it would be buried by almost thirty feet of snow.

"How's Pete Carlsen know this?"

"Well I'll tell you, you let me talk. Cripes."

"Go on."

"Shuf and Armand haul the beef and the carcass up to the granary, see? And they hang it. Next day, before breakfast, Shuf sees Nels come over to grind feed and runs out in his long underwear."

Nels Carlsen, Pete's brother, and a neighbour of Shuf's.

"So Shuf—dumber 'n a hitchin' post—asks Nels to help Armand 'cache' the meat."

"He does?"

"In the snow."

"The snow." All winter, you cursed it. Then, when it was hotter than a two dollar pistol in July, all you wanted was the snow's cool, damp breath.

Hector, his arms crossed under his head to pillow him, said, "One of 'em talked."

Those days, boys hungered for the ten and bacon they earned every month, for that poky feather bed, for the blood steak on butchering day. And yet, Cousin Hector told, within days, the cached meat was known to Harry Dunford, another of Shuf's neighbours, who always wore overalls and had two prized roosters that reared a terrific flock of Rhode Island Red hens. Dunford was always winging about how he'd "lost stuff" since the day he came back from war and got his section next to Shuf.

"I suppose Dunford followed the sleigh tracks in the snow to the fence by the granary, and stole the stolen meat. Three quarters anyway."

The story was like piano keys. As she gave Cousin Hector a hand up and then a leaning shoulder, she'd take two steps and think back on one detail or another, the double trees and chains, the red-raw beef thighs in the icy snow, the cut-out hide tossed in the snowbank.

Her eyes were on their boots, the dirt, but something called her to look up. There, by the corral and the faints of sun were those damn colts, their dark tails swaying in the morning wind.

$25 REWARD

For one bay mare, weight 1200, branded
LE right shoulder and WF (F attached to
bottom of W) left hip. The only horse in
the country with these brands—
Frank Hill, Maple Creek, Sask.

26

1924

SHUF LOOKED A SMALL MAN as he stood a half-foot away from his horse, straightening the reins. He wore a beard, never gloves. He was leaving.

She was standing on the porch, behind her wooden bed of crimson and white sweet williams.

You small man, you jowly man, you coward man. She wanted to say, *Even your horse snubs you.*

His was a fine blood bay, getting whiskery but still fine. The wind tousled its mane, it blinked back dust.

George and Cousin Hector had guessed it: the colts had scrabbled back up to her place again and now, indeed, their hips had been seared with her half-circle *TU.*

Sure as shit if Hector and George were on a run to Ravenscrag. And Shuf had a lead and a halter on the red dun. It looked at her solemnly, unblinking.

"Might be I know more 'n you think, Mrs. Kinnick."

“You threatening me?” She walked toward the column, the steps. She was feeling territorial, animal. Her very blood cells chanted: *Fight!* “Because I might know a few things myself.”

Shuf looked up, kept his small man frame facing south, his horse. He gave a knowing smirk.

He saw it and she saw it: that time Shuf and Bill got in a fight over that damn buckskin and in Belle Jane’s attempt to club Shuf, she’d nearly killed Bill. Never did find out who it was, running like a headless chicken up the hill when she was ordering Shuf off the place.

Now, above them, the sky was dark, smoky clouds crawling hither. Just a few weeks ago the Farwell flooded so bad Shuf’s chickens flew off the roost and landed in a foot of water, and he’d joked at the store about getting out the boat. Belle Jane was glad she’d had Hector do the lightning rod on the roof.

“Hands talk, don’t they Frank?”

Now he turned.

You beady-eyed man. You pocket-gopher man. You vulture. What enraged him so about a woman getting by like a man?

His horse stepped back. A beautiful chestnut bay, hide was dust-caked, looked like it hadn’t been curried in a coon’s age.

You small man, you coconut-cake-baking man, you in-a-yarn-about-the-flies man. Ordering parcels and cheating at whist. Nicking yearlings so he had enough grub for his hands. At least her gang had the sand to move them on, make a profit.

(Also, Shuf played the violin finer than anyone near and would soon build a two-wheeled cart for a Shetland pony so his three children, Lewis, Ruth and Bun, could ride to school rather stylishly and comfortably.)

“That’s about right, Mrs. Kinnick,” he said with a salty smile. He took a few steps toward her, close enough she could eyeball the size of his boots, a puny seven, and smell his coffee breath. “Hands *do* talk.”

Since that June day when Pete came for the colts, Pete and Hector’d become friendly. Griping about shovelling shit, fixing fence, ninety-six in the shade and you gotta do it. Weren't they *macs* sharing bottles and stories at the stampede. Now, Belle Jane let herself question, what had *Hector* told? The irons? The bunches that Old Angus had his boy Joe run here to overnight, the barn and coulee a kind of port, next stop the States or the Kinnick chopping block and then the ice cars for beef at the Ravenscrag station? The thirty feet of quicklime they'd poured in the well to stay the rot of entrails, and the flies and coyotes?

Shuf shook his head, squinted at a pierce of sun in the black sky and rode off wearing that same beady-eyed spook. He hollered to her and the wind: "Might be trouble you don't get back the other colts you're keeping."

Belle Jane threw the only thing within reach—a Dixie cup with the verbenas she'd grown from seed and was going to plant next to the clump of bearded iris.

The cup crashed softly, denting only at the lip, and the soil spilled out reluctantly. There were the tiny magenta petals. There was the low breeze, the black soil, rising.

*

Belle Jane woke not a bit startled by the dream:

She tip-toed around the snake, though it was dead, sliced in two, longways. She peered at the white muscle flesh, the perfect half rings. Where was the head? The teeth? She thought to touch it: Would it be cold?

She felt a rubbery thing beneath her heel: a black garter snake with yellow stripes, butchered lengthwise as well. Curled up to a rock: a red-bellied snake with both its parts splayed like husband and wife on a cot. She marvelled at the precision of the job. No blood, not a thread of tissue. Where were the eggs? At the corral post were the lithe halves of one that resembled the bovine intestine, sickly and gray and blind. She rose tall, left hand on her hip, and surveyed the drawn and quartered bodies tossed about.

Oh, dear. She has grown a garden of headless snakes.

She rode the mile west to Justin Arnal's, thinking, High road, Belle Jane. It might not kill you.

It had rained some overnight, and the grasses were punched up with themselves: their earthy scent and pea-green blades. The sun was nowhere yet, but it was a half day in already for country folks.

She could be playing the piano on her porch, she could be kneading dough with painted cheeks. She could be washing her hair with rain water and drinking tea till her curls dried. But here she was, a dog with a bad name riding over on George's saddle horse to say a strange word.

"Go to Canada they said . . ." Her voice was like an old miner's at the bar, bellowy and unruly.

She guffawed. The horse nodded, and how?

"Raise horses they said. And beef!"

Oh but it was good, to deal out a little blame. And yet, she could only call up the image of her younger self. What would she tell the Belle Jane of nine or nineteen or twenty-nine? No use, but it was as that glorious rebel Belle Starr once spoke: *I regard myself as a woman who has seen much of life.*

The horse kept trying to nose south, over the wild barley and greasewood and sea blite, to the creek or town or the Legwin pasture lands where the horses ran, the cause of all this neighbour trouble.

Now she spoke in a high-whiny voice meant to be Annie: "Trouble always knew where to find *you*, Belinda Jane."

Two years of it already with Arnal's colt alone. Dang animal insisted on running with her herd, eating her feed hay, it was going to get branded eventually.

As the shadow of Justin Arnal took shape in his yard, all hat and skinny arms swinging, she told herself: That'll do. Be calling you crazier than a biffy rat too.

Of men she didn't care for, she always tried to remind herself, he was a babe once. His mother couldn't kiss him enough.

Whistling was what she heard, what drew her nearer and nearer as Justin's shadow tucked off and reappeared. Finally, there she was and there he was, fitting a harrow to the horse. It shat.

"Justin?"

He carried on with the leathers and buckles. Didn't even look her way.

"I have that colt. Have you lost a colt?"

He sniggered.

"If I've branded it, I made a mistake. Before you go making trouble about it, I can make . . . arrangements . . . to settle with you. You can take it. It was me, I branded it myself."

Her damn tongue. Had she been the one? Her mind was sand, most nights she checked three times that she'd locked the barn.

Justin snarled, "Well I owned it myself."

What good was it to him, a colt with her half-circle *TU*?

Justin waved her off. "I don't have time. I'm plowin'."

Belle Jane felt the cinch of the spin: the blue grama grasses, the breeze and the rain, the stars invisible. Was she running? Were the clouds always this whisper-close?

She was a badger in the woodshed. They had rifles.

Belle Jane rode home with maggots at her ribs and her wrists like white feathers.

Her fingers hit the hot metal latch of the biffy, and she screamed.

*

Belle Jane was on her knees on the dirt, pruning her yellow rose bush by the porch when she sensed the rising of dead things, bad things. She sat on her rump, shears in her hand as she wiped the sweat off her forehead. Squinted her brown-black eyes, to see. Who? What now?

A man on a horse. A man she did not know riding a tall buckskin.

The sky was blue, that's all. Blue. And the sun was the sun.

Time slowed. It was as if she were the lady-tiger in the ring, and he the top-hatted master circling the edges of the crowd.

The stranger wore tall boots, a thick moustache. The stranger wore duty. It was in the angle of his jaw, the steely gaze of his eyes, the gait of his horse, trained for war. For them, the grasses parted. A Mountie?

Well, Belle Jane thought, she ought to stand. Forty-something and still she had those legs. Those breasts. No bat wings at the arms for her.

"Afternoon, Mrs. Kinnick."

Not a question, a declaration. Where had she seen this man before?

Over by the creek, a band of swallows flew low and high like a quilt on the line. They were dozens as one. She was a woman, one.

She thought of those cowards shooting Belle Starr in the back while she crossed the South Canadian. The splash of her body—*I want to die in my boots*—in the muddy river, heard only by Belle Starr's sorry mare, her poetless killer, and a dagger-billed green heron nesting in a River Birch tree.

The stampede, that's right. His slate blue eyes, his curls, his hands. Craggy and calm and uncaring about the others, a cactus.

She drew up her most charming smile. "The roses sure like the sun well enough."

He got off his horse, walked toward her verandah and the hitching post as if he were one of the boys.

Would she fall from standing too? For real?

Belle Jane fought the urge to glance at the biffy, the barn, the well. For a moment, she thought, I will make coffee.

Also: *I had no part in the thefts.*

She had gleaming sugar-frosted doughnuts, hips that'd birthed nine-pound sons, two upright pianos and sepia photographs of Irish aunts tough as old boots. The Mountie, he'd ride off drunk on her pollen.

*

The sky was a dark sea, an eddy swallowing puffy cloud fish. On the other side of the whorls of darkness—for the sky was bright as noon day on either side—arrows of lightning. They struck sideways, across the ribs of the cloud-sea, lit it scarlet, white-pink, blueberry blue. The crickets cared not. It was dusk, their little lungs would *crick-crick crick-crick* as they must.

Two days after his first visit on horseback, Hillock held the wheel with one hand, peeked back with those eyes, that moustache, to see all was right: Cuff on door, cuff on hand. He'd joked, on clasping the cool metal around her wrists, "I got to, Mrs. Kinnick." Again, she'd felt it in his grip, the warmth of a fresh laid egg. He'd winked. "I know how fast you can run."

Well, I have heard about it and you know, I'm full glad to tell you myself. There's a colt, just there, wearin' my brand but do you know, oh, I think there'll be trouble over it—Can I get you a glass of lemonade? That sun today.

Wouldn't her other boy be just like this? Gentle and fair. Fair, above all. Did Hillock say her name like there was a chance of redemption? That she was a good, innocent woman and the Justice of the Peace, that horse-toothed Major Moodie, would wave the charges off snorting at the thought, pass Belle Jane her apron, wrinkled and dark and stiff as a dead rose, and say, "Be on by. Better get your dinner on"?

The trouble about it is, George and I, that's my son, we only branded the four colts come spring. Two browns. Two bays. Well, that colt's wearin' my brand but we only branded the four. I don't know how to say it quite, but I've had some troubles with a neighbour. Shufletofski.

Her hands stopped shaking. She'd fallen away from worrying about the simmering stew in the pot, the engorged udders of the milk cow, the heat-spawning blood mites biting at the hens' necks, the headless recipes by the sink (what did it say about her, that she almost always skipped titling them: *GOLDIE'S APPLE SAUCE CAKE, MRS. BACON'S CHICKEN PUDDING*?).

Lightning catching the buckboard afire while the boys slept, flames licking at the barn roof, horses bucking at their stalls to escape. She did not wonder, how the others had fared, which neighbours would be her neighbour again in those cells. How did they do it, with women? She'd worn a crochet shawl. She'd treat it like a holiday. She didn't have to feed every little thing or clean every little dish. Might be just what she needed. What do you say, legs?

That colt was looking for its mother. The creek, there's no fences at the creek. That's how.

As the car's tires kicked pebbles and dust south and rumbled north, away from the coulees and toward the golden flats and town, she felt her body undressing its worries. George and Hector knew what needed doing, they'd do it. She'd be gone a day, two at most.

The colt of Justin Arnal's? Pete Carlsen came up and picked 'em out, the three he said were Shuf's—strays as far as my range was concerned—the one of Chaleur's, and then Justin's, yes. I had no objection. Charity, feeding 'em when I can hardly feed my own. And how often do you think I get to town to place a notice? There's boys five years old around here who've never been to town. You know what we use the paper for out here? Out here, you got a problem with a neighbour, you ride over.

A spill of rain at the tail of the storm, making its way toward them. Thunder, crawling the earth.

Ha! Belle Jane thought. Even the skies should like to thwart her capture. She'd felt it too, as gopher holes and rocks'd chomped at the hoof of Hillock's horse on down-up mile-long valley ride beside Farwell Creek to Chaleur's corral.

I make the T with a bar, not a letter T.

Mrs. Kinnick, you see these irons fit this brand exactly?

Yes, it must be.

The car shook as it sped another five, ten miles an hour. "Hold tight, Mrs. Kinnick."

Mr. Kinnick? Wouldn't I like to know. You heard that saying: A man loves his sweetheart the most, his wife the best, but his mother the longest? Well, two out of the three are in Montana. Be my guess. Left me quite a mess. So I'm not counting the days, am I?

"Oh, I don't mind." Her voice was a throaty whisper. It was as if she hadn't spoken in years, hadn't heard herself aloud in so long. To George, she'd pantomimed and mouthed: *The ledger, burn the ledger*. She'd tell them she didn't know the exact number of horses and cattle. Heck, she couldn't remember family birthdays. Wasn't room in her thinker; she had one hundred beasts and plants to keep alive, until she killed them.

She did like to go fast, more than anything she liked to go fast, even, perhaps especially, toward danger. As a girl Dad George liked to say Belle Jane was a bull, and anyway most things in life you can't go *around*, you have to go *through*—but tonight, she begged the Lord for time to slow. Oh, what if she had been born with a cock? Where would she be in the world just now? In the field, cool breeze on her dick.

This part of the country, this July night, the crops were tall, their heads like the fists of babies in the family, ready to open and pop whatever brother struck next. Mostly around here cereals froze or got hail-stomped before they were ready to harvest. When the car met with the downpour, Hillock pulled over but kept the engine running.

Rain crashed over the car in sheets. Spits of water trembled in through crannies in the roof and doors. The perfume of rain—woodsy, *female*--cloaked the car. An emerald-winged moth woke from its slumber and shivered at the window: *Out!*

Of all the thousands of unlawful acts on that ranch . . . she was getting arrested over a few well-fed, wobbly-legged foals come for their mama? That fucking Shuf.

The moth couldn't breathe, the air too thick with wet, she knew. But she resisted the urge to help it, as she had once with her apron for an ugly, stick-looking moth stuck in the kitchen.

George, who had a tremendous collection of moths, "an eclipse," had scolded her: "Ma, *don't*! Don't do that. They lose the dust on their wings, they can't fly. Good as a robin's breakfast." How many times had Belle Jane seen a severed wing, spat out on a rock, for creatures only ate the head? Wasn't that life?

The creek, that's how. There's no fences . . . and the mares are all about the place, they travel in the bunch all winter . . . The colts find their mothers. Always, if they can.

The downpour passed like a dream, fitful at first, then faint. When it was over, Hillock got out, rubbed the windshield with his arm, got back in, saw the fog on the glass from the inside, wiped it with his other arm, and put his boot to the pedal.

Oh, but in the yard, as Hillock led her off, George's last glare at her: *Damn you, damn you to hell, doing this to us.*

A darkly comic thought, another of Dad George's sayings: "May you be at the gates of heaven an hour before the devil knows you're dead!"

The moth's thready legs slipping at the trails of water on the window glass. Out!

By the time Belle Jane could see the long neck of the brick post office, she was dizzy with her new lightness. *She* was a fluttering emerald moth lost in the light in the day. She was a flyleaf, a blank page at the back of a book.

THE MORNING LEADER

REGINA, SASK.

CATTLE COUNTRY AT LAST RID OF GANG OF CATTLE THIEVES

Six of Band Who Operated for Years Are Jailed After Sensational Trial

Joe McDonald—Five years. Three years for cattle stealing and two years for defacing brands. Nine counts.

AP McDonald—Three years, on six counts of stealing horses and receiving stolen horses.

RT "Buck" Drury—Three years for stealing a horse and receiving stolen stock.

Charles Drury—Three years for stealing five horses and for receiving stolen stock.

Frank Shufletofski—Two years for stealing a steer and for receiving a stolen animal.

Belle J. Kinnick—Twenty-three months for stealing two colts and for receiving stolen stock.

During the period 1914 to 1924, residents of the country south of Maple Creek estimate that from three to four thousand head of cattle and horses have been stolen from that district. But, for a hundred miles east and south and west, reports of stolen and missing herds have been frequent for years. The number of horses actually taken, rebranded, killed or driven on the hoof to markets or "disposal ranches"—in some cases many days' journey distant—will never be known.

Among the heaviest losses in the Maple Creek District are:

Joseph Wylie—Former member of legislature and now one of the largest livestock operators in the southwest.

Gilchrist Brothers—Holders of immense grazing concessions in the vicinity of Cypress Lake.

Isaac Fleming—Rancher in federal forest reserve area, south of Maple Creek.

William Small—Horsebreeder in the Fish Creek district south east of Maple Creek.

Justin Arnal, John Chaleur and many others are listed among victims of the "rustlers."

STRAYED OR STOLEN

One bay gelding with star on head, one bay mare with blaze face branded SO on right hip, a black Shetland pony. $10 reward. Gilchrist Brothers.

27

1960

THE LITTLE BELLS ON the back of the door clattered with joy: *Vis-it-or!*

Belle Jane had just been fixing herself a cup of tea. The little wooden desk clock with the silver face and black numbers admitted, here it was, four o'clock, and she'd forgotten to have any tea herself. It happened that way, most days. She meant to and she meant to, but the hours got away. She set down the kettle, glanced at the door. The blue kerchief, the perfume so many of her ladies wore: a pass of carnations and peaches, then the heart notes, the cheek-kiss of rosemary and cloves. *L'Air du Temps*. Had any other scent quite declared, "To heck with all that, let's be girls and flirt and eat cupcakes. Give me *two*!"

"That you, Mrs. Mutch?" Belle Jane was careful to sound welcoming, even delighted, rather than tired, disappointed, but she'd just read for Mrs. Mutch, was it yesterday? Monday? Maybe it was last week. Anyway, Belle Jane knew well that beatific face, that salmon pink lipstick, those *Oh-what-do-you-see?!* gray-blue eyes. Last time, it was the orchard. Barney, Mrs. Mutch's son, wanted her to sell, had brought the pen to her fingers.

"Mrs. Dale, oh Mrs. Dale, I'm so glad you haven't closed."

Four, that was usually when she locked for a few hours and came back just as folks were trickling out of restaurants holding hands, happy as dogs to be on vacation, drinking wine, here.

Already, the old woman was unknotting the silk kerchief wrapping tight the curls that carried the ammonia smell of a permanent. The Moderne Beauty Shop was the other place Mrs. Mutch visited at least once a week. Would Belle Jane even be in business if it weren't for Mrs. Mutch and her friends, and the swarms of tourists who could smell ways to spend money?

To know where Starr Tea Room was, you had to be walking down Main Street and notice the sandwich board with the crimson peony or get a tip from your hotel lobby boy. She fed those skinny, homesick young men lunch once a week to drop her name, and she tipped more for widowed sisters. For the door opened to the alley, to the rear of The Jewel Box and the parking lot used by folks heading to Simpson's Order Office and The Capitol Theatre. The other side of the brick wall were the cooks and clanging and laughter of the diner, Breakfast Matters, Lunch Too!

The Starr Tea Room was hardly bigger than a bedroom and only two tiny windows let in light, so it always appeared darker, more mysterious inside. To that Belle Jane said, "Let the dust be sacred!"

On a display table she'd painted pink, Belle Jane sold her crochet shawls and collars and gloves. The white gloves with butterfly top wings and antennae at the wrist had been the thing for a while but now only older women about ten years behind in the latest fashion bought them, often for daughters who would probably never wear them, and that left Belle Jane nervous about moths nibbling at the threads while the gloves lay solemnly in drawers, like casket samples. Would the fingers crumble like the shells of ant eggs when the daughter of the daughter picked through granny's things to take after she died?

The walls were also stacked ten high with Belle Jane's framed paintings of the lake at sunset, always a fragment of home at the edges: the lonely picker's cabin on an orchard, grand Ponderosa Pines watching over saplings like cow boys on the range, a sailboat seeming to look backward as cloud slivers blacken.

But what most entered The Starr Tea Room for was her tea leaf reading. Her ladies were new empty nesters afraid of time, and the white-haired set with plenty of time and pin money, and tourists with bill-stuffed purses at the start of the trip, still stupefied by this heaven place. As soon as they stepped off the boardwalk and set foot on the sand, saw the radiant blood-orange sunset and felt the tucking in of the valley ridges, the lake that seemed to never end, they'd declare, "Oh, I want to come back!"

To get here, some drove up from Washington State, through that queer desert of Osoyoos, but most drove down through Summerland then Peachland, along a highway that so tightly hugged Okanagan Lake and the fruit orchards you imagined sticking your hands out the window to swim your fingertips in the lake or yank a peach right off a tree. And then here you were, Penticton, with its thighs of lakes, the Skaha and the Okanagan. The sun. Apples and peaches and cherries to feed the world, and did. You could tell the pinched, cabbage-white faces of first-timers a few days in to their trips, in July, the height of cherry picking, for they'd gone too far, gobbled too many, and the bowels were determined to cramp and splatter, cramp and splatter.

Belle Jane hobbled (Get going, legs!) to the front of the shop and reached for Mrs. Mutch's navy-coloured rain shawl, damp with a light spring drizzle that'd been over before it started. Even the rain here was meek.

"Oh, that rain," Mrs. Mutch said, to the sky beyond the window, as if scolding a boy stepping in the house with muddy boots.

"Won't it make up its mind?" said Belle Jane, and to herself, Piss or get off the pot!

Belle Jane remembered the downpour that fell her first night in jail, in Maple Creek. The lightning, all night, the chill of the stone bed, the smell of fresh coffee brewed by the inspector's wife. How an orange ladybug wandered down a crack, said: *It'll be all right.* Thirty-odd years ago, and it was fresh as yesterday, the hearings, the trials, first, on stealing the colts of Chaleur and Justin Arnal.

Constable Hillock's voice was an old campfire. Steady, gentle, nothing to prove.

. . . I questioned her as to what brand she used. I asked where she kept her irons, she said in the house, and asked if I would like to see them. In the woodshed of the house I found at least twelve or fifteen irons, branding irons of different characters.

Quite a collection.
She did not claim to be running a branding iron store?

And that smug, hairy-eared agent of the attorney general, Rose.

You said there was hair on one of these branding irons.

Burned hairs.

Her own voice was another woman's, a mama coyote's. Breathy, steady. Snow was all around, snow was falling on her lashes and there was the gaze of man and where was her pack? No mind. She had legs, teeth. This was her country.

You told the constable you don't know
where some of the brands came from.

I don't know where a good many came from.

Whether they dropped down at night, or
whether someone climbed up in the window
and left them, or if Santa Claus left them there.

No.

Have you anything further to say?

I don't know if the colts are mine or not.
There were 250 head of horses running
through our land last winter . . .

I had my twelve in my corral which I
figured was mine. I told Mr. Arnal I was
sorry if I made a mistake . . .

I had not enough feed for my own colts,
why then would I figure on stealing another
man's colt, especially a neighbour that's never
done me any harm in any way, and never
had a grudge against each other?

Belle Jane pulled out the chair for Mrs. Mutch and saw her nails had been painted coral, just a shade darker than her lips.

"Oh, thank you, Mrs. Dale."

"Of course."

Belle Jane walked over to the wooden door with the glass plate, turned the lock, and flipped the sign that said, TEA LEAF READING IN PROGRESS, PLEASE CALL AGAIN. As she did so, she heard the voices of two women in alley: “How can she *heal* with all those *smokestacks*?” “You’re right, she can’t. I told her, Come out here, to the *woods*.” “Yes, trees are *healing*. You should write to her and say, ‘Do you want to come out here to heal before or after you die?’ D’you get it?” “Oh, before or *after* you die, funny!”

Mrs. Mutch had her eyes set on her nails, her gold wedding rings, the mottled age spots. Belle Jane could sense it: that sickness of excitement and regret, ahead of regret. She struck a match at the sisters of candles on the table, said, “I’ll get the kettle going, Mrs. Mutch.”

“Will you do the Jasmine today, dear?”

“No,” said Belle Jane, a bit too quickly. With this type, the only thing they liked better than telling others what to do, was to have someone with authority on a subject instruct *them*. Yesterday, Mrs. Mutch hadn’t let on, at first, that there was a specific question troubling her, and Belle Jane questioned now what she had seen in those swollen clumps of leaves: a hummingbird (or a gun?), a hand saw (those nosy neighbours, the Oxleys, asking about her Saturday night visitor), an archway (maybe there would be wedding bells or a trip abroad yet). Today, however, Mrs. Mutch wanted to know: Should she sell the orchard like Barney wanted, or like he didn’t? “We’ll do the gunpowder green.”

Gunpowder green tea, so called for the leaves like pellets, painted the boldest shapes. It was her go-to for one-question readings.

“Would you know, Barney comes over last night, just before supper, of course. I tried that pineapple upside down cake you clipped—”

“Did you do the cherries?”

“I did. It was *div-ine*.”

"I think it's the sliced pineapples, baking up from the bottom, makes it so moist. But you have to eat it quick or keep it in the refrigerator, if you've room." And Mrs. Mutch would have room. Might be the type with two refrigerators, maybe three. One in the kitchen, one in the billiard room with bottles of soda pop for the grandchildren, another in the barn where the late Mr. Mutch would've kept some on hand for himself or to celebrate a good day's work with his foreman, maybe a regular picker. Belle Jane herself had only wanted an ice box (for her mint juleps!), but the last time George was here, he'd insisted. They drove from her two-room house at 289 Conklin Avenue over to the PENTICTON PLAZA, that sign like a rocket, in George's big fat Buick, size a churches in her day, and bought a Coldspot Refrigerator in Hawaiian aqua. Belle Jane had come to love the minor chords of its thrum, the little shake it gave when it needed to emit freon to cool and tick toward thirty-five degrees, the blink of its wands of light when she opened the steel handle, the smacks of condensation on her milk bottle like dew drops; and in the freezer compartment, the tiny ice cabinet, the coat of glittering frost. The fifties, her seventies, the South Okanagan, it was a woman's Neverland. Never need to walk to the creek with a pail for cool water, never need to keep quarters of beef cold in the snowbanks.

In response to a lawyer man, Belle Jane could still hear Nels Carlsen's salty retort:

Are you telling this court that Shufletofski
was fool enough to tell you he killed
another man's steer?

I think he is fool enough
to do almost anything.

How did it happen that you were helping to hide this meat?

I did not know it was stolen.

Why did you help hide it?

Because he asked me.

Wanted to be a good neighbour yourself.

And then the laughter again after they heard from Harry Dunford, who'd followed the sleigh tracks to find the cached meat.

. . . *Why did you take this meat?*

I thought I should get even with him. I have lost stuff ever since I have been in that part.

Those suits, fit to be tied. Just couldn't get it. Flummoxed them too, how the rolled-up Gilchrist hide wouldn't get flea-bitten through months of being buried under three feet of snow, wouldn't unfurl on being tossed twenty feet to a bush, could even be rolled at thirty below, though that Constable Hillock, on the stand, tried to help the lawyer man understand:

If the hide was not tied up when it got to the bottom it would spread out.

I don't know. If the animal was killed in the winter time and the hide was rolled in the morning.

If the animal was killed in the morning
and the hide taken away in the
afternoon it would not be frozen.

Yes I have seen the freeze
while they were killing the beast.

How could you roll it up if it was frozen?

They could roll it up
as they skinned the animal.

Never need to go months not seeing another woman. Probably, Belle Jane figured now, she'd spent most of her thirties afflicted with prairie madness caused by the extremes of relentless, thrashing wind, and then, total silence (the beasts and the fork scrapings and weather talk of the boys did not count). And then, during her three years at the Prince Albert Penitentiary, the "PA Pen" as it was commonly known, Belle Jane'd had to steel herself to walk the yard and carry her porridge tray and tea as one among almost two hundred women criminals who'd embezzled, shot the boss, shot the death shot in a lover's quarrel, poisoned a husband to take another, gave ammonia to a cheating son-in-law, hid the booze in the root cellar, slit the throat of the jitney bus driver, twice. A few months after the train ride up from Regina, shackled in the cars with the Ravenscrag five and likely fewer comforts than the cattle being shipped to market at that very moment—

SHIP TO CHICAGO

Melstone, Nov. 8—(Special)—James
Shaw and W.R. Kinnick, two early day
ranchers of the Grass Range country,
accompanied by several other ranchers
of that section brought in nine cars

> of heavy cattle this week and loaded them here for the Chicago market. The cattle were driven overland from Grass Range, a distance of nearly 100 miles. It required one week to make the trip.

—Belle Jane got into a kitchen shift and started cooking (she worked up from chopping onions to boiling soups to roasting mains—meat, if there were some). It was better, having tasks that amounted to something and sharing the long days with Mrs. Holweg and Mrs. Physick, the older women who told tales of families of seven (plus a calf and two hens) sharing a tar paper shack over six winter months, the husband who made the son go the next winter without shoes. Wasn't this a holly-day?

The younger ones were too needy, couldn't let go of pining for lives just as they used to be ("Harry and I would be married now! I had my dress hanging on the closet." Or "This'd be Girlie's first Christmas." Or "Be just a Sunday like this, I used to shell peas with my sisters"). The older women in her kitchen gang, the "pea grannies" as they were known for their most prolific ingredient, though Belle Jane was only in her mid-forties then, they hoped not for what was, but for a candle in the darkness. On their unapproved breaks, "a sit" they would call it, when lunch dishes had been dried and stored, and before they got to the supper chopping, they drank tea. It was old Mrs. Holweg who had to do the brewing (one more for the pot!), and first asked Belle Jane, would she like to have her tea leaves read?

Today, the kettle was whistling and there was Belle Jane, with the tray: pot, teacup, saucer, cloth napkin, and her pointing spoon. Mrs. Mutch was gazing out the window, said: "Can two old people run away to Tahiti?"

Ahh. So. Who was it? Some childhood sweetheart recently widowed? One of the hands?

"Mrs. Mutch, I think you earned the right."

Sometimes, as Belle Jane well knew, you had to kiss a few frogs. To find your prince.

Her mind called up Gilbert, before his skin had softened with age. Nights, they drank wine. Only a glass or two. A bottle a night, at most. Sometimes she sat right on his lap, and fed him her stories, the truths and the lies. "My robber bride!" he'd cheer, and kiss her. She could feel his whiskery jaw yet, on her lips.

There it was, that beatific face: I can? And then the truth: I *can*.

"Oh, why do I say such things? You must wonder at me."

Black tea, black tea would've been better for questions of the heart. But, here Belle Jane was, pouring. Being loved, loved perhaps more, for every truth and scar and sorry thing, she was still walking on clouds. Nothing mattered. Everything was beautiful. Almost. Most days.

"Well, that's my job, dear, isn't it? Now, drink your tea."

Mrs. Mutch leaned in and whispered, "That's all I was going to have for my dinner, the pineapple cake and some slices of ham from Sunday—"

"Why not?" Widowhood: the joy of eating cake for dinner!

"—Pour some syrup and there I go. Till Barney peels up the drive in that *Pontiac*."

Everyone was going in for the biggest, the shiniest. Cars with three rows, overcoats with shoulder pads, ovens and deep freezes a child could get lost in, king-sized mattresses that'd fit the whole family. Don't get her started on *teevees*. How many times had she seen Mr. Berdine climb his house like a cat to tip the antenna so the picture didn't fizzle? They were even building a plaza called Cherry Lane to house the shops under the same roof so folks could buy *buy buy buy* without having to go out of doors. Belle Jane was in her seventies now, too old to become acquisitive, and anyway, she knew: more was not more.

BELLE J. KINNICK – sworn
Examined by Mr. Burnett

We have a few head.

What do you mean by a few?

I cannot say exactly.

Could you give me an idea,
within a hundred or so?

I think we had 45 or 50 head of cattle.

How many horses did you have?

At one time we had 60 or 70 head.

When was that?

I would not state exactly, I would not
know exactly. I cannot say. I would not
know the number, I don't know that.

Belle Jane and Mrs. Mutch were almost past the niceties. What her ladies really wanted was for someone who did not need them whatever to say, *Here is your lamp and here is your mirror.*

"—So Barney says, 'Oh do you know I forgot to turn off the sprinkler and here it'll rain and I tried to ring you, Mother,' but I watched him wrench it off by my gardenias before he drove off. Oh, shoot, I cut you a lovely bunch, I must've left them in the car, well . . . so he comes back and he says, 'Mother,' he says, 'I been thinking and I think you're right, after all. Let's not sell. Things are really coming up. Might be we get a better price down the road. Well, that's got me thinking, is he monkeying with me? Pardon my talk, but I know you don't mind."

"No, I surely don't."

The Leader-Post

W.M. Rose, whose work as crown prosecutor played an important part in the bringing of the gang of rustlers to justice and their convictions by a King's Bench Court jury, expresses the opinion that Mrs. Kinnick was one of the best witnesses he had ever cross-examined. Her manner and personality made a distinct impression and she used correct, refined language.

This is contrasted with statements of other witnesses at the trial who swore that around the ranch Mrs. Kinnick was domineering and possessed vocabulary of invective comparable with that of a captain of a pirate ship.

"I think he's going back on what he said to make me want to go the other way now, to sell, like he wants?"

Belle Jane understood perfectly, the tides of sons and land. How you can give and give only to let them break your heart, again, and yet, you could never let go. You think you could never let go. Five quarters, Belle Jane had in the end, and could not bear to sell. For all the misery, there was glory, too. And what had she ever had, but that land where the horses ran wild? She'd rented it out to the Schweigerts and then the Richardsons in the thirties; the Henrys in the forties, the Girvins in the fifties. Through those years, George drove up every June in his big black Chrysler, always a black car, to check on the place—leaving Mrs. Doris Willard and little blue-eyed Juanita, and, later, Mrs. Marion Willard, behind in San Rafael or Corte Madera, California, so he could make the drive in peace, alone. Belle Jane went to the farm Septembers. She'd turn up at the Ravenscrag stop, no longer a station but a stop, and she'd have sent a telegraph to Clement Arnal to pick her up in his '29 Model A, her and all her trunks. "You movin' back?" Clement had asked, the first time. Belle Jane opened the trunks: tiny T-shirts and button shirts and long underwear and coats with zippers and winter boots—gotten at the Salvation Army thrift store in Penticton for all the children of Ravenscrag, for boys and girls who'd never been to a shopping mall and who still wore the felt boots of their fathers, if anything. Well, there would not be any more trunks, any more visits.

Just a few years ago, '56, Belle Jane finally sold, to Mottie Gallot, a student of hers in another life. If she were a cat, she'd about had her nine lives.

Mrs. Mutch would always draw out those last sips. You had to leave just a sip before you flipped the teacup over, to see how one's *aura* cast the fattened leaves to illuminate gifts and troubles to come. It was a tight window, this kind of divination. You only saw weeks, months at most, ahead.

Belle Jane saw in her mind the first cup that old Mrs. Holweg had read for her at the spice table (as it was called, for the three lowly spices on a shelf above it) where Mrs. Holweg did her ordering and her writing out the week's menu each Sunday. Beans, money problems. Grass, time to move on. The letter O, they couldn't guess. No sign of a turn of luck, of that silly wish of hers: the gates, the look of recognition, that moment. Such depressing, unsurprising foretellings, it was a wonder Belle Jane'd let Mrs. Holweg read for her again, never mind teach her the art of tasseography.

Two slivers of leaves had crawled to Mrs. Mutch's top lip. Belle Jane thought to ignore it, Mrs. Mutch always worried it was like orphaning a child from the family. No, Belle Jane reassured her. They were meant to be somewhere else. Is what she'd say. She'd tell her later, after.

The last sips, the tea cup flip, the scatter of the leaves: Belle Jane thought of it as a ballet on stage: the curtain, the slippers prancing like squirrels in the dark to their places, and then, the lights. The slipper-leaves freeze and the scene is revealed: a passing storm, a bulbous maple tree, a hopeful lady bird perched on its branch. Where is he? Almost always, in Belle Jane's own cup, the perched morning bird, waiting for news.

"All right then," said Mrs. Mutch. How gleefully she flipped the cup, let the tea soak the napkin. What fun! Mess-making like a child. We become children again, don't we?

It was a letter about money that led to the taking down of Buck (Russell Thomas) Drury, their Wembley cow boy, and his poor father, Charles Drury, on whose land some of Buck's "sheep-sheared" Gilchrist-stolen horses had ran.

New York
May 23, 1924

Dear Joe,

As I did not see you before I left I did not get much money.

I wish you would leave that money with Dad so he can send it to England to me. I have figured it out that you owe me $37.20 now as this was a business part. between you and I.

Please fix things up.

R.T. Drury

Ted Eldridge, that war veteran turned ranger of the forest reserve, had been out on a ride on a rosy-skied June night near the scrub at the head of Davis Creek when he heard the scuffle of hooves, branches clicking. He put the cool metal of his field glasses to his eyes to study the horses, must've been almost twenty-five. Weren't they Smalls' stock? He recognized them, but the tails and manes had been roached. As Eldridge rode closer, a rider fled the brush. Was that Joe's tall hat and slunked shoulders, that bull-chested saddle horse? Eldridge thought to give chase, but the horses. He got off his saddle, walked closer. The horses were not shy, and as he approached, he saw more clearly that on their hips there was just the tip of the P of the Small brand. Where the rest had once been, now, either fresh pink wounds or long-healed scars, both with stitch marks that made the shape of a pine tree.

Folks in the court heard Eldridge would report this to the authorities the next morning, but now, now he would ride to get help. In the near dark again the next night, Irving Fleming and Babe Wylie led the meek horses, like beaten, starving dogs, to the ranch of Charlie Smith at the heel of Maple Creek (the watershed, not the town). The Smith ranch became the headquarters of Constable George Hillock, acting as a range rider, a part he'd played since boyhood, since his foster parents, the Osinskis, left the Dakotas for a section at Bow Island, Alberta. Hillock, now three years into his Mountie career, began weeks of night ridings and visits to lonely hired hands desperate to confess. He even took in the Murraydale Rodeo, offered to be a pickup rider. He'd felt sorry for Mrs. Kinnick when, at the end of the ladies' race, that big-boned bird bit the dust.

How irritated John Chaleur, star witness in the trials of Joe and Old Angus and Belle Jane, became with the lawyers' ranching ignorance:

How was McDonald dressed?

I cannot say. He had a hat on him.

And boots on him too.

I guess he had boots all right!

Do you know how he came there?

No.

Do you know if he came on horseback
or in a wagon?

I told you, I don't know if he came
in an aeroplane.

Belle Jane, as if she'd never seen the tea dance, felt herself grow rosy-cheeked, her fingers trembly.

Wasn't it something, to feel the chords of the universe, plucking at the valve-strings of her heart, the veins in her fingertips, as if she were a harpsichord? It *was* music, a message in the medium of vibration, those trees, the birds' lungs, these leaves.

Mrs. Mutch waved her gloves at her face. Pits of sweat rushed to her hairline. "Havin' a flash. *Par-don* me." She looked away, at the paper-thin window, the alley, the last hours of the sun. The sky darkened so much earlier on summer nights, in the mountains. The Prairies in July, you were naked until eleven. The pale, wonderful moon was summoned, shyly, only for the mid-night hours. What a life Belle Jane had lived, those hours, those years.

"Well?" Mrs. Mutch eyed the pointing spoon.

"Hold tight, Mrs. Mutch." Belle Jane half-dreaded the spoon, the lights: her fat-knuckled arthritic fingers, always in the arch of coming to grips with something.

"Do I want to know? Maybe I don't want to know. Do I?"

At the bottom of the cup, an umbrella, opened just so, troubles that will pass. Was that a feather on a hat, on a man? A perfect square dangling by the feather? The son. He wasn't telling his mother everything, was he? Oh! And a chubby tree. Mrs. Mutch's wish, whatever it was, would come true.

While Belle Jane was in jail, she missed the funeral of Annie, buried in the Live Oak Memorial Park in Monrovia, Los Angeles. After Belle Jane left the Pen with her suitcase and a train ticket, she kept house for a year for the Stewicki family, neighbour friends of her Aunt, Mrs. Story, on Patricia Drive in Toronto.

She shared a bug-ridden bed with a sometimes ranch foreman that George'd worked for one summer, Arthur Powers, and let herself be called Jane Powers for a few years. She wept at the funeral of Dad George, who'd been living with her sister Alice in Great Falls and willed them all his "library." And she wept when she held George's baby, *Yawny Juani*, her white-blue eyes, those rolls at her feet (what made one want to gobble at a baby's fat like a bridge troll?!).

Then it was cooking in lumber camps (still, in every man's dirty face, *Are you my son?*), the tender grip of the widow hard rock miner Gilbert Dale. He said he loved her nipples. He said holding her would never get old. At age fifty (fifty-five, truth be told), to a fifth man, on the eleventh day of January 1935, she said I do and I will.

Foggy mornings in Vancouver, they made love like half-drunk teenagers, grumbled about hips and backs and new moles, and drank black coffee naked, in bed, where they read the paper, always, still, with an eye to her fellow criminals and sons and husbands, and to the many names of Belinda Jane.

Now they called her Mrs. Dale. Folks called the ranch the Dale Place or the Dale House, or, after she stopped coming with her trunks, Robbers Roost. Right up until she sold, she still had her rose bushes, her boxes of sweet williams on the porch, where she was photographed once, dark eyes and broad shoulders and her baking apron, with George Arnal, his wife, Doris, and their little boy, Clarence. She let her breasts hang low now.

To celebrate their first anniversary, Belle Jane and Gil went to the island, to an ocean town called Duncan. At the shore of Willows Beach, she gave not a second thought to unrolling her stockings (for Gil to hold in his pocket), stepping barefoot in the wet sand (how extravagantly it shone), and closing her eyes as the ocean rushed her ankles and toes. She was blind, she was a girl with a feather-light heart. *I want to die in my boots!*

Gil died. They were the age, now, everyone did it. Twenty years together, they had. She said, "Legs, where will we go?!" And her legs, her strong, beautiful legs, took her through the woods, west, toward the convent but not too close, to the paradise place where the son would surely wander. *Here, if any place, here if anywhere, surely.*

Forget the tourists, tonight. It was too hot. Belle Jane longed for her bare legs under her silky muumuu, rocking on her shaded porch with a cool mint julep in her hand. Mrs. Mutch offered Belle Jane a ride. On the slow drive from Main to Conklin, they let the windows down, let their hair and cheeks be tickled. Mrs. Conklin, at the wheel, too slow for Belle Jane's taste, said, "Well, I feel right as rain now."

Belle Jane smiled. It was moments like this, a little knowing, a little wind. A good, good friend. *Let us be girls and eat cupcakes. I'll have two!*

A star to wish on, already in the sky, whispering: *I see him! He's on his way.*

George Willard's car drew streaks of dust as he and Juani drove backroads to get there. Mrs. Mutch had called. Said, "Your mother . . ."

Belle Jane's last breaths were giddy and frightened, canaries in the cave. But she herself was unafraid. In her mind's eye, she saw her pet duck, Old Rocco at the bar, Belle Starr's starlight-etched boots, the blood-laden heels of the boy, Jane Nash coming up the walk, George crawling under the table and looking up at her, lovestruck, Gale's thick wrists at the gun, Judith's snow-glittered legs, her dry August roses, the Mountie on horseback, the perched bird. Just now, the house sparrows trilled. To her sons—the one she'd given away, the one she'd held too close—she mouthed: *Never goodbye.*

CAME TO MY PLACE

Sec. 1-14-25, one bay gelding branded OI left shoulder, hobble marks on front legs – Apply to Henry Bollinger, Piapot, Sask.

EPILOGUE

1960

IT WAS JUANI—early bird Juani, Juanita Willard, "bride-elect of John Leach," Mrs. Leach—who rose on the banana-shaped sofa in her grandmother's house, to hysterical sparrow-song in the trees. She'd fallen asleep wearing those pearl-drop earrings, there were pinches on her neck but she did not slip them off her earlobes. She made coffee, she sat on her knees on the sofa, leaning in to the bay window, the sun riding over the hills. She was warm, she wore her grandmother's zipper robe, its sleepy fragrance of lavender talcum. At the edge of Juanita's periphery, a shadow, pacing steadily. Her heart quickened, until she saw, it was just the mailman holding out a skinny envelope. As he ambled happily up the shiny sidewalk, he noticed her, gave her a nod and a smile. Oh! She can be seen. She gave a half-hearted wave, waited until he must be a dozen houses on, to fetch the letter. It felt peculiar, opening mail addressed to *Mrs. Dale*. Her mind said, Remember, the stone at Lakeview Cemetery?

DALE BELINDA JANE

1879–1960

IN LOVING MEMORY

The wild lake water beyond and those pines, the caretakers of secrets, and on a branch, a black- and white-feathered sapsucker, pausing as the pastor led the prayer. Prettiest burying place anywhere. Mrs. Mutch's embrace, what had she meant, a squeeze-your-lungs hug like that? The other name on the envelope, written jaggedly in blue ink by a man with shaky hands: *GEORGE HILLOCK.*

> *Dear Mrs. Dale,*
>
> *I think it's been forty years, but I'm afraid you will remember me. I helped you up at the footrace at the Murraydale Stampede. Also, I was the Mountie who drove you to Maple Creek.*
>
> *I write because my mother just passed. My foster mother, in fact. She loved me enough, but of course I knew, she'd taken me in when my folks met with a train accident. I have the strangest memories of that time, alone on a cart in the yard with the dog, a priest's blessing, the dog's cries. They turn up, like perfect fossils, don't they? Like the dinosaur jaws farmers from your country dug up, holing for water.*
>
> *I am carrying on. I will get to my point. Well, as my wife Betty-Mae was sorting through Mother's effects, really, one drawer, she came upon two letters. The one*

Rap, rap.

A knock at the door? Oh, why don't they go away? All these disturbances, these strangers, when a grandmother dies. *Shoo!*

Juanita's coffee was about cold and the sun already trickling over the crochet doilies, the dusty maple table, and this letter . . . The writer, she already felt a kinship with him. She had experienced that very feeling, prying through Grandmother's bedside drawer, the land titles, the crinkled newspaper clippings (plucked from Annie Corneil's "death drawer"):

> Miss Belle Corneil arrived in this city
> Wednesday from Rossland, BC, where
> she has spent the past six months. After
> visiting with friends here for a few days,
> she intends to go to Butte and there take
> a course in the business college.

Now, in the thick, lazy slough of daylight in her dead grandmother's parlour, every inch decorated with quilted afghans and knitted coasters, tight-fisted doilies and redheaded glass ducks (what would they ever do with it all?), Juanita kept her head ever so still as she goosed her eyes to see who it was.

The knocker now had his face at the little window at the top of the front door, his hands cupped at the edges to better see inside. It was not the mailman, it was some other man. Curly, dark hair. Stars of dark blue eyes, scattering across the room.

In the other direction, her ear heard footsteps, the click of a doorknob in the hall, her father. Hadn't said but two words the last few days, other than that call he made, to the Arnals of Ravenscrag. "Well, thought you'd want to know . . . Yes, I surely will . . . I will. You as well."

Rap, rap. Then fingers, a strong man's fingers, tapping at the glass.

"Daddy? Daddy, will you get the door?" But her voice was a whisper. She was in a housecoat yet.

George stole out of the hallway in his black jeans, sliding his arms into a collared shirt. "The door, Juani."

But he did not even glance at her, couldn't see that she couldn't.

"The heck?"

Oh Lord, she thought as her father reached for the handle. It's him. The door opened slowly, then all at once, there they were. Juani in the bedroom scrambling for the trapeze dress, for buttons, fingers shaking. Oh! The baby, the buds of toes fluttering under her navel, ears wading in his mother's thoughts, her *son* (as the long-whiskered man at the fish market wrapped her California halibut last week, he'd pointed at her belly and declared: "Boy"). And on the floral chesterfield, strangely loud, then quiet, George Willard and George Hillock.

"When did she . . . pass?"

They had the same eyes, sweet and sorry and sea dark. That was how you knew.

"Tuesday."

"Uh-huh."

Juanita stole into the kitchen for any little thing, coffee, milk, a window. Air!

Tears nooked in the corner of George Hillock's eyes as he peeked about the parlour, the photographs, of white-haired Annie and Dad George in a bowtie, of George Willard in a nappy in the dirt half-strangling Good Sir the collie, of Belle Jane, in her curlers and boots in her garden.

Outside, the song of the sparrows swelled until the only sound was the odd chitter of a nestling as the sun rose high.

ACKNOWLEDGEMENTS

I am so very grateful to Ann Saville, the woman who compiled and edited *Between and Beyond the Benches: Ravenscrag*, as well as its many contributors. It was through Ann's own words in this gorgeous pioneer history book that I first discovered the formidable Belle Jane. On the first of several research trips to the area, I was delighted to learn that my guest ranch host was Jim Saville, Ann's son. Thank you, Jim, for your charming retreat and your hospitality in giving me a tour of your country.

A handful of women at the Provincial Archives of Saskatchewan assisted in my requests for materials over the years. Thank you for your efforts and thank you to the archives. I also owe thanks to my local librarian, Peter, for assisting in making it possible to borrow newspaper reels from the archives.

Thank you to Pamela Johnston for the McGuinness family lore and encouragement.

Historian Donny White at the Jasper Cultural and Historical Centre in Maple Creek was most generous with his time and knowledge. A handful of horse and farm women featured at the centre and in other records, and several women in my own life, served as inspiration. What strength and pluck.

As I was writing, I often listened to the music of Max Richter. A handful of his song titles found their way to characters' mouths: "Never Goodbye," "The End of All Our Exploring," "Full of Stars" and "I Will Not Forget You." The title of a beautiful book of Prairie poetry by Lorna Crozier—*The Garden Going On*

Without Us—also inspired a line from Belle Jane. "Rinsing his dick in the sink" was spoken similarly once by Pamela Anderson. The phrase that starts with *A cow and a calf, if separated . . .* was adapted from a line in *Cowboys North and South*, by Will James. Such a diatribe about the etymology of the word *luna* was given by my son Bennett.

I am so very thankful to my gracious and thoughtful first reader, Kerry Gilbert, and to the rest of the beautiful Spokes—Hannah Calder, Michelle Doege, Kristin Froneman and Laisha Rosnau—for all the laughter and words of encouragement.

For their faith in this story and their great care in bringing it to light, I would like to thank Kate Kennedy, Tori Elliott, Nara Monteiro and Senica Maltese.

Thank you to my mother and to all the Allen women for your example of fortitude, family and love.

And to my own family—Noel, Bennett, Eddie—I love you I love you I love you.

Natalie Appleton studied journalism at the University of Regina and creative writing at City University London. Her literary travel memoir, *I Have Something to Tell You*, followed publication of an essay in *The New York Times*. Natalie has won *Prairie Fire*'s Banff Centre Bliss Carman Poetry Award and *Room* magazine's Creative Non-fiction Contest. *I Want to Die in My Boots* is her debut novel. Natalie lives in the Okanagan with her husband and sons.